THE
CURTAIN
FALLS
IN
PARIS

THE CURTAIN FALLS IN PARIS

An Aria Nevins and Noah Roche Mystery

VICTORIA ZACKHEIM

LEVEL
BEST BOOKS

For Michele Zackheim and Anne Perry, with love.

Praise for The Curtain Falls in Paris

"The setting, Paris theatre, is sharp and real. The crime is dramatic, and the resolution even more so. But above all, I care about the characters and watching their relationships grow."—Anne Perry, international bestselling author

"Zackheim's stunner of a second novel, set against the glittering backdrop of the Paris theater world, reveals a devastating opening-night murder, the desperation of a disgraced reporter to regain her reputation, and the tumultuous mystery of love, revenge, and secrets."—Caroline Leavitt, *New York Times* bestselling author of *Days of Wonder*

"I loved *The Curtain Falls in Paris*. From the enigmatic Chief Inspector Noah Roche and his nemesis, American journalist Aria Nevins, to the rich descriptions of Paris, a glorious old theater and a grisly murder backstage, reading this novel was like the joy of watching a play unfold. Zackheim's writing is vivid, passionate and always entertaining."—Robert Dugoni, *New York Times* bestselling author of The Tracy Crosswhite Series

"*The Curtain Falls in Paris* by Victoria Zackheim drew me in. Rich with sensory detail, Zackheim evokes the intriguing story of Aria Nevins, a disgraced American journalist's last chance assignment in Paris, and Paris Inspector Noah Roche. Against the backdrop of the theatre world, they grapple with the police investigation she's assigned to cover, facing moral dilemmas and politics in the police force. The Curtain Falls in Paris paints their evocative journey."—Cara Black, *New York Times* and *USA Today* bestseller, recipient of the 2024 Médaille d'Or du Rayonnement Culturel

"Zackheim spins a fascinating tale of mystery in *The Curtain Falls in Paris*! Her depiction of Paris and the theatre make the setting come alive in this must-read work!"—Charles Todd, *New York Times* bestselling author of the Inspector Rutledge Series and Bess Crawford Series

"A tale of suspense written with verve and elegance."—Sulari Gentill, author of the Roland Sinclair mysteries

Chapter One

It had been several years since Aria had visited Paris, and that was to celebrate her mother's eightieth birthday. Today, it was to save what was left of her career. As a journalist, how could she say no when she received that letter from Georges de Charbonnet, the head of France's National Police, offering her the assignment? The meeting with him a few hours earlier had made her uncomfortable, but she understood that this could be her last chance.

She took a few steps away from the Hotel Esmeralda and raised her hand to get the attention of a passing taxi. As it pulled up to the curb, she thought of her friends and how it drove them batty that the harder it rained, the faster she found a taxi. And here she was again, a steady rainfall and her taxi karma working. Too bad she didn't have man karma as well.

They drove through what soon became more a mist than a downpour, the flashing lights of police cars reflecting off the bridge's stone barriers as three policemen tried to direct traffic across Pont d'Arcole.

"I'll never get there in time," Aria said, her words lost under the radio's lilting Arabic music and her driver's animated phone conversation.

"You will," he said, glancing through the rear-view mirror. "I'll see to that!"

They broke free, drove along the quai, and then zipped past the Hôtel de Ville, the lavishly illuminated city hall of Paris. The cab barreled up the rue des Martyrs, where women lined the sidewalks, rain puddling around their ankles, garbage slapping against their bare legs. The older women did their business in reeking alleyways shared with rats; the younger women were invited into cars, or a room in some fleabag hotel. The Basilica of Sacre

1

Coeur sat at the top of the hill. It was bathed in a heavenly light that ignored the girls and women lurking in its shadows.

As the taxi turned onto the little street leading up to the Théâtre Junot, Aria told herself to make the most of the evening. Chief Inspector Noah Roche was not an easy man to read, but did that matter? Based on their first meeting, after she had left de Charbonnet's office, she would place him in the not-easy-but-not-impossible category. Certainly, she could tolerate one social event and a week of dogging his team. What she could not tolerate was the feeling that de Charbonnet had commissioned her to document one week in the life of a homicide team because he intended to humiliate Roche for his own gain.

And Aria was no stranger to humiliation.

As a respected journalist, she had been writing a series on the opioid epidemic in San Francisco. With three articles already published and a fourth about to come out, newspapers around the country had picked up the series. There was even talk of a Pulitzer. While she was finalizing the last article, she heard about a woman who had run a red light and struck a car, killing a young mother and her infant child. A friend inside the police department told her that the driver, Adele Jameson, was probably on opioids. He wasn't sure, but they were running toxicology tests, and everyone seemed to agree. Although Aria had a rule never to write anything unless it was one hundred percent verifiable, for the first time in her career, she broke that rule. She wrote that Adele Jameson was *suspected* of driving under the influence of drugs. The article was published, Jameson was arrested and jailed, and the Jameson family was hounded by every gossip rag and website, with the public calling for the death penalty. While Jameson sat in a jail cell, her car and home were vandalized, and there were death threats against her family. After days of unrelenting attacks, Adele Jameson hanged herself in her cell.

Two days later, the lab and autopsy reports came back. There were no drugs in Adele Jameson's system. She had suffered a stroke while driving and had lost control of her car.

Aria was overwhelmed by guilt and shock. In addition to being held responsible for a death, she lost her job and her reputation.

Even if this Paris assignment were more suited to an entry-level journalist, the letter from Georges de Charbonnet gave her hope.

As the taxi approached the theater, Aria took a deep breath. Her mother was supposed to have flown to Paris with her to attend this play. She had known the actors and the director for more than a half century and was heartbroken when she took ill and her doctor forbade her from traveling. When Inspector Roche had voiced his regrets that all the tickets for this play were sold out, Aria handed him the ticket meant for her mother.

And now, here she was, embedded in Chief Homicide Inspector Noah Roche's team, and she already sensed that they were not off to a good start. Why in the hell had she given Roche that ticket? She could imagine him seated next to her, silent and sullen.

The taxi squealed to a stop in front of the theater. Aria paid the driver, thanked him, and climbed out, stepping into a large and boisterous crowd. A young woman was admonishing everyone to stay off the red carpet leading up the steps and into the lobby. "For the dignitaries!" she kept repeating, but no one paid her any heed.

Aria stepped onto the carpet and, despite the rain, paused. Celebrity or not, she was feeling particularly stylish. She was wearing one of her mother's designs, a suit that showed off legs that still turned heads. She almost pitied the paparazzi who would rather photograph Lady Gaga in an old bathrobe than Aria Nevins in a Delphine Nevins suit.

A few of those paparazzi raised their cameras, but quickly lowered them when a man announced, "Don't bother, she's a nobody."

In the lobby, Aria spotted Noah Roche. He was dressed in a tweed jacket, jet black and deep cocoa. She was tempted to touch it, ask if she could take a swatch, and have a suit made for herself. She wondered how such an attractive man could be so aloof. She looked into his eyes and thought of the Mediterranean, but these waters were cold. His hair was dark, cut short, gray at the temples. A bit of George Clooney, but without the warm smile.

Even if Roche proved to be a cold fish—and he had given her no indication of being otherwise—she could lose herself in the drama of the play. Then she would go backstage, hug the lead actors, her old family friends Solange and Bertrand Gabriel, give director Max Formande—known to Aria as Uncle Max—her mother's greetings and apologies for her absence, and take a taxi back to the hotel for a much-needed sleep.

She shook hands with Roche and felt not so much scrutinized as probed, as if he were looking into her mind. One week and then home. She could do this.

"Nice jacket," she said, giving no resistance when he took her by the elbow and guided her toward the inner door leading to the theater. She guessed his height to be around six feet. Without her heels, she was a few inches shorter.

Aria thought of her mother and how she should be the one complimenting this stranger on the fabric of his jacket. If she were here, she would be gazing around, attempting to appear modest while half the audience recognized her as one of France's legendary couturiers. She would have appreciated this moment far more than Aria did, having seen the original performance of this play a half-century ago. And she had a long history with its stars, the venerated Gabriels. As for the director, Max Formande—whether or not her mother and Max had once been lovers was an unanswered question.

She pulled out her phone and took a few pictures, hoping not to be too obvious, too—American. When she returned home, she wanted the pleasure of regaling her mother with every detail, including these elegant Parisians milling around in their theater finery.

She glanced at Roche. His eyes were alert, darting around the lobby. She respected men who were curious, yet warned herself to be careful, to keep her distance. This was not a warm man, someone with whom she could build trust. They would watch the play, perhaps get a snack, and then revert to their business relationship. The inspector didn't strike her as a star-struck fan. Still, introducing him to Bertrand and Solange Gabriel might win a few points with him. Anything to make this assignment successful.

An elderly man rushed by. It took a moment for Aria to register his face. "Uncle Max!" she declared, her voice rising above the din.

Max Formande stopped and turned. It took him a moment to recognize her. "Aria!"

They hugged quickly, and then he looked around. "Your mother?" he said, his voice suddenly filled with worry.

"She's fine, Uncle Max. A bad cold that went to her chest. She's better today, but the doctor was adamant."

He smiled. "And she obeyed?"

She turned to Roche. "Inspector, Max Formande is the director of this play...and my uncle."

The two men exchanged polite greetings.

Aria gave Max's arm a squeeze. "My daughter hid her passport. Mama sends her love. I'm here to write about a French homicide unit, and Chief Inspector Roche is showing me the ropes."

After exchanging another quick hug and a promise to meet before she returned to the States, Max rushed off to check on his actors.

"Is there anyone you don't know?" Roche asked. "Famous actors, directors—"

"I've never met Simone de Beauvoir."

He stared at her. "She's been dead for years...decades."

She returned his stare. "Ah, then that would explain it."

Their seats were in the third row, the first two on the aisle. She left the aisle seat for the taller Roche, settled in, and used her mobile to take a photograph of the empty stage. She nearly took one of Roche, but decided against it. She felt him watching her.

"Did you know that this is the last performance in this theater?" he said. "Its swan song, if you will. In a few days, the wrecker's ball will take her down, and Montmartre's new cultural center will be built. A theater, a four-plex cinema, and a big café. Just what Paris needs: another café."

She gazed around them. "I didn't know, and...how sad. It's elegant, and with so much history." She loved that there was no curtain separating the audience from the stage, making the comings and goings of stagehands and technicians visible to all—a proximity that suggested a kind of alliance.

A young man crossed to center stage and looked up into the rafters. Then, after repositioning a chair, he raised a thumb to someone standing on the overhead catwalk and disappeared into the wings. Within seconds, the theater dimmed to black and fell silent.

It was nearly a full minute before the lights came up and an elderly couple made their way onto the stage. For a moment, there was no reaction, and then the audience stood en masse and erupted into applause. There they were, Bertrand and Solange Gabriel.

She stood, sharing this massive wave of adulation that wrapped around the couple. To the public, the Gabriels were idols. But she had known them her entire life, and it wasn't so easy to worship someone when you have slept in their home, used their bathroom.

As Solange and Bertrand Gabriel took their bows, Aria was struck by how small they were. Solange was barely five feet and bird-thin, her wrists like those of a child. Her hair was short, that shade of blonde-white that older women prefer in order to cover all signs of gray. Bertrand was nearly as small as his wife, yet carried a bit more flesh on his frame. Born a redhead, age and vanity had changed his hair to faded strawberry. There were few wrinkles on his face—it was likely that a surgeon's skill had taken care of that, and more than once.

It was another few minutes before everyone settled back into their seats. By that time, Aria had read the program. The Gabriels were Claudius and Gertrude; Camilla Rodolfo was Ophelia. She was the A-list actress rumored by the tabloids to be Bertrand's love child. Or was it Solange's? Hamlet was played by Anton Delant, a film star with a reputation for frequent visits to posh rehab facilities, and Linné Colbert was Camilla's understudy, which Aria thought odd, given her recent success at Cannes. Certainly, she was far enough along in her career that her understudy days were over.

The first act began. Bertrand and Solange became ageless, loose jowls and rheumy eyes disappearing as they transformed themselves into characters possessing agility and power. Aria was sufficiently familiar with Shakespeare's *Hamlet* to appreciate the creativity of this spin-off story. She marveled at the Irish playwright's ability to take one small scene from a play written more than four hundred years ago and develop it into this drama. It was genius.

Camilla Rodolfo, Ophelia, entered with an air of humility, yet a tension that foretold evil. She announced her belief that Hamlet would never ascend to the throne, and then she exited on the arm of Hamlet's father, Claudius, Bertrand.

Nearly forty minutes into Act One, Solange Gabriel stood alone and delivered Gertrude's first soliloquy. The queen was expressing her fears, her rage, but Aria felt them as her own. These past months had been fraught with so much drama and humiliation. She was grateful for the distraction when Bertrand, as Claudius, reappeared at the edge of the stage and declared his Gertrude magnificent.

Aria realized she was holding her breath. Letting it out slowly, a thought came to her. Though she tried, she could not push it away. Gertrude had Claudius, Solange had Bertrand, but who did she have? There was no one there for her, no partner to keep her safe from the onslaught. This feeling was made even more poignant because she was sharing an armrest with a man who seemed to be leaning away from her, keeping his distance and yet, for this moment, was playing an important role in her life, perhaps in her future.

As Solange and Bertrand were speaking, Aria watched how he, the old king, approached his wife and extended his hand. She took it and, after holding their poses for a long beat, and in choreographed perfection, they whipped around and exited the stage, heads high and shoulders squared in a most regal manner.

The audience rose, roaring for the couple's return. After minutes of steady but unsuccessful applause to call them out for a bow, the lights came up.

"We have thirty minutes," Roche said. "If you like, there's a very nice bistro nearby. I'm meeting an old friend there."

It was so tempting to say to this aloof man, "Oh, you have friends!" Instead, she nodded. What she wanted was to return to the hotel, sink into a hot bath, and then burrow under the covers. But no, she was here, and he was being kind. "Sounds good, thank you,"

She stepped into the aisle and nearly tripped over a foot extended into her path.

"Sorry," said the man seated directly behind Roche.

Aria saw that he did not have long legs, but there was almost no room between the rows. She guessed he was around forty, but with a shock of white hair, she would expect from someone far older.

She followed Roche as he maneuvered through the crowd and onto the street. There was one moment, navigating a particularly crowded patch, when he took her arm, which she saw as the gesture of a man well taught.

The bistro was hardly larger than a sidewalk kiosk. They ordered jambon-fromage crêpes and grabbed a table while a young man prepared the food. Sitting in silence, Aria could not find words.

Their number was called. Roche jumped up, collected their order, and returned. "Jean-Philippe should be here soon," he said.

"Is he with the police?" she asked, unfolding the little napkin.

"Theater critic." He put the plates on the table and sat down.

Aria took a bite of her crêpe. The ham was thick and sweet; the cheese managed to be both creamy and pungent. "Delicious," she announced, wiping oil from her hands with the minuscule napkin. "I didn't realize how hungry I was."

They ate in silence. When Aria finished her crêpe, she asked him about his work.

Roche looked at her. "I see dead people."

She smiled. Was there anyone in the world who hadn't seen that film, *The Sixth Sense*? She was encouraged. Perhaps he had a sense of humor after all.

Roche scanned the entrance and glanced at his watch. "It's not like Jean-Philippe, he's never late."

"Perhaps something came up and—"

"Not for a theater reviewer. The first to arrive, the last to leave. And the second act begins soon."

Aria retrieved the recorder from her bag and placed it on the table.

"I'm not allowed to eat without that?" he said. Any semblance of calm between them quickly evaporated. "A recorder? Really? I would have thought a big journalist would record on her phone."

"I find this more dependable," she said.

He remained silent.

"I'm here on assignment, remember?" she went on, her voice cool.

"And what do you need to know on assignment? Our last case, the shopkeeper whose son died? That one's wrapped up. Or would you like me to conjure up a steamy, ghoulish murder for you? Or," he quickly added, "I could describe the crêpe."

"I have a few questions," she persisted, leaving the recorder untouched.

Roche gave her a hard look, pulled a handful of euros from his pocket, and tossed them onto the table. Without a word, he stood and stalked off.

Aria grabbed the recorder and followed, anger energizing her step. They were about to enter the theater when a man rushed up to them.

"Sorry!" he said, giving Roche a quick kiss on both cheeks. "I forgot to feed the parking meter, and I've been towed twice this month!"

Roche laughed. "Some things never change." His face turned sour. "Aria Nevins, meet Jean-Philippe Mesur, my old friend and esteemed theater reviewer."

"Older by three days!" complained the man.

"Three days older is old in my book, Jean-Philippe." He gestured towards Aria. "She has graciously allowed me to stand in for her mother tonight."

The warning light flashed.

"Let's meet after the play," said Mesur. "We can argue over the absurdity of casting Camilla Rodolfo as Ophelia."

"You find that odd?" Aria asked.

"Not odd, bizarre. Why wouldn't Max Formande, a director known for brilliant casting, give that role to the younger and more gifted Linné Colbert? And to make Colbert an understudy? What was he thinking?"

"So, age is your criteria?" challenged Roche. "That a woman of forty can't deliver like a woman in her twenties?" Before Mesur could respond, he added, "And let's not forget, my friend, that it was illegal for women to act in Shakespeare's day. So, having a woman of any age on the stage would have been shocking."

Aria watched the two men, amused by their verbal sparring.

9

"And yet," teased Roche, "you're over the moon about Solange Gabriel, a woman playing a character half her age."

"Solange Gabriel is ageless!"

Roche's laugh filled the space around them. "My God, man," he declared. "She's in her eighties! Not even a makeup artist can hide that."

"Solange at eighty is more vibrant, more alluring than most women of forty," Mesur said.

The warning lights flashed again. Roche gestured for Aria to enter the theater. Turning, he said, "We can have this conversation later. Brioche Café?"

The audience settled down quickly.

The house lights dimmed to black, and a spot came up on the stage. Solange, Queen Gertrude, made her entrance, this time to silence. She crossed to the chair positioned directly under the spotlight. Her posture, the way she held her head, suggested that some kind of inquisition was about to take place, and that this chair was, in fact, her throne. She said, "Have I not performed like a mother to her?"

Her lines spoken, she fell silent. Seconds passed, nothing happened. "Have I not performed like a mother to her?" she repeated.

Again, nothing. After another pause, she stood with effort, crossed the stage, and disappeared into the wings.

There was a heavy silence, followed by a rustling of movement. Aria felt tension make its way through the audience, until a white noise of whispering filled the room. Roche looked around, as if the missing actor might be seated nearby.

Max Formande appeared at Roche's side. His face was pasty, his brow lined with concern.

"Uncle Max, what is it?" Aria asked.

His eyes never left Roche's face. "You must come with me," he whispered, his voice nearly a cry. He was so distraught that he didn't glance Aria's way.

Roche stood at once and followed him up the aisle.

Aria rose and ran to catch up as the men raced through the lobby.

This was big. She could feel it in her bones. For the first time in months, her heart was pounding the way it did whenever something unknown, challenging, exciting, even dangerous lay ahead. As a journalist, she had felt this rush many times.

They passed through a door that opened onto a dimly lit corridor. There were several more doors, all closed but one. Aria saw that Max was about to enter that room, but was stopped when Roche placed his hand on his shoulder. "Let me," Roche said gently.

Max resisted, and then his shoulders—his entire posture—suddenly sagged. In the next moment, Aria was at his side, her arm across his back, and she held him there while Roche stepped into the room. She moved close enough to peer inside.

Camilla Rodolfo was on the floor. The gash in her throat was so deep she was nearly decapitated. A pool of blood had formed around her head and shoulders. Sprays of blood ran in little rivulets down the mirror attached to a dressing table, and more blood covered some of the overturned bottles. Aria tasted the crêpe she had eaten only minutes earlier.

Roche moved closer and then knelt, a man who had done this before—many times.

Someone was retching, and she turned, expecting to find Max unable to tolerate the gore. Instead, it was Roche's friend, Jean-Philippe. He was gripping the door jamb with one hand, the other hand pressed against his mouth. Roche quickly stood and went to his friend, taking him by the arm and leading him into the corridor. Turning, he called out to the gathering crowd of actors, staff, and crew, "No one is to enter." Then he gestured to Aria, who walked Max back several feet.

In that moment, a thought struck her: as long as she was helpful, she could stay.

Chapter Two

Roche would have preferred to be alone in the dressing room with the mutilated body of Camilla Rodolfo, but this journalist would not leave his side. So far, she was not in the way, and she seemed to respect the protocol required at a crime scene, but he still wanted to send her off, banish her. And wouldn't de Charbonnet love that! Roche wasn't deceived by the bastard's insistence that Aria had been brought here to write about the excellent work of a homicide team. The man wanted Roche out and replaced by someone more fitting. That is, more socially prominent and well-connected. Someone who hadn't grown up on a pig farm.

He knelt, peering at the wound, while at the same time taking out his cell phone and hitting the button that connected him to the precinct. "I need Forensics at Théâtre Junot," he said. "The full team. That means detectives Kumar and Berglof. I don't care what they're doing, find them."

He moved to the dressing table and studied the bottles, their contents still dripping onto the floor, and the pattern of blood spatters on the mirror. A wig hung from a wall hook next to the mirror.

He stepped away from the table and began to circle Camilla Rodolfo, careful not to step in the blood pooling around her. It was too easy to contaminate a scene, especially during that first look, when emotions are running high and the clinical mode has not yet clicked into place.

The room was stifling, the air heavy with death. He knelt again, taking a closer look at Camilla. In life, she was a beauty, lovely and purported to be charming. Not so in death. A towel was stuffed into her mouth, distorting her disfigured face even more.

He leaned closer. The flesh across her neck was hanging open, revealing her hyoid bone.

Twenty minutes later, while Roche was still examining the corpse and the contents of the dressing room, Anuj Kumar appeared. He had been part of Roche's team for several years, a transplant from Bombay who brought a keen and sometimes creative perspective to their work. In the short time that he'd been working under Roche, he was proving himself invaluable. Where Roche could be abrupt, sometimes to the point of rude, Anuj remained calm.

"Ah, good," Roche said, standing with some effort. "Anyone call the prosecutor?"

Anuj nodded, saying nothing, his eyes riveted to the body as he handed nitrile gloves to the inspector. His focus was so intense that he did not notice Aria standing nearby.

"Thanks," said Roche, pulling them on as he peered even closer. As team leader of this homicide squad, he knew better than to make a move without a prosecutor present. Unlike U.S. law, the prosecutor attends crime scenes and is not adversarial. Roche welcomed this presence. His team did things by the books, and the prosecutor would note their attention to procedure and defend the team, if accusations of misconduct were made.

Roche watched Anuj circle Camilla and then crouch down. He was reminded of a giant spider, legs spindly. After a moment, Anuj bounced back up. Youth, he thought.

"What do we have, Boss?" he asked, pushing a shock of black hair from his forehead.

Before Roche could respond, Tenna Berglof rushed in. She gave Aria a brief glance and a nod, pulled on her gloves, and squatted onto her haunches.

Tenna was the other member of his team, and quite different from Anuj in several ways. Where he was tall and lanky, she was short and stocky. Not overweight, but her body was strong, the kind of musculature required of a police officer who restrained people. Where Anuj had straight black hair, hers was Scandinavian blonde, and pulled back into a long braid. Tenna was more talkative than Anuj, often thinking aloud with no awareness of others around her. When it came to high tech, there was no one better. Roche knew very little about her private life, other than she was married and had two sons in boarding school in Sweden. She and her husband had moved to Paris from Stockholm, and he was working for one of the Swedish agencies at NATO. Like Anuj, her French was excellent.

Roche saw that Aria was pressed into a corner with Max Formande, whose back was to the room. Roche guessed he was in shock. But then he saw the little green light emanating from Aria's hand. It seemed that, even if he threatened her, nothing would stop this woman from activating her recorder.

"Nasty," said Tenna, shifting her weight to study the body from another angle.

Roche knew it was purposeless to respond. When Tenna was laser-focused, she heard nothing.

"Give it a good look," Roche instructed his team. "Let me know any observations you make before Forensics arrives."

He noted how quickly Anuj joined Tenna, both of them squatting, one on either side of the body, murmuring to each other.

The low hum of voices and movement was interrupted when Max stepped forward. "Inspector?" He was cupping his hand next to his eye, head turned away.

Roche glanced at Aria, who, like Max, seemed to be awaiting his reply. "This is a crime scene, sir," Roche told him. His voice was measured, calm. The old man had experienced enough trauma; he didn't need to feel badgered by this detective.

"Yes, well, that might be," said Max, pulling himself up to full height. "But you know what they say, Inspector: the show must go on."

Roche looked closely and noted how pale Max was, how his hands trembled. "Seriously?"

"I could not be more serious. We have a full house, a full cast, and only one night to make this play memorable."

"And a dead woman," Roche reminded him.

Max gave him a long look. "That's what understudies are for."

Before Roche could respond, the director turned and left the room. The inspector glanced at Aria, who gave him a wide-eyed look, suggesting she was helpless to control the man.

Within one short minute, the speakers in the building came alive.

"My friends," said the voice of Max Formande. "Due to unavoidable circumstances, the role of Ophelia will be played by Linné Colbert. Enjoy the performance."

One by one, doors to the line of dressing rooms opened, and the actors appeared.

"For Camilla!" Max declared, gesturing down the hallway. "And to the memory of this noble theater!"

Solange and Bertrand moved slowly towards the door leading to the wings. Behind them was a young woman Roche had not yet met, but he guessed she worked for the Gabriels, judging by her proximity to the couple. The Gabriels were followed by Anton Delant, recognizable to Roche from magazine covers and tell-all newspapers. Behind Delant was Linné Colbert, the film star who was understudy to Camilla Rodolfo. And in their wake was Max Formande, clapping his hands and calling out, "Take your places, we're finishing this play!"

Chapter Three

Aria remained in the room, the smell of blood and excrement all around her. She watched Anuj and Tenna working together, a team in harmony. She tried to quell a growing excitement. She was watching a major story unfold, something more memorable than a series on opioids, and certainly more fascinating than following a homicide team around and putting up with its boss. As much as she would love to walk away from this assignment, return the generous fee paid by de Charbonnet's office and focus on this story, she saw no other choice.

She directed her recorder toward the young detectives. The last thing she wanted was to miss even one word. At the same time, her eyes were never still, always moving, scanning. She pressed her back against the wall, hoping this might make her invisible to Roche, who was going through the drawers in the dressing table. Aria had no doubt that he was unyieldingly harsh with anyone hovering around his crime scenes who had no solid reason for being there. She tried to catch Tenna's attention, but the woman was studying her clipboard.

"We need a list of everyone in the theater," Roche said, his eyes never leaving the contents of the open drawer.

Before Tenna could reply, Anuj said, "You're asking that of Wonder Woman?" His eyes were almost laughing. "The woman who effortlessly gathers data that mere mortals struggle to find?"

Tenna looked up from Camilla's corpse, but said nothing.

"Every team needs its tech guru, right?" said Aria.

Anuj turned to Roche. "This goes beyond a crime of anger, don't you

16

think? I'm a detective, not a psychologist, but—"

"Those two aren't so different," said Aria. "I've watched those disciplines cross over many times."

"Oh, you've met my mother!" said Anuj.

"I'm not sure what—" began Aria, but she was cut off by the young detective.

"She's a psychologist who fancies herself a detective, and swears I fancy myself a psychologist."

"If you'd stayed in India and stuck with psychology," Tenna said, "you'd be making more money and sleeping longer hours."

"If I'd stayed in India," he countered, "I never would've met Maryam."

Tenna turned to Aria. "The love of his life, stuck in Ethiopia until her travel visa comes through."

"You'll have to watch Act Two without me," Roche told Aria,

She nearly laughed when she caught Anuj and Tenna exchanging glances, their expressions announcing *Whoa, wait a minute! He was in the theater with her? Like...a date?*

"Come back and tell me how it ends," Roche said, his voice almost wistful.

"It's a spinoff from Shakespeare," said Tenna. "Everyone falls in love, commits adultery, then dies."

Max Formande entered the room. "Thought you'd want to know, we're about to start Act Two."

Roche turned to his young inspectors. "Make sure no one leaves the theater after the play."

"You're joking, right?" said the director. "To even consider keeping the audience—"

"Not the audience," Roche said, cutting him off. "The cast, crew, and your staff."

Formande shrugged and left the room.

"What about the audience?" Tenna said.

"Get names and contact information as they leave the theater. With a hundred seats, it shouldn't be difficult. Be sure to check their tickets and note where they were seated."

Aria wondered how this murder would be viewed by de Charbonnet. And would it matter that Roche was in the theater when it happened? Judging by the condition of Camilla and the hubbub sure to take place when her murder was publicized, Roche might have a reason to worry. Would de Charbonnet dwell on the convenience of it, especially if he was looking for cracks in the inspector's armor? If he found any, that could make Roche vulnerable, even replaceable. Not that he would think Roche in any way involved in the death, but there would be newspapers hounding him for information. He would be the central focus of what could be the most dramatic crime in decades.

If there was one question that niggled at Aria after that meeting with Georges de Charbonnet, it was why he was so determined for her to write these articles. Did he want to support Noah Roche…or bring him down?

She almost felt sorry for Roche, having to deal with her, an American journalist who didn't take nonsense from anyone. If she were Roche, she would fear that her weaknesses might end up in one of those articles. And if Roche feared this, it would certainly heighten the tension between them.

She adjusted her thoughts, telling herself that no matter how calculating de Charbonnet might be, he couldn't possibly see Roche's presence in the theater as anything more than a coincidence. She could always put in the article how fortuitous it was that Roche was at the scene when the murder was committed, how this allowed him to close off the area, get the names of everyone in the building, and begin the investigation at once. She could spin it.

As much as she wanted to resist Roche's tough demeanor, nothing would be served by antagonizing the one person who, at the moment, was deciding her fate.

"Go watch the play," said Tenna, a hand on her arm. "There's nothing we can do until the science squad shows up. I'll fill you in, if anything happens."

"Thank you," Aria said. She handed her recorder to Tenna.

"I'll get it all," she said, making a show of holding it towards the room.

"Everyone," the inspector announced. "It's going to be a long night, and we have a job to do."

"I'll call Klemens," said Tenna, punching a button on her mobile phone. It rang only once before everyone in the room heard the man's voice. "An all-nighter," she told him.

Aria watched Tenna's face shift to something she couldn't read.

"It's my job," Tenna said. "Yes, I know we're out of coffee. Could you please pick some up?" She listened to his response. "Fine, no problem, I'll do it, just not sure when." The man's voice rose in volume. "Gotta go," she said, and ended the call. "He hates it when I'm home late. And the more important the case, the angrier he gets."

The room fell eerily quiet. Aria thought this was the best time to return to the theater. She suspected that Tenna was right, that until the forensics team began working, nothing could be done. She'd seen enough crime scenes to know the procedure.

As she was leaving the room, she nearly ran into Jean-Philippe Mesur.

"Still here?" she heard Roche ask.

"I'm a theater reviewer, remember?" he said.

"So, shouldn't you be in the theater, watching the play?"

"The drama isn't on the stage."

With that, Roche took his friend by the arm and walked him into the corridor. Turning back, he entered the crime scene and firmly closed the door, leaving Jean-Philippe and Aria in the hallway.

"I guess he told us!" Jean-Philippe said, extending his elbow.

Aria linked her arm through his and they made their way to the wings, stage left, where they could not be seen by the audience or the actors, and Aria could easily rejoin the team without causing a disruption. From her vantage point, the faces in the audience were illuminated to a soft glow.

There was a buzz running through the audience, and it continued until Solange Gabriel made her entrance and repeated her lines. This time, it was Linné Colbert who entered from the wings.

Aria studied the actors, then the audience. A frisson ran through her: there was a killer among them.

The actors moved around the stage delivering their lines, fully engaged in the story, but Aria had no such focus. "Sorry," she murmured to Jean-

Philippe. "I can't do this." Before he could respond, she turned and walked away.

As she approached the dressing room, a pain ran through her jaw. Tension. The need to prove herself. She was no fool: Roche wanted her to leave. But if she walked away from this assignment, what did that say about her?

Inside Camilla's dressing room, she found Roche inspecting the drawers in the vanity, pushing around the contents, reading labels.

He looked up, saw her, and released a sigh.

Anuj was using a fountain pen to push through stacks of papers, envelopes, and little porcelain knick-knacks that sat in a bookcase wedged next to the vanity. Tenna was holding a jar of makeup in one hand and jotting down notes with the other. A man Aria had not seen before was standing to the side, his back against the wall. He was watching everyone's movements, his head turning to catch each comment, each conversation. It took Aria a moment to realize that this was the prosecutor, an essential element during the study of a crime scene. She nearly approached him, but he pushed away from the wall and left the room.

She walked over to where Tenna was going through a wardrobe closet. "Thank you," she said, when Tenna handed her the recorder.

Aria moved to the side, out of the way, and watched how everyone was moving with caution, a reminder that forensics experts didn't appreciate a policeman's DNA contaminating the evidence.

As much as she fought the impulse, her eyes were drawn again to Camilla. More than anything, she wanted to cover the woman's face, give her the respect and dignity she could not demand for herself. But she knew this was about protecting evidence, and until the forensic work was done and the pathologist had made a thorough on-the-scene inspection of the environs and the victim, the body would remain where it lay.

The body.

The victim.

Camilla Rodolfo.

At least here, there were no onlookers, but she knew very well how quickly word of a high-profile crime could spread, and she didn't doubt that a phalanx of reporters and photographers was pressing to gain entrance to the theater. What a coup, if one of them could capture the image of the disfigured face of the woman considered among the most beautiful in Europe.

Aria raised her phone. If anyone was going to take the photo that would be shared with the world, why not her? A shudder ran through her. She lowered her phone and drew her eyes away from the massive wounds and the blood-soaked gown. She wondered how many people were walking outside the theater, locals and tourists sauntering along rue Junot or the busy rue des Abbesses, without any knowledge of this historic play, or the fate of Camilla Rodolfo, her face displayed on the billboard at the entrance to the theater; or the elderly couple repeating the roles they had performed a half century earlier.

Aria was worried about that couple, the Gabriels, who would be exhausted from the performance and the death of Camilla. Soon, they would be in their dressing room awaiting word that they could go home.

"Where's Tenna?" Roche asked.

Aria looked around. "She was just here."

"I passed her down the hall," said Anuj. "She's talking to—" He checked a little notepad. "Sashkie Ferrer, Solange Gabriel's assistant. I believe she's known as her dresser." Almost as an afterthought, he added, "It seems her boss can be...challenging."

Aria nearly responded, but what would she say? That Solange was easy? That she was kind?

A crescendo of noise rose around them.

"Sounds like the play's over," said Anuj. He suddenly dropped into a squatting position, peered at Camilla's feet, then rocked back on his heels. "Boss, where are her shoes?"

Aria looked around and saw them under the vanity. Not side by side, as they would be if Camilla had slipped them off while seated at the table, but with one shoe upside down, and the other shoved against the wall.

"Wearing them when she was attacked," Anuj said.

"Looks that way," Roche agreed.

Anuj moved closer, his mouth pursed. "So, she's seated here, touching up her make-up for Act Two. Someone comes up from behind and slits her throat."

There was another roar from the theater, robust and joyful, in sharp contrast to the mood in this room.

Three faces appeared at the door. Before Roche could speak, a woman and two men were pulling white garments over their street clothes, white booties over their shoes, and snapping on white latex gloves. They strapped on white oversized safety goggles, then pulled on white bouffant scrub caps.

Aria watched them prepare for their examination of the crime scene. Their appearance brought to mind the Michelin man.

After a flurry of movement that included opening large boxes with honeycomb-like compartments, the forensics team went to work.

Tenna walked in and gave a quick look to the scientists. "The night has just begun."

"And a long night it will be," said Roche. "Let's leave them to their work and grab a bite."

Aria rushed out of the room for a quick visit to the bathroom. When she returned, Roche and the others were gone.

She wasn't hungry, but that didn't diminish her sense of being left out. Had they intentionally done that? Perhaps they thought she'd be close behind, or that she had heard the name of where they were eating and would join them. She tried to shake off this feeling of being excluded and refocus on what lay before her, but it persisted—like barnacles affixed to her skin.

She reminded herself that she was in the middle of a story to which no other journalist had access. Not in France; not in the world, and it was imperative that she stay close to this team.

Noises in her stomach told her that she needed to eat, if only for the fuel to keep going.

She walked into the hallway, now eerily quiet, all onlookers gone, and followed the route that returned her to the lobby and out the front door, where she was accosted by a noise level she found deafening. A collection of journalists and photographers were pushing and shoving to enter the theater. When they saw Aria, they began to shout, "Who was it?" and "Is it true that one of the actors was murdered?"

When she said nothing, one man called out, "And who in the hell are you?"

She elbowed her way through the crowd and rushed off. When she was halfway down the block, she looked back and was relieved that no one was pursuing her.

There was a neon sign flashing in a window, and she was relieved to discover that it was a café. Standing at the entrance, she wished they served something other than falafels.

The place was the size of a closet, with two tables, one of them unoccupied. She gave her order to the old man who greeted her, and then she sat down. Despite the hour, there were people wandering about the street. A couple dressed in matching sweat suits was trying to read a map of Paris, using the light from their mobile. Americans they were, Southern accents and all. Aria nearly stepped outside to help them find their way, but she couldn't muster the energy.

Several people passed by, some holding hands, others walking alone. One man was being pulled along by a very large dog on a leash. He gripped the leash with both hands, green plastic bags hanging from his pocket. Watching all these people made her wonder if her life would ever return to normal.

A teenage boy arrived with a plate of falafels, humus, and two pitas, their aroma suggesting they were fresh from the oven. He presented it all with a flourish, a coveted prize.

She ate so quickly she hardly tasted the food.

When he returned, there was surprise on his face. Who could possibly consume so much...and so fast?

"A thief," she explained. "He grabbed my food and escaped."

The young man smiled. "And did this thief desire coffee?"

"As a matter of fact," she said, "espresso, a double shot. With a touch of steamed milk."

She loved this city.

The waiter arrived a few minutes later with her espresso. He tossed her euros into his apron pocket. "Did you hear about the excitement at the theater? We have our share of murders, but this one—"

"A terrible thing," she said.

"I hear someone broke in during intermission and killed one of the actresses. Probably a robbery gone wrong."

Aria wasn't surprised that the news had hit the street. How long before this young man, working a short distance from the crime scene, would be approached by journalists demanding *What do you know? What did you see? How would he respond, when offered encouragement—perhaps in the form of a pay-off?*

It was such a delicate line between truth and supposition. She thought of her first meeting with Noah Roche only hours earlier. After the events of the past few hours, it felt like days ago. In any case, it had not gone well, not well at all.

Her arrival in Paris that morning was followed by a quick stop at the Hotel Esmeralda on the Left Bank and then a taxi to her meeting with Georges de Charbonnet, the man who had orchestrated this writing assignment. She was disappointed that the headquarters for the Regional Directorate of the Judicial Police were no longer at 36, quai des Orfèvres, a building that always made her think of Inspector Maigret. Today, nearly all police-related departments were in the new building located at rue du Bastion, in the quarter known as Batignolles, a short distance from the Porte de Clichy. The venerated old headquarters was wistfully referred to as *Thirty-six,* whereas the new center was simply *Bastion.*

She was concerned about being late, with traffic delays as common as boulangeries.

Her taxi pulled up before the six-story, glass-walled building. It was undoubtedly high-tech to the max, but it was no Thirty-six. Inspector Maigret wouldn't have been caught dead here.

Despite the letter from de Charbonnet explaining the reason for their meeting about an assignment that required she fly nearly six thousand miles, she had little idea of what awaited her.

There were several security checkpoints, each one more restrictive than the one before, and taking up so much time she feared she would be late.

After she was given a badge, her purse was returned, and she walked across the lobby.

The half-dozen people on the elevator stared at the ceiling.

The door slid open, and she stepped into what appeared to be an anteroom. There was a wall of thick glass—bulletproof, no doubt—with a sign above it that announced *Criminal Brigade*.

The woman seated behind the glass was gray-haired, her expression steely. Aria wondered if she ever smiled. "Aria Nevins. Georges Charbonnet is expecting me."

The woman adjusted her headset and punched a few numbers into the phone. "Your appointment is here, sir." She reached under her desk.

Aria heard the click and pulled open the door leading into the main office.

The receptionist held up a hand. "If you want to start on the right foot, my dear..."

Aria felt her jaw tense. "Yes?"

"It's Georges de Charbonnet. He's very particular about the *de*. Aristocracy and all that."

Aria smiled and mouthed a silent "Thank you," chastising herself for having judged this woman unkindly.

She crossed the threshold just as a man appeared, his hand extended. She shook it, his grip so firm she nearly winced. She hoped he wasn't noticing how she was bending a bit to match his height.

"Welcome to Paris. I hope you find your hotel accommodations satisfactory." His eyes almost sparkled with conviviality.

"I was there long enough to drop off my bag, Monsieur de Charbonnet, but it seems lovely, thank you."

He smiled. "Please, you can dispense with the *de* part. I find it pretentious. You were undoubtedly warned by my keeper of the gate. She's the only one who's impressed. Using my full family name makes her think her boss is aristocratic. I assure you, that is not the case." Without awaiting a response, he turned and walked away, as if certain she would be close behind.

They crossed the room, following an aisle that passed a dozen desks, the men and women seated at them wearing business suits and looking more like corporate attorneys than police officers. "A small part of my staff," de Charbonnet explained. "We do it all here, from PR to legal. Under my supervision, we oversee all divisions that come under the homicide label. I allocate the cases; my team makes sure investigations are properly executed. Protocol followed, everything by the law, fair and equitable. When there's doubt, we have an oversight group that steps in, and public relations experts who know how to put out fires."

On the door leading into his office was *Director of National Police*. Her research had informed her that his job was to allocate criminal cases to the units under his supervision. She also learned that his senior criminal unit supervisor was Noah Roche, and it had been several years since he was promoted to head the famous Criminal Brigade, one of the investigation units, and the one in charge of the most sensitive cases.

The office was a private space separated from the main room by a wall of glass. It was nearly identical to the office of Izzy Martinez, her former boss at the San Francisco newspaper. He was the managing editor who had done everything possible to save her job, but had failed.

She shook the thought away and sat in the only uncluttered chair. The other three held stacks of folders, books, a few laptops, and assorted articles of clothing.

"Now, Madame Nevins—"

"Please, it's Aria."

He leaned back in a chair that was elegant, leather, and well-worn—the kind of chair one takes from job to job. "First, I want to thank you for coming all this way. San Francisco is the other side of the world. Also, allow me to commend you on your elegant French."

"My parents are French, and I've lived here throughout parts of my childhood," she said, warmed by the memory. "I attended university here for two years, and I still have family scattered around the country, including a brother living in Paris. How could I resist?"

"How, indeed," he responded.

Her eyes never left his face. He knew. She had come to France because it was the only job anyone had offered—this is what happens when you fall from grace.

Seated across from him, she searched for signs of judgment, but he wasn't easy to read. "How was it that you chose me?" she asked. "France is brimming with outstanding journalists."

"When I was looking, it had to be someone not living in France. How better to avoid even the suggestion of bias? A colleague had read your work and recommended you. You are fluent in French, and also comfortable with the nuances of our language, those little phrases and inflections that differentiate so many innocent statements from something derogatory or hurtful."

She certainly knew about derogatory and hurtful. Hate mail, messages left on her phone at the paper, even at home. Did de Charbonnet know about her name being removed from potential Pulitzer recipients? Of course, he did.

"I realize that we discussed this over the phone," he said. "But it's important that you have a full grasp of my purpose. We've recently had, shall we say, bad press. A very difficult case that has threatened to tear at the heart of the city. A young man died while in custody, a Senegalese immigrant suspected of running an illegal gambling house."

"And was he?" Aria asked.

"I beg your pardon?"

"Running an illegal gambling house. Was he guilty? I'm no stranger to charges of police negligence, even brutality. You said he died in custody." She saw his expression change, harden, and she quickly added, "We're none of us exempt from those claims."

He made a sound under his breath.

"So, to be clear," she said quickly. "I'm to become part of your team, observe how all of you respond to a crime. Focus on your interactions, and how your team works under duress. Is this correct?"

He shook his head, made a little *tsk-tsk* sound, and ticked his finger back and forth, characteristic of the French way to announce that something has been misunderstood. "I am not the subject of your observations. No, you will be with the team of Chief Inspector Noah Roche. I won't give you any background on him, other than to say he worked his way up through the ranks, starting at the bottom. He's not from a prestigious family, nor is he the son of a high-ranking officer, yet his success rate for solving cases is the highest in Paris, perhaps all of France. He's closing this case—the young Senegalese who died in our jail—and is now with the boy's father, a storekeeper in Chateau Rouge. You know the neighborhood?"

"In the 18th Arrondissement, near Montmartre, yes?"

"Right." He looked away. "No doubt, he'll resolve it well, as he always does. In fact, he's wrapping it up as we speak."

Aria wondered if Roche's success disappointed de Charbonnet, because he looked less than impressed. "And his team: do I include them in my articles?"

"Roche has put together a rather eclectic team," de Charbonnet said. "Two young detectives—one from India, the other from Sweden. They're both very capable, and seemingly indispensable to Roche. This has not made them popular among their fellow detectives, as you can imagine."

"Because they're foreign?" she asked.

"I prefer to say it's because they are not French-born."

Aria was tempted to sing *tomato, tomahto,* but reminded herself that it was almost comical for an American to judge anyone who cast doubt or suspicion upon the immigrant population. In the States, racial stereotyping was uglier than it had been in decades.

She nearly told him that she, too, was not French-born, and that she felt as if she were the interloper, the American writing about the French. Instead, she said, "This investigation...into the death of this young man..."

His expression stopped her cold. "There were multiple departments involved, from homicide to community relations. He was killed by another inmate. The victim was Senegalese, his killer from Algeria. Always a delicate matter, potentially explosive. But then, being an American, you understand all too well."

Aria felt the verbal slap, but said nothing.

"One thing I do want to stress," he said. "You must go into this as a neutral observer, someone who knows nothing about any previous cases. Yes," he quickly added, holding up both hands. "You're a journalist, and I read something about a Pulitzer—" He left the sentence hanging, as if certain she would get his drift.

She had no way of knowing if he was being kind or crafty. What she did know was that there weren't many investigative journalists mentioned as a possible Pulitzer recipient and then removed from the list, a fact she expected to be mentioned in her obituary.

She was in the office less than five minutes and was already regretting having taken this assignment. Had she been fully engaged at the newspaper, swamped with work, she would have remained in San Francisco. But there was no job, no projects, not even the promise of any, not until his offer arrived. Anyway, this was Paris. She could visit old friends, perhaps bury the hatchet with her brother. She and Martin had never been close, but he was her only sibling, nearly four years younger, and her mother was desperate for them to have a loving relationship. Aria would settle for a short, polite meeting, but even that felt like a stretch.

She also intended to spend more time with Bertrand and Solange Gabriel, as well as Max Formande. He, too, was an old family friend and was directing the play she was seeing that night. The Gabriels and Max were woven into her life like golden threads in a tapestry.

She realized that de Charbonnet was speaking. "Forgive me," she said. "Being in Paris is like coming home, with wonderful memories rising to the surface."

"Inspector Roche is expecting you tomorrow morning," he said, crossing to his office door. "If you run into any problems, you know where to find me."

"Tomorrow?" she repeated. "I'm ready to begin now."

"They're all at the Chateau Rouge site, so, I'm afraid—"

"Give me the address and I'll find them," she said. "I'm ready to work." She patted her bag, sure that he'd understand that whatever she needed was at hand.

"He won't be pleased," de Charbonnet said, a tinge of warning in his voice. She was too tired to argue, but there was no way she would back down.

"If I don't begin now, I'll lose a full day of observations."

He shrugged. "Have it your way. Please keep in mind that you're documenting how the team works together, nothing about this case with the Africans. We've managed to calm those choppy waters." He turned back to his desk, jotted down an address, and handed it to her. "He should still be there. It's the shop owned by the young man's father."

He led her through the large room and stopped near the receptionist's desk. "You have one week to follow the team," he said. "And I'll expect to read your first article two weeks from now." He shook her hand and turned to leave.

"One more thing," she said, causing him to swivel around. "Where will this series run? And how many articles are you expecting?"

He stared at her for a long moment. "At least four, and I've no idea where I'll have them published."

"But I'll have a say," she stated, hoping her voice sounded professional, free from the annoyance creeping into it.

"Actually, I'll decide after I've read your work."

Aria's mouth formed a tight line. "So, you'll have full editorial control."

"Did you not read the contract that you signed? You're being paid generously, all living and travel expenses included. It's only logical that I…we…own the results."

Aria watched him walk away. She had a growing suspicion that he had hired her for a specific reason, perhaps an ulterior motive, but she had no idea what that could be. At least, not yet.

The elevator carried her to the ground floor, and she left the building, fatigue pushing her into a cab. She gave the driver the address in Chateau Rouge and leaned back, hoping to regain even a fraction of energy during the short ride.

"Ah, the African quarter," said the cabbie, his voice suggesting they were about to enter a foreign and not necessarily friendly country. "Big trouble, dangerous." He glanced at her through his rear-view mirror.

The man was white, middle-aged, and soft around the middle. Obese, in fact. She had no desire to get into a verbal jousting contest.

"The Blacks," he went on. "What was our government thinking?"

Aria bit back a response. Arguing with this guy was useless. "Could you please turn on the radio?" she asked politely.

She nearly laughed when Stevie Wonder's voice filled the cab.

Twenty minutes later, they stopped at the foot of a narrow road, made impassable by the vendors' stalls erected along the cobblestones. "There," said the cabbie, pointing up the little road. "And good luck."

Aria paid the fare and climbed out. The neighborhood was alive with activity. There were window displays that looked like vibrant paintings, and behind the panes of glass were row upon row of goods. One shop sold spices, saffron, and turmeric, their vibrant yellows and oranges reminiscent of still-life paintings. There were deep, rich tamarinds and clusters of cilantro so green they had to have been harvested that same morning.

Across the way was a fish shop, the day's large catches suspended on hooks from the ceiling. And fruit stands with every kind of fruit, including a few she had never seen. And the vegetables!

But it was the textiles that caught her breath. Florals and geometrics, from subtle to vivid. If her mother were here, she would keep the vendors racing around, gathering bolts and measuring off lengths. What fashion designer would not love this neighborhood?

Aria checked the slip of paper offered by de Charbonnet and found the shop, its window displaying what she thought must have been every imaginable gadget and adornment for sewing. She stepped inside. The place looked small at first glance, but then she saw another room triple the size of this one and separated by an archway. She approached the larger room and stopped. Three people were seated with an old man, their body language suggesting they were protecting him. She remained where she was, out of their line of sight, yet able to hear the conversation.

"What will happen to the man who killed my son?" asked the old man, his voice pleading. "My boy wasn't a bad person; he didn't deserve this. He was a good boy!"

"We're doing what we can." The speaker was young, his skin dark.

Aria recalled the conversation with de Charbonnet and assumed this was the detective from India.

"You know how it goes, sir," the young man continued. "If you're from the same country, it's like family. Everyone protects everyone else, guilty or innocent."

The old man squeezed his hands into fists and banged them against his knees. "But he was being held for gambling! Why would someone want him dead?"

"The judge will consider all the facts," said the woman, her voice warm, her long braid swinging against her shoulder as she spoke.

The Swede, Aria decided, still holding back from making her presence known.

"We'll do what we can," repeated the young man. "Won't we, Inspector?"

The shopkeeper turned to the man she was certain was Chief Homicide Inspector Noah Roche. "He was a good boy," he repeated.

Without a word, Inspector Roche touched the old man's shoulder, stood, and walked towards the shop entrance, his young detectives close behind.

Before they had passed into the front of the store, Roche turned back. "I know this is difficult," he said, his voice softer. "We'll do everything we can."

The old man shook his head, gave a little wave of his hand, and disappeared through a door.

As Roche and his two officers moved towards the street, Aria approached them. "Chief Inspector Roche?"

"Do I know you?" he asked, but he may as well have said, "Who in the hell are you!"

Aria introduced herself.

"You were expected in my office tomorrow morning," Roche said. "Please meet me then." With that, he opened the front door and stepped onto the sidewalk.

She followed him. "That may be," she said, "but here I am. So, let's not waste time." She tried to smile, but failed. Aria had met more than a few tough nuts during her long career, and one of her great challenges—in truth, one of her great pleasures—was her ability to crack them.

"We're going back to the precinct," Roche said. Was he hoping to dissuade her? He made no effort to introduce the others.

She gave him a long look. "Lead the way."

Chapter Four

Noah Roche preferred not to ride in the passenger seat of a police car. It brought back memories of being a rookie, a junior, the rough-hewn kid who never belonged. However, as he was climbing into the driver's side, his glasses fell onto the road and the temple piece broke off. Without a word, he handed the keys to Anuj and walked around to what the Americans call the *shotgun seat*. He considered this propitious: it would give him time to think about how he would handle this Aria woman.

Tenna was seated in the back with her. He didn't ask for her, and he certainly didn't want her around. With Anuj and Tenna by his side, they would make sure this interloper watched her step. But really, how difficult could she be? He had faced off with some of France's most notorious criminals, killers all, some of them devilishly cunning, employing firearms and arson, poisons and letter bombs. There was the occasional garroting, and the mundane, such as a pillow pressed over a face. Some crimes were memorable. At the top of his list, and likely to remain there, were the teenage brother and sister who took her science project—a guillotine similar to those used during the French Revolution—and tested it on their parents. It worked!

During his career, he had faced the lowest, the slyest, the most manipulative killers, but they seemed to lose their threat when compared to what was facing him now. Wasn't he in charge? The big cheese? Perhaps, but he was not prepared for the bomb that de Charbonnet had dropped on him. A journalist with carte blanche? An American journalist? And a woman!

And now here she was, and he already sensed trouble brewing. He saw it in the set of her jaw, the way she looked at him. Those intense hazel eyes. Or were they green? What did it matter! And he much preferred long hair on a woman, feminine and chic. Hers was short, almost what they called a pixie, popular thirty years ago, when it was fashionable.

Being a policeman meant being observant, often making quick judgments. When he had first seen her, it registered that she was only inches shorter than his six feet. And those eyes were looking right through him. Into his thoughts. He would have to be careful.

Had anyone else assigned this woman to his team, he might have felt less suspicious, but it wasn't just anyone: it was de Charbonnet. The man might be the head of the investigative units, but he wasn't the marionette master he thought he was, someone who could pull the strings and make others follow his command. Roche reminded himself of this again. So why did he feel like a damn puppet?

Roche had joined the force as a traffic cop, barely twenty and working the streets. It had taken more than a decade of hard work and little sleep—while ignoring the needs of his wife and child—to prove himself worthy of sitting for the exams to become an inspector. And now here he was, commander of what was undeniably the most successful homicide unit in Paris. He knew de Charbonnet wanted someone he could manipulate, and knowing that Roche would never bow to his command, what better ploy than to plant a journalist in his team and hope she would uncover the fodder to discredit him? Wouldn't de Charbonnet love that!

Roche grimaced. It would not happen, not on his watch.

There was pressure built into this job. Public recognition, for one. His face was often in newspapers, occasionally on television, and his opinions were printed and repeated as the final word. For most men in his position, it would be great for the ego, but not Chief Inspector Noah Roche. Dozens of people wanted his job, including two of de Charbonnet's buddies who headed their own units smaller than Roche's and without the celebrity that came with it. Both men were vocal about their feelings: they felt cheated that such a nobody could rise to his rank. Were they not from the best families, and had they not attended the most elite schools? And yet here they were, jockeying for his position. What nobody understood was that this post was Roche's ultimate goal. Unlike his detractors, he sought no ladder leading up the hierarchy to some cabinet position, or even higher.

He thought of Judith, his ex-wife, and how she believed that his laser-like commitment to his job had cost them their marriage. Four years after the divorce, and he still struggled to understand. And Luc, their son. Would he ever drop that attitude of entitlement and accept his father? He was nearly thirty, too old for all this adolescent resentment. Perhaps if he found a job—and stuck with it—he wouldn't see his father as little more than a living, walking ATM. He wondered if Judith felt the same, then reminded himself that Luc and Judith were close. She was the parent Luc turned to when needing emotional support. And when he needed money? He didn't play favorites. Whoever came up with the cash was the preferred parent. That is, until the next time.

They pulled into the parking garage. Anuj flashed his badge for the security guard inside the kiosk and then parked the car.

"Anyone hungry?' Roche asked.

With unanimous consent, they crossed the street, entered a little café frequented by all levels of police personnel, and took a table.

There were few words spoken as they read the menu on the chalkboard hanging on the wall behind the bar.

"Suggestions?" Aria asked.

Roche was tempted to say, "Yes, I suggest you leave." Instead, he said, "The chicken sandwich is edible."

"I agree," said Tenna, her French tinged with a Swedish lilt. "But I strongly recommend the Mediterranean dish, Madame. Perhaps..." She paused, as if unsure about something.

"If we're going to be sequestered for a week," Aria said, "please call me Aria." She turned to Noah Roche. "And may I call you Noah?"

He thought: journalist, clever, good with words and innuendo. "In my capacity," he said, "it's important that I'm called Inspector Roche. I'm sure you understand."

She smiled again. "Whatever your team calls you works for me."

Perhaps this wouldn't be as difficult as he had feared. He was relieved when the waitress approached and his two young officers made inquiries about the menu. It gave him time to think about how he would handle this. He had briefed his team about Aria Nevin's arrival and had said nothing to discourage them from accepting her. In truth, he counted on them to stay close and help him deal with this encroachment. "So, now you've met my team," he said. "Our very own version of the Mod Squad."

The young detectives exchanged smiles and remained silent: they had heard this before.

Roche made a little steeple with his fingers. His former wife had pointed out that he did this before making what he considered to be an important statement. Pontificating, that's what she called it. Perhaps this would go more smoothly if he formally introduced his young detectives. "Tenna Berglof has been on my team for two years, a transplant from a homicide unit near Stockholm."

"And charmed by this city," said Aria.

"More like a husband who's charmed," said Tenna. "He accepted a position with NATO, and I followed."

"That can't be easy," murmured Aria.

"Change never is," said Tenna, wrapping the end of her braid around her fingers.

Roche watched Tenna closely. He had learned long ago that, unlike men, two women could meet and within minutes share secrets reserved for trusted friends. Roche had men friends for twenty years who knew little about his private life. Nevertheless, he was quite certain that Tenna would not reveal how her shit of a husband insisted their young sons remain in Sweden, rather than being exposed to the depravities of Paris.

"Two boys," Tenna said. "In a boarding school near Stockholm. Not my decision."

"I have a daughter," Aria was saying. "Lexie. She's nearly thirty."

Roche felt his control slipping away. "And this bright-eyed young man," he announced, "is Anuj Kumar." He watched Aria's expression as she did a quick study of Anuj.

"What a lovely name," she said. "Anuj. It's poetic."

Anuj reached over and shook her hand. "A rather common name in India. It's Sanskrit for *younger brother*, which I've always found interesting, since I'm the only child in the family."

"Are they here?" Aria asked. "Your family?"

"Everyone's in India," he said. "Mother, father, three grandparents, six aunts and uncles, and more cousins than I can count."

"I envy you," Aria said. "I always thought being part of a large family would be wonderful. All that support and love."

Anuj laughed. "Support, love, yes, and also a lot of noise and too many people giving advice, whether I want it or not. Over a family dinner, when I announced that I was moving to France, there were so many relatives swarming around me with warnings and accusations of abandoning my parents and my country, I felt like an invading enemy brought up before the United Nations on charges."

As he spoke, Aria reached into her bag and removed a small recording device. When Anuj saw it, he fell silent.

"We need to discuss this," said Roche.

"Yes, let's," she said.

"What do you hope to…accomplish?" Roche asked.

"Well, when I met with Monsieur de Charbonnet—"

Tenna released a groan. "Ah, yes, de Charbonnet," she repeated. She looked at Roche. "Sorry, Boss."

Roche sighed. She still had much to learn about discretion.

Tenna turned towards Aria. "Need I say more?"

"Please do," responded Aria. "The more I understand about this assignment, the better."

There were glances exchanged between Roche and his team. He knew the American was watching as well. A muted alarm rang in his head. "As I understand it," he said, looking directly at her, "you will join us from our arrival each morning and will remain with us until we leave for home, whenever that is." A thought jumped into his head, and he nearly smiled. "Of course, we sometimes work late into the night. On rare occasions, all night, into the next morning. When that happens, I let my team run home, change clothes, and return to continue the investigation. However," he added, "we rarely do all-nighters."

"I'm not worried," said Aria. "As a journalist, I've had my share."

"No doubt," Roche mumbled.

"About the recorder," she said. "If I have to write my observations, or a recounting of your conversations, I run the risk of getting it wrong. Recorded, that risk doesn't exist. I'll be able to replay conversations, listen to the facts, even get the nuances. It will make for more accurate articles."

"I realize that you must write what you see," said Tenna. "But what if you write something that's not accurate, or that you've misinterpreted?"

"Good point," said Anuj, leaning forward in his chair. "You might assume something that isn't so."

Roche was pleased that his young detectives were asking questions. Better it came from them. If he were asking, it might sound aggressive.

"So, what are you saying?" asked Aria, looking at both Anuj and Tenna. "Are you asking me to let you read the articles before I send them in? To have you as fact-checkers? Or, perhaps, to argue my interpretations of how the three of you relate to each other? Or approach findings? Or even more important, how you conduct interrogations?"

An uncomfortable silence was broken by the arrival of four plates of fried rice, onions and chickpeas stirred into a spicy tomato sauce.

Roche nearly spoke, but reminded himself that if he said nothing, and if his team said nothing, she might provide information about herself. It was an old interrogation technique.

"I can't do that," she said, proving him right, and then waving her hand in the air. "Wait, let me back up. I can certainly check facts with you, but when it comes to how I see your interactions, the way you work together, the way you deal with suspects, or people who might provide information, this must come only from me. Any input from you would be viewed as influencing my impartiality."

"Can anyone really be embedded within a team for a week, get close to the members, and remain completely impartial?" asked Tenna. "I sure couldn't."

Aria tipped her head, which Roche interpreted as tacit agreement. "I do my best," she admitted. "But what's most important, at least for you to know, is that I've always focused on being fair and unbiased."

Roche worked hard to keep his expression unchanged. If he looked directly at her, would she realize that he knew about her past? She must know. Even the head of a homicide team, a man considered by younger officers to be from the Stone Age, was proficient with search engines. Whether he was researching a suspect, getting background on a witness, or going into the case archives to study a specific crime, he did his homework. However, when it came to Aria Nevin's transgression, he had decided that she must be the one to bring it up. "We understand," he said.

Anuj sighed dramatically. "Boss, does that mean we have to hide our brass knuckles and billy clubs?"

Roche smiled, then looked at Aria in time to see her exchange glances with Tenna.

"We just closed a case," Tenna said. "The final days are always exhausting."

"Very sad," Anuj said. "You saw the father. His son died in custody. He was pretty brash, but harmless."

Roche saw Aria put her finger on the recorder button. Before turning it on, she looked at him. He nodded, and she pressed the button.

"Go on, please." She leaned back in the chair and waited.

"Not much to tell," said Tenna. "The man was arrested, and then killed in his cell by a rival who will probably stay in prison for life."

"I'm afraid you've arrived after the excitement," said Roche.

"We're in a lull, but they rarely last," Anuj added.

Roche wanted to be certain this woman understood the rules. She might not like his repeating them, but that was her problem. "You'll stay close, record everything, but share it with no one until it comes out in your article. I'm concerned that you'll slow us down."

"I'll go at your pace," Aria said, looking at Roche. "And the reason I asked about late nights was because I have a ticket for the theater tonight, so I need to leave my hotel by seven. If I don't show up, I'll have to bear the weight of my mother's wrath. Which is no problem, since I'll tell her it was your fault."

He was too tired to engage in any sort of humor, but when she mentioned the play, he felt as if every cell in his body had switched on. "Hamlet's Father?" he asked. He would have killed for a ticket, as would every theater aficionado in France. And he had tried for months. The last thing he wanted to do was share his personal life with this woman, but he couldn't suppress the excitement in his voice. There was only one performance, and in a theater with a hundred seats. "It's easier to book a private dinner with the Pope," he told her.

Aria reached into her bag and pulled out her wallet. Opening it, she slipped out a ticket. "I have two," she said, handing one of them to the inspector. "I'm sure Maman would love you to use hers. Solange and Bertrand Gabriel are old friends, like family."

Without missing a beat—without *oh, I couldn't,* or *are you sure?*—he snatched it from her grasp, slipped the ticket into his pocket, and offered her a brief, but grateful, smile. If getting the ticket meant putting up with this outspoken and pushy woman for a few hours, so be it.

Chapter Five

Roche and his team stood in a hallway of Théâtre Junot so dimly lit they strained to see each other. It ended at a heavy door, black and scarred from a century of use. He rapped on it. "Solid metal." He put his shoulder to it and gave a hefty push, but it didn't budge.

"Let me give it a try," Anuj said. Two shoulder bumps and the door flew open.

They stepped outside, into a passageway that was damp and barely wide enough for two people. Garbage bins were shoved against the opposite wall, each one covered with black grime, and giving off a stench so powerful that Roche stepped back.

"Bacterial stew," Tenna said, retrieving a handkerchief from her coat pocket and pressing it over her nose and mouth.

"Too narrow for deliveries," Anuj said.

Roche craned to see where the pavement ended.

"Hell if I know how these bins get emptied," Anuj said. He studied the door for a moment. "Anyone having business with the theater must know about this door."

Roche gave it a closer scrutiny. "Definitely forced." He pointed to the lock. "Here, see? Someone's altered the faceplate."

Tenna moved closer. "Looks like a screwdriver's been used to pry it loose."

"An outside job?" Anuj suggested.

"Or someone wants us to believe it is," Tenna said.

Aria stepped into the alley and made a gagging sound. She pressed one hand against her nose and mouth; the other hand gripped the recorder, its light glowing in the gloom.

"Eau de Paris," Anuj said. "Aromatic and memorable."

"If you're thinking of buying me a bottle," Aria replied, "save your money."

Roche watched this exchange. Aria seemed respectable enough, reasonable, but could he trust her? He saw her take a few steps toward the bins, step on something slippery, and nearly fall. He grabbed her arm, and she mumbled her thanks.

He turned away and gave the alley a closer inspection, starting with the faceplate on the door.

Tenna was right beside him. She pulled out a little flashlight and bent for a closer look. "I'm betting someone tampered with it to mislead us. You see, here?" She pointed. "Forced, but not enough to disturb the locking mechanism."

A rat raced out from under a garbage bin. Before anyone could respond, there was a second rat, this one even larger. Roche saw Anuj pull his jacket around him, his shoulders trembling. "Let's go inside," the inspector said.

They retraced their steps through the warren of passages and into Camilla's dressing room. Roche did not have to look to know that Aria was behind him. Not lurking, just following closely. He reminded them to discard their gloves and pull on new ones. There was much in that alley that could contaminate the room.

The forensics team was nearly finished. With Camilla Rodolfo still on the floor, there was little conversation. A sign of respect, as well as intense concentration. They all understood that after her body was moved, much of the evidence would be lost.

Roche saw that the pots of makeup, creams, and brushes of various sizes had been bagged and labeled. It bothered him that Camilla had not yet been moved, and relieved that someone had placed a square of sterilized gauze over her face.

"A stabbing is one thing," said Tenna. "But this speaks vengeance, deeply personal."

"I have to agree," said Anuj. "What thief takes time to do...this?"

Roche watched Tenna lift the gauze and study the wounds. He had to give her the same credit he gave Anuj. No matter what her struggles were at home, she performed her work in exemplary fashion. Exemplary fashion? Why not get to the guts of the truth? Tenna Berglof was damn good at her job. She was meticulous, smart, curious, and she always wanted to know more. If Anuj and Tenna were the future of police work, there was hope.

"There's certainly nothing random about this," said Tenna, replacing the fabric.

He saw Aria nearby, watching while her little machine captured every sound, including her own voice whispering observations. Was she also recording judgments about his team? *Concentrate*, he warned himself. *Stay focused.*

"Remarkable," said Tenna, as one of the men picked up something so small it could be seen only with a magnification lens. He slipped it into a clear envelope and held it up to the light, but even then it was not visible to her eye.

"Almost ready for us?" said a familiar voice from the doorway.

Roche turned. "Rafael! Why must we always meet in the most unpleasant circumstances?"

"The nature of the beast," said Rafael, shaking Roche's hand.

Roche heard Tenna explain to Aria that Rafael headed the collection team. "You know, from the morgue."

Rafael glanced at the women. "*Collection team* is a delicate euphemism for *body snatchers*."

"You look far too young to be a body snatcher," Aria said.

"Closing in on fifty."

Roche laughed. "Easy to look young when you've never married or had children."

Rafael grimaced, but his eyes sparkled good-naturedly. "Never too late."

Roche had always considered Rafael to be one of the good guys, a man who cared about the bodies under his command. In the many years they had worked together, he had never seen him lose his composure, nor treat a victim disrespectfully.

Rafael stepped aside to make room for two elderly men pushing a large gurney into the room. "Nasty work, this," he said to Roche, glancing at the corpse. "We don't get many mutilations, thank God." He knelt, removed the gauze, and peered closely. After a moment, he leaned back on his haunches. "Noah, isn't this—?"

Roche felt a tightening in his chest. "Your attention!" he announced, demanding the ear of everyone in the room, down the hallway, and behind closed doors. "If I see one image of this woman's body in the paper—one photo online, on YouTube, social media, anywhere—I'll have your job and your career. Do you understand?"

The words were barely out when it struck him that Aria might capitalize very nicely, both financially and professionally. He glanced over and saw that her recorder was still running, picking up every word he was saying. God, what if she went on one of those talk shows? "The moment you step outside," he continued, "you're going to be approached. You'll be offered money, a great deal of money—as much as a year's salary, even more—in exchange for one photograph of Camilla Rodolfo."

"I'm off to Tahiti," quipped one of the pathologists, his attention never leaving a clump of hair he was placing in an evidence bag.

Tenna shifted closer to Camilla and knelt. "Boss?"

He moved in as she pointed to a smudge on Camilla's sleeve.

He turned to one of the forensics people.

"On it," said the man.

The smudge was pale brown and thick. "Theater makeup," said Tenna. "Now, look at her face: it's not the same shade."

Aria moved into Roche's line of sight. He watched her, expecting her to deliver a swift opinion. She said nothing.

"Well?" he finally asked, more out of curiosity than hoping to gain insight.

"I agree with Tenna," she said. "It's shades lighter than what's on her face."

Roche asked for the evidence bag holding the jar of makeup. "Take swabs," he ordered. "Gather all the makeup in the building. Can you get DNA off that?" he asked the senior member of the team.

"We're swabbing it now," he said. "And yes, we'll do one specifically for DNA." He took what appeared to be a small surgical knife, cut away the fragment of sleeve in question, then passed it to the woman. She smeared it onto a paper-like strip, slipped it into a vial, capped it, and wrote on its label. It joined dozens of samples already stashed in the box.

He turned to Tenna. "Good eye."

She flushed, clearly pleased.

Rafael and his men spread a body bag on the floor. With his guidance, they gently placed Camilla Rodolfo inside and zipped it closed. The sound of that zipper was the final act. The bag was hoisted onto the gurney and rolled out of the room, leaving bloody smears on the floor, some of that blood forming the outline of a woman who had dreams she would never fulfill.

The room was silent for a few moments, everyone needing time to bid *God speed* to Camilla Rodolfo.

Rafael followed the gurney, giving a little wave over his shoulder as he left the room.

The forensics team collected their tools and stuffed all the gauze and tissues into a large bio-hazard bag.

Roche blinked hard against the chemicals in the air. "We're all tired, I know that, but we can't let everyone leave the theater. Not just yet."

"At least the audience is gone," said Tenna. "Keeping them here—"

"An uprising, to be sure," said Anuj.

"You got everyone's names, seat numbers, and contact information?" Roche asked Tenna. When she nodded, he asked, "When? You've hardly left my sight."

"The director's assistant," she said. "Laurene. She'll get the printout to me soon."

Max Formande appeared at the door. He looked drained, all sprightliness gone. His jowls sagged, and his eyes were bloodshot. "Inspector, really."

"I'll make this quick," Roche promised. "We'll speak to everyone now, in their dressing rooms, but they have to return in the morning." He waved his hand, expecting his team to follow, and then stepped into the hall. Behind him, he heard Max mutter to Aria, "Doesn't he realize it's already morning?"

The first dressing room they reached was filled with period furniture, including a sofa that spanned the length of the wall. Stretched out was Bertrand Gabriel, his eyes closed and his skin alarmingly pale. Solange was seated at a vanity covered with bottles and assorted containers, but there was no stage makeup—that had been collected for testing. What looked like a flower vase was filled with makeup brushes. Her eyes were riveted to her own image in a large mirror as she ran a tissue across her skin. "Did you come to give us a hall pass?" she asked, leaning closer to the mirror and dabbing makeup from the corners of her eyes.

There was no humor in her voice, nor did Roche expect any.

Bertrand sat up slowly, and with obvious effort. "Max?' He turned to the director.

Max crossed to the sofa and sat. He took Bertrand's hand and held it.

Roche was moved by this. Two men who shared a history and were there for each other to protect and defend. He thought it touching, but it also made him sad. He saw that Aria was also watching. In her eyes, he sensed the same wishful longing.

She stepped forward and put her hands on Solange's shoulders. "I know this is difficult...and exhausting."

"But we must question all of you," insisted Roche.

Solange raised her eyes and stared at him through the mirror. "Because one of us killed the poor girl?" And then she looked at Aria.

For a moment, Roche thought Solange might laugh. Instead, she went back to removing the heavy makeup. No matter how he approached her, he feared she was going to be difficult.

"You can ask us anything you wish," said the actress. "I'm sure our attorney will guide us through your questions."

"Do we need him?" Bertrand asked, looking utterly defeated. His voice suggested that all this drama was too much for a man of his age. "And must we do it now? Can't it wait until tomorrow?" He glanced at his wristwatch. "My God."

Solange dropped the cloth onto the floor, certain someone would retrieve it. No one did.

"Madame Gabriel," Roche asked. "Where is your assistant?"

Solange turned slowly away from the mirror. "Sashkie? I sent her home."

Roche felt heat rise in his face. "I was very clear," he said, swallowing his anger. "No one was to leave."

This time, Solange laughed. "Oh, pish-posh, the girl needs her sleep. If you want her here in the morning, I'll have Bertrand text her."

Her husband looked at her reflection in the mirror. "You're removing that makeup only now, my dear? You know how it ravages your skin."

Solange smiled, and Roche half-expected her face to crack. "You're right, Bertie, but after Camilla's...well, you know...I looked ghastly, and the makeup helped."

Roche tried to follow her reasoning. She cared how she looked, with someone murdered in the next room? And why in the hell had she sent Sashkie away? Probably not so far away, he reasoned. To their Paris apartment? Whether he questioned her now or a few hours from now, what difference did it make? Sashkie could wait.

He took a few steps closer to Bertrand. "There's no need for an attorney. We'll be questioning everyone who was in the theater."

He turned to Anuj and Tenna. "Ticketholders included." To the others, he said, "I want cast and crew here at eight. Staff, too." It was spoken more as an afterthought, but his objective was to test his clout.

Solange's mouth twisted into an unpleasant grin. "Eight? In the morning? Bertie and I will be here at ten. With Sashkie."

Roche was about to protest, but he was stopped when the old woman raised her hand.

"And," she added, all humor gone from her voice. "You won't get a word out of me unless Aria's in the room."

He felt Aria's eyes on him and willed himself not to look at her.

"Don't worry, Solange, I'm not going anywhere," Aria said.

He had been so close to asking her to leave. Now, he had no choice: she had to stay.

Chapter Six

Aria watched as the early morning sun cast its glow across the cobblestones outside the café. She had nearly finished her espresso and croissant when a voice said, "Join you?" Looking up, she saw Tenna.

The detective pulled out a chair and settled in.

"Nice to have the company," Aria said. "I usually can't eat when I've had so little sleep, but I'm starving."

On cue, the waiter rushed up and whipped out a little notepad.

"Please, another espresso," Aria said.

"And another croissant?" he asked sweetly.

"A baguette," she said.

"No butter, right?"

Aria gave him a wide-eyed look. "Heavy on the butter, raspberry preserves on the side."

Tenna ordered the same, and he rushed off.

"What's it like, working with Roche?" Aria asked, taking her recorder from her pocket and placing it on the table.

Tenna looked at the device before she spoke, as if making sure it was not running. "He can be gruff," she said. "But he's always fair. Not," she quickly added, "like Klemens." Her voice took on a hard edge. "He's always waiting for me to say something he can argue. Or worse, mock."

Aria removed her hand from the recorder. This was personal. Tenna needed a friend, a kind ear, not someone who was recording her every word.

"It's our jobs." Tenna twisted her mouth. "His career path is horizontal, although you'd never hear him admit that. He's not liked at work, and I'm quite sure he's not respected, so advancement is unlikely."

"And he has a wife who's praised," said Aria. "And liked by others, advancing through the ranks. He must feel threatened."

Tenna leaned in closer. "Am I supposed to ignore my dreams, stay on the bottom rung of the ladder to satisfy his need to feel superior? The higher I advance in the department, the more I'll earn. Nice, yes? Not from his point of view. If I'm earning more, he sees that as a threat. It means I can take my boys out of that damn boarding school and bring them to Paris." She leaned back. "Sorry, I get riled up when I think about them."

"Do you have photos?"

Tenna reached into her bag and pulled out her mobile phone. A few taps and there they were, blonde-haired, blue-eyed boys with their arms draped around one another. "Axel is seven, Hugo is nearly nine." She gazed wistfully at their faces. "My heart. I miss them." She replaced the phone in her bag and sighed. "My husband insists that living here will hurt them. But tell me, what hurts children more than being separated from their parents?"

"Can you reason with him? There must be a Swedish school somewhere around Paris."

Tenna chewed on the inside of her lip. "That would mean he'd have to give in. Klemens Berglof has never given in to anyone or anything. He sets his mind on something and it's unchangeable, no matter what."

"Maybe he will, in time." Aria said the words, but she did not believe them, not with someone as self-centered as he seemed to be.

"I've wanted to take the exams to improve my rank, but I can't bear the thought of how he'd react."

That second espresso was the jump-start Aria needed. The caffeine hit its mark, and the baguette gave her a sense of having eaten something substantial. She took out her wallet. When Tenna reached for hers, Aria gestured it away.

"I didn't expect you to pay," Tenna said.

Aria touched the woman's hand. "Next time, it's yours."

50

They left the café and turned onto the little road leading to the theater. When they arrived at the entrance, Aria stopped. "It's painful to know this will soon be gone."

Inside, they found an empty lobby, a dramatic contrast to last night's crowds. With the paparazzi and the excitement now a memory, the place felt eerie.

A young woman appeared, clutching a clipboard to her chest. Aria recognized her as Max's assistant, and had a vague memory that her name was Laurene. She had been given the unenviable task of guarding the red carpet. Was that only just last night?

Tenna thanked her for helping with the patrons.

"Check your email," Laurene said.

"We're meeting in the rehearsal room," Aria told her. "But I've no idea how to get there."

Laurene smiled, turned, and walked away. "Follow me," she called over her shoulder, leading the women through a door.

Tenna and Aria stayed close, as they wended their way through a maze of hallways. "One could disappear here," Tenna said, "and never be found."

"It took me days to learn how to navigate this jumble," Laurene said. She stopped at the open door of the rehearsal room. "My boyfriend suggested I use breadcrumbs. You know, to leave a trail."

Aria laughed. "A wise man."

Laurene released a little snort. "The bread crumbs were an excellent idea, but the boyfriend was a disaster."

Aria noticed how Tenna joined in the laughter, but there was sadness in her eyes.

Roche and Anuj were with the cast and crew, everyone seated in the first two rows of the mini-theater. Anton Delant was doing what Aria thought was his best impersonation of boredom, tapping his fingers on the armrest and humming just loud enough that others could hear. Linné Colbert was crossing and uncrossing her legs, and then shifted until she was ramrod straight, chin high.

To Aria, the scene was almost humorous, watching players in an unscripted drama of suspense, all of them anxious not to appear guilty. She studied their faces, wondering what guilt looked like.

"Is everyone here?" Roche asked Max Formande.

"We're missing Solange," said the director.

"She's resting," offered Bertrand. "You might say I'm representing both of us. But she's here," he quickly added. "In her dressing room."

"That won't do," said Roche.

"Really," Bertrand said. "Must you—"

Roche cut him off. "There's been a murder."

Aria nearly defended Bertrand, but thought better of it. Perhaps something else was bothering Roche. He was sounding rather cruel.

Just then, a man she didn't recognize sidled along the row of flip-down seats and settled next to Anton Delant.

She scrolled through her memory, but couldn't find his face. She turned to Tenna.

"Darwin McAfee," she whispered. "Anton Delant's understudy. There's a picture of him in the program."

The man looked at Tenna and gave a little smile.

"Old friends?" asked Aria, pushing her elbow gently into Tenna's ribs.

"In another life," she said, and then giggled.

Aria saw that Max was watching these exchanges, the pallor of his skin telling her that he was suffering distress as much as fatigue. At the same time, she was quite certain that if someone handed him a bullhorn, he would rise to the moment and announce "Quiet on the set!"

Laurene approached Max with a plastic container. He fumbled with the lid, and she tried to take it back.

"I can do it," he insisted, twisting and pulling.

Aria expected him to fling it across the room.

"Childproof, my ass!" he declared, surrendering it to his assistant, who removed the lid, shook out a pill, and dropped it into his hand. From the pocket of her jacket came a small bottle of water. "Next time," he insisted, "I'll take a 1985 Maison de Vignes Bordeaux. It's perfect for washing down my meds." He turned to Aria. "Age, my dear, is hell. Sheer…hell."

She gave him what she hoped was a comforting smile. "Time has a way of rushing by."

He sighed dramatically. "Time, the greatest thief of all."

Roche leafed through several papers. He asked Aria, "Would you please go to Solange Gabriel's dressing room and accompany her back here?"

With Laurene pointing the way, Aria followed a passage leading directly to the dressing rooms. When she reached the one with *Gabriel* on the door, she knocked.

"Yes?" came a voice from inside.

Aria opened the door and crossed to where Solange was reclining on the sofa. "You're needed in the rehearsal room."

"Not going to happen," said Solange, gesturing for Aria to take the chair near the sofa.

Aria pulled the chair closer and sat. "None of this can be easy. Camilla's death; the effect it's had on the performance."

Solange shifted her body so she could face Aria. "My dear, have you seen this morning's papers? The best reviews I've had in years. We were already delivering a memorable performance. Camilla's death pushed us even further, to higher levels. I can't speak for the others, but I was brilliant!"

Aria reached out and gave Solange's arm a gentle squeeze. "Yes, you were. But you really must join the others." When Solange nodded, she helped her off the sofa and draped a silk scarf around her neck. "The rehearsal room is chilly."

Solange clung to Aria's arm, and they made their way to the rehearsal room, where Bertrand stood and guided his wife to her seat. Aria wondered if this was devotion, or was it a role they were accustomed to playing?

Max took the seat next to Bertrand, looked at Aria, and said, "I can't help staring, you so resemble your mother."

Aria dipped her head. "Maman is smaller, and far more delicate."

"But you have her eyes," Max said. "And the same coloring." He checked his wristwatch. "Shall we call her later? I want Delphine to know how much she is missed."

Roche cleared his throat, causing everyone to focus on him. "Perhaps we can get this done," he announced. "With your cooperation, we might even get it done quickly." He made a point of looking at the light now burning brightly on Aria's recorder.

Aria commanded herself not to laugh, and wondered how much longer he was going to play this infinite-patience game with her. It was already getting old.

"Let me add," said Roche, "that Aria Nevins is not with the force. She is a journalist documenting our work, our processes."

Aria heard the unspoken part, *now you know, end of subject*, and she saw how he shifted his gaze from face to face, as if hoping someone would insist she turn the damn thing off. Perhaps he intended to make them nervous, or even turn on each other. She wondered who would reveal that critical piece of evidence that would bring this investigation to a satisfying conclusion. In their fear of being accused, perhaps they would hurl accusations, or would they rally around one another? There might be old grudges hovering overhead, secrets about to be exposed. She told herself that this situation was serious, yet a little voice was chortling in her head.

Max stood. "May I?" The inspector nodded, and the old man stepped up onto the stage. "As all of you know," he said, "my dream was to send this jewel of a theater to the gods after directing the greatest production of *Hamlet's Father* that Europe has seen in more than fifty years. In the days leading up to last night, I wasn't easy. I refused to mollycoddle you, no matter what your star power, and I came down hard on you, never covering for your lapses in rehearsals. You were ready last night, and you performed brilliantly." A plaintive note crept into his voice. "I only wish—" He shook his head, unable to continue.

A sadness swept over Aria. This last performance would be remembered not for the brilliance of the play, but for the tragedy that had befallen it. That would be his legacy.

"Thank you," he said. "All of you, thank you." He stepped off the stage and took the seat at the far end of the row, away from the others, isolated. There was a brief applause.

"That's our Max," mumbled Anton Delant. "One of the great bullshit artists of the day."

"Be kind," said his understudy, Darwin McAfee. "Can't you see he's flattened by this?"

Delant gave the man a long look and turned away. "Why, exactly, are we here?" he demanded.

Aria watched how Roche moved forward a few steps and then stopped. It struck her that it was his turn to deliver the monologue.

"You are here," he said, "because all of you have information that will help our investigation." A murmur rose from the room. "Whether you're aware of it or not."

The murmur died out, replaced by the sounds of bodies shifting in spring-loaded seats.

"We're asking for personal information about Camilla Rodolfo," he said. "Conversations you might have had with her, discussions overheard." He paused, presumably to give everyone time to consider this. "And let me add that everything you tell us will be in confidence."

Aria looked at the two rows of suspects. Even the lighting and sound technicians were working to look innocent, which made most of them appear quite guilty. She held up her recorder, aiming it directly at Roche. She did not intend to miss even one word.

"We understand, Inspector," said Anton. "And God knows we all miss Camilla."

Aria heard what struck her as genuine grief. She hadn't considered that the man had known Camilla before this play, but it made sense. The theater and television communities in France were small; actors had many opportunities to cross paths.

"But does it have to be now?" Anton continued. "Today? We've had no time to feel the loss."

Perhaps his grief wasn't genuine after all, judging by the number of people rolling their eyes. Aria wondered if it was Anton, and not Max, who was the bullshit artist.

"The longer we wait," Roche explained, "the more difficult it will be for you to recall the sequence of events before her death." He took a sip from a paper cup and frowned.

"Then ask away," said Anton.

Roche walked over to a trash basket near the door and dropped the cup into it. His walk back to center stage was more a stroll.

Aria exchanged glances with Tenna again. The woman was clearly fighting back a laugh. Aria was dying to interview her, this officer who knew Roche so well. How did he use time and pacing to unsettle someone being questioned? Had she seen him accomplish this with criminals, as well as with innocent people who had information they preferred not to share? What about his interactions with attorneys and other police officers? At the moment, he reminded her of a cat stalking his prey, about to pounce. And a few of the people in the room reminded her of frightened mice.

"So," he said, his voice suggesting that the conversation was at an end, rather than a beginning. "Perhaps someone can explain why Camilla left a brilliant career in the theater, a successful place in French film, to do a television series?" Before anyone could answer, he rushed forward with, "Which I gather has done very well, but—"

"Ka-ching!" declared Anton.

"Anton, really!" said Solange. "That's vulgar."

Anton swung around to face the woman. "Oh, please, Solange. Everyone knows she needed the money."

"Anton—" It was McAfee, the understudy. "Please."

There was a sudden hush in the room. Two thoughts raced through Aria's mind. First, that no one with such a constant presence in entertainment should need money. And second, how could Anton Delant possibly know this?

"Needed money?' asked Roche. "Why?"

"Why?" the actor repeated, as though a more stupid question had never been asked. "Well, let's begin with that bastard of a husband. Not the first one, he was a pussycat. But the second one? He gambled away everything she had. Terrible debts. Big, mean people pounding on her door and demanding payment. What was she to do?"

"Divorce him?" suggested Linné.

Aria craned to get a better look at the actress. She was lovely, to be sure. Who could forget her in that blockbuster movie that had made her the darling at Cannes? After she had won the award for Best Actress, Aria had rushed out to see the movie. Brilliant. Memorable. And now here she was, this amazing actress, seated only a few feet away. Such fame, yet she seemed down-to-earth, no signs of grandstanding. Not like Solange and Anton, who could breathe only if at the center of attention.

"Divorce him? She did that!" Anton said. "But he left her drowning in debt."

Aria saw how Solange was fidgeting, one hand squeezing the other. She wondered why the woman was so agitated.

"We'll get through this, my dear," murmured Bertrand. He leaned closer and kissed her cheek.

The gesture reminded Aria of how sweet love could be, but then Solange ran a hand across her cheek like a petulant child.

"Of course, we'll get through it," she declared. "But are we expected to mourn? Rend our lapels and cover the mirrors? That woman tried to upstage me every chance possible!"

"If Padraig Finnegan were here," said Max, "he would celebrate last night's performance."

Solange laughed, the sound pure and clear. Youthful. "If Padraig Finnegan were here, my dear man, we'd be the victims of his wrath!"

"Solange is right," said Bertrand. "Slashing that interminable scene in act two was treachery enough, but casting a man in his eighties to play a man in his forties? No, I think we're all safer with our playwright dead and buried. And let's not forget," he added, warming to the drama. "Fifty years ago, when Padraig's response to each little edit suggestion was *Drop dead, shithead*, he left little room for negotiation."

Laughter ran through the group. The only person not laughing was Darwin McAfee. Aria could see that, unlike the others, he was taking this seriously. Had he known Camilla?

Solange began to cough, the sound hardly louder than a whisper. Her assistant, Sashkie, materialized out of nowhere, rushing forward with a glass of water. Solange took several sips, then returned the glass without looking up.

Aria studied this hovering young woman at Solange's elbow, like a waif ready to serve. If she had to describe her, she would have to say mousy. Fair skin, average height, stocky. Her hair was frizzy, dark blonde tending toward brown, pulled back into a ponytail, with wisps falling over her forehead and ears. She was wearing the baggy shirt and pants favored by women convinced this makes them appear thinner. All told, she was not attractive; there was nothing remarkable or memorable about her face. And the hard line of her mouth did not help. Aria wondered if the girl ever smiled. Or was she always like this, rigid and grim-faced? But then, in all fairness to the girl, there was little to smile about.

"We are prepared to interview all of you," Roche announced. The room fell silent, and everyone's focus shifted to him. "And for as long as it takes."

The atmosphere turned so quickly that Aria thought of a sunny day replaced by a solar eclipse. Everyone sat up straighter; some even folded their hands in their lap.

She looked at Bertrand. Unlike the others, his posture had wilted. Eyes that had been flashing in anger were hooded and blinking rapidly.

As for the assistants and crew members, they struck Aria as more wary than fearful. They would either be forthcoming, or they would hold back and give up only what was necessary.

"Will you interview us, Inspector, or interrogate us?" asked Anton.

"Before anything goes forward, we'll need your passports," Roche said.

Again, the room fell quiet. When a voice was heard, it was the man Aria knew only as Joseph the electrician. "Our passports?" he asked. "Mine's back at my place. Should I go home now and fetch it?' It was no challenge, simply a question.

Roche took the clipboard from Anuj and scanned the names. He looked at the electrician. "Joseph, yes? After we've spoken to all of you, and if you're removed from our list of suspects, your passport will be returned." He glanced toward Anuj and Tenna. "Collect them when we're done here. Anyone who doesn't have it handy, get someone to drive them home and wait for it."

"If?" Anton repeated. *"If* we're removed from your list of suspects?"

Aria had been a reporter on the beat long enough to understand that, in a murder investigation, that little distinction was the difference between freedom and life in prison.

Chapter Seven

Noah Roche sat on the bench in the little plaza near the Metro entrance, leaves from the horse chestnut trees shimmering with the breeze. This was a rare event, being outside and alone, taking time to enjoy a break from the stormy weather, and even stormier suspects. This morning, nothing was interfering with the moment, except for his father's voice buzzing through his mind.

"Get out of here while you can," the pig farmer had insisted. "Before the stench of slaughter is trapped forever in your skin."

He had heeded his father's warning. He got out and had excelled. Now what?

A crowd of travelers was emerging from the Metro tunnel, maps of Paris being shared between them. He thought about his work, and how it demanded constant communication with his team. Moments of non-communication were rare. It was no surprise that he had developed an aversion to phatic communion, idle chitchat. While his friends dreamed of villas on the Riviera, winning the lottery, or waking up to discover they were twenty years younger, Noah Roche desired one full month without having to speak to anyone. No colleagues, no family, no friends. Just silence.

His mind jumped to something one of his superiors had said after his last promotion. "The thing is, Roche, you didn't pursue this position as much as it pursued you."

One decade later, and he still wasn't sure what the man was saying. From his vantage point, being named Chief Homicide Inspector was one of those situations where he had worked hard to achieve a goal, succeeded at it, and then wondered why in the hell he had wanted it in the first place.

"So, when is this brilliant, calculating homicide inspector going to figure out who murdered Camilla Rodolfo?" It was a long moment before he realized he had spoken those words aloud. When had it come to this, what he considered the first sign of old age? His next thought was, *So...who did kill her?* Followed by *Ay, there's the rub!* Anyone could have committed this murder. If it had happened during the intermission, his suspects included actors, crew, staff, even someone in the audience. But it had to be someone who knew their way around the hallways, and this narrowed the field. Tenna had suggested they eliminate all female suspects, but Anuj quickly pointed out that it took little strength to come up behind a woman and drive a knife across her throat.

Roche pushed himself off the bench and walked towards the theater. That damned theater! Not exactly the second home he had imagined. That fantasy was restricted to ski chalets and seaside cottages. He would be relieved to get this investigation away from the theater so he could continue his work at the precinct.

He opened the door to the lobby, and Aria was there. She was another enigma, like a case he expected to solve, but could not. For the moment, he had more important things to do than allow her to be an obstacle.

He watched her approach, surprised by the dread that ran through him.

"Good morning," she said.

They crossed to the corner of the lobby.

He smiled, but it was forced.

She looked at him, her brow creased as if not sure how to proceed. "I'll be honest with you," she finally said. "The Solange we're seeing is not the Solange I've known most of my life."

He felt a door blow open, but was reluctant to step through it. "The arrogance?"

"No," she said. "The cruelty. Arrogance doesn't faze me; I've lived with that." Before he could respond, she said, "My mother's not as haughty as Solange, but she's proud and quick to judge. But she's never cruel. I've always thought they were alike, that two-peas-in-a-pod thing. I was wrong."

"You can see this already?" he asked. "We've just started."

"I've seen enough." Her voice was low.

They walked down the corridor and into the room set aside for his team. It felt closed, stuffy, and barely large enough for the table and four chairs.

"Where are Anuj and Tenna?" Aria asked.

He began checking that none of the chairs was unsteady. Even the smallest thing could sabotage an interrogation. "Tenna's running the names of everyone who was in the theater, ticketholders included, and Anuj is talking to local shopkeepers."

He thought this was a good time to remind her of the rules. What she could say and what she could not. He pointed to one of the chairs. "I talk, you observe. No questions, no interruptions. If you think of something, write it down and we'll discuss it later." He pulled the recorder from his pocket and placed it on the table.

She sat down, took out her recorder, and placed it near his.

"I prefer you keep it out of view," he said. "One is expected; two can be intimidating."

Without a word, she slipped it onto her lap.

There was movement at the door, and then Sashkie Ferrer entered the room.

"Miss Ferrer," he said. "Right on time. I was about to send for the Gabriels."

She took a strand of hair and ran it across her mouth. "It's unfortunate that you've put them first, Inspector. Madame Gabriel is not yet fully awake from her rest. As you know, this drama has exhausted her. I'm to tell you that she needs another hour or two."

Roche gave her a long stare. "Then I'll question you." He pointed to the chair across from Aria.

Sashkie's eyes grew wide. "What could I possibly—?"

"Please…sit."

She took one step closer to the table. The recorder's red light was glowing. "I'm quite sure I can't help you."

He took the seat next to Aria, so Sashkie would have to face both of them. Then he crossed his legs and leaned back, relaxed, his eyes never leaving her face.

Sashkie's attention shifted back and forth, Roche to Aria: a pendulum.

Roche wondered if she was trying to determine which of them was safer. He kept his face inscrutable and saw that Aria was doing the same. And then he wondered if another tact might be more successful. That was, to be less of a policeman and more paternal. It wasn't easy being questioned, especially by a senior inspector, so how could he not feel a smidgen of sympathy for her? But there was another way to look at this: Would she lie to protect the people who paid her salary and provided her with a home?

He pushed a button on the recorder, and the red light turned to green. Such a small device, yet the source of such anxiety, even fear. "Interview with Sashkie Ferrer," he began, and then gave the date, time, place, his name, and Aria's.

He looked directly at Sashkie. She was chewing on a cuticle. When she pulled her hand away, her thumb was bleeding.

"You work for Solange and Bertrand Gabriel," he said.

"No," she said. "Only Madame Gabriel." She slipped her hand onto her lap.

Aria reached into her bag and removed a tissue, which she placed on the table. Sashkie stared at it for a moment, and then picked it up and wrapped it around her thumb.

"Not her husband?" Roche asked.

"He's very independent."

"Meaning?"

"He chooses his clothing and prefers to handle his affairs. If he needs something, he usually gets it himself. I can't remember the last time he asked for my help."

"And Madame Gabriel?"

Sashkie made a snorting sound, which she immediately tried to cover by pressing her lips together.

"Miss Ferrer?"

"How much of this are you repeating to her?"

Roche leaned forward, elbows on the table. "Not one word. Everything you say is confidential."

"And recorded," she said.

"Only for my use," Roche responded.

Sashkie studied his face. "I hope so. If not, I'll end up on the street."

"You have my word."

The girl looked at Aria. "Madam Gabriel has me do everything but wipe her ass."

Roche nearly laughed, and a quick glance at Aria told him that she was in the same state. "So," he said, composure regained. "She's dependent on you."

"Dependent? Inspector, I was hired to be her assistant and her dresser. When we're in production, I work day and night. I even live in their home, that's how demanding she is."

"And what was your relationship with Camilla Rodolfo?"

Sashkie stared at the recorder. "My—?"

"Relationship," repeated Roche. "Were you acquainted with her before this production? Perhaps you were friends? Or became friends?"

Sashkie made another sound that struck him as derisive, almost obscene. "We were never friends. It's not my place to be friends with the cast."

"But you were in a position to observe exchanges between Madame Gabriel and Camilla," he suggested.

"Madam Gabriel is rarely out of my sight. My job is to be there, always."

"Which means being at her side," he continued. "Did you witness any harsh words between them? Any indication that there was jealousy or anger?"

Sashkie took her time before responding. "Jealousy? On whose part? Camilla is—was—younger and beautiful. Madame Gabriel is an icon, worshiped by fans all over the world, which doesn't change the fact that she's in her eighties. I guess one could have desired what the other had, but I never heard either of them express this. No," she added, her voice suddenly quiet, yet firm. "It's not Madame Gabriel you should be asking about."

Roche felt a change in the air. He saw that Aria was about to speak, but held back. No matter that the Gabriels demanded she be included. If she took one step into interfering with this session, he'd send her packing. "I see," he said, leaning so he could rest his arms on the table. "So, someone in this theater has had words with Camilla." He tilted his head, indicating that it was now her turn to speak.

Sashkie sat in silence, her fingers playing with strands of her hair.

"Miss Ferrer?"

"I may as well tell you, but you didn't hear this from me."

Roche paused a long moment. "I've given my word. But let me remind you that this is a murder investigation, not an exchange of gossip on the school playground."

"If Madame Gabriel learns that I've blabbed, even about other actors, I'll be dismissed."

"Miss Ferrer," he said, the edge in his voice turning sharp.

"If she fires me, no one will give me a job. She'll see to that. And believe me," she added, her eyes brimming with tears. "If the great Solange Gabriel tells them to shun me, they will. You have no idea how powerful that woman is."

"Unless we need your testimony in court," he said, "this remains between us. But some things will be out of my control. You do understand, yes?"

Some of the tension in her face slipped away. "Yesterday afternoon, Linné and Camilla got into a terrible row. I'm not sure what started it. But when I passed Linné's dressing room, I heard Camilla boasting that she'd earned her leading role because of her talent."

"And how did Miss Colbert respond?"

"Oh, she was not at all happy being the understudy, and she said so." Sashkie leaned so close that he smelled the scent of coconut shampoo in her hair. "Do you blame her?"

Roche did not respond, reminding himself yet again that silence was often the best prompt to getting someone to deliver the goods. And here was the proof. One minute earlier, Sashkie had refused to speak. Now, he was wondering if he'd be able to silence her.

"Think about it," she continued. "Camilla might be a big name, but she was getting old." Her mouth twisted into a smirk. "I can't swear to it, but there might have been a mention of Camilla winning the role on her back."

Roche considered protesting that forty-something was far from old, or debating her suggestion that some women attain their status using their sexual gifts. The thought that Camilla might have seduced Max Formande to get this role was laughable. He made a concerted effort not to look at Aria. God only knows what her face would reveal.

"Linné is young," she continued. "And not just young, but more famous than Camilla will ever be. You can't pass a magazine stand without seeing her face on at least one cover. How could Camilla not be jealous?"

He thought about the confidence of youth. Like his son, always certain his parents would jump into any mess he had created and make it right. "Is this the only incident you recall?"

"Incident?" repeated Sashkie.

"Any other conflicts that someone under this roof might have had with the deceased—with Camilla Rodolfo."

Sashkie blinked hard and looked away.

Roche wondered what she was withholding. "Miss Ferrer?"

"No, only that one moment," she insisted. "And it could have meant nothing." She raised her chin.

He pushed the STOP button on the recorder. "We'll continue this conversation after I've spoken to the actors, crew, and staff."

He stood, walked Sashkie to the door, and held it open.

Before she could cross the threshold, Bertrand Gabriel appeared.

"I was told to expect you in several hours," Roche said.

"I was able to convince my wife that sooner was better."

"It took some convincing," said Solange, stepping into Roche's view.

Without another word, Sashkie slipped out the door and disappeared into the hallway.

Roche studied the Gabriels. Was it true they only wanted to be done with this unpleasantness? Or did they have something to hide? If so, making themselves available could be a ploy to have Roche think they were being cooperative. He stepped to the side and gestured them into the room.

Aria stood and embraced them. As if by mutual agreement, they went directly to the table, taking the two chairs across from Aria and leaving the one next to her for the inspector.

Roche took his seat. In a move he hoped was intimidating, he pressed the button on the recorder, its green light indicating that they were now being recorded.

"Our agent normally demands a contract before interviews," quipped Bertrand.

Roche gave him the courtesy of a smile, while feeling uncharacteristically apprehensive about what lay ahead. He usually reveled in these interviews. He was good at nudging, urging, sometimes even threatening to get answers. This morning, however, he wondered if these two might fabricate their responses with the same expertise they had recited their lines the evening before.

He was recording the names of those present, the time, date, and place, when he noticed a stark change in Bertrand. The man was staring at Aria. Not a vacant stare, more a quizzical one, like someone whose memory was trying to kick in.

Aria leaned forward and took his hand. "Uncle Bertie," she said, her voice low and soothing. "Do you need to take a break?"

Solange released a hissing sound and turned to her husband. "My darling," she murmured. "This is Ariadne, do you remember? Aria? Delphine's little girl?"

Bertrand studied Aria's face for a long moment. "Yes, of course I remember, my dear. It's just that I am so very, very tired."

Roche couldn't decide if this was acting or an old man trying to shake free a memory trapped in his mind. To forget was tragic. He had seen it with his mother. The lost word, the precious incident no longer remembered. Finally, a tabula rasa, all memory wiped clean.

Bertrand suddenly grinned, making his face younger, more alive. "Delphine! Didn't she play the role of—"

"You old fool!" Solange snapped, and then quickly looked away. Tears filled her eyes, and pain stretched across her face. She looked at Aria. "He goes in and out. This play was his last; we have no choice."

Roche felt his chest tighten. Bertrand Gabriel was perhaps thirty years his senior. If he could get to his eighties before showing signs of forgetfulness, he could accept that.

Solange waved her hand, shooing away a bothersome fly. "Delphine is not an actress." Her voice became gentle. "She was Max's girlfriend before the war, remember? And then she became a dress designer. We had that garden party, Coco was there? That's when she admitted she was jealous of Delphine's work."

"Coco Chanel?" Aria declared. "I never knew."

Solange tipped her head. "It's possible I forgot to mention it."

Roche was certain she had withheld praise because she considered Delphine competition. Was every woman her rival?

Bertrand suddenly slapped his hand on the table, his eyes again bright, the sun discovering a path between a mass of dark clouds. "Of course!" he declared. "Delphine the designer! And this is her Ariadne! My dear, you came to our home and we swam in our pool. You climbed onto my shoulders, and I pushed myself out of the water so you could dive in. That was you!"

"I recall those moments with great pleasure," Aria said. "That was when you first insisted I call you Uncle Bertie."

Roche wanted this little stroll down Memory Lane to be over. He wasn't sure what he expected to happen next, but it was not Solange taking her husband's wrinkled, darkly veined hand and pressing it to her lips. The gesture was so tender, so natural, that a wave of longing swept through him. He cleared his throat. "May we proceed?"

"Is it necessary?" asked Solange, directing a look at the recorder.

"The older I get," said Roche, "the more I depend on technology."

To his surprise, Solange laughed. "Then record away!" she announced. "After I'm dead, you can sell it on eBay."

Roche resumed his questioning, glancing at Aria from time to time. In all his years as a homicide inspector, he had rarely questioned his tactics or his techniques, yet her presence was making him do so. Anyone who worked with him knew he was respectful, even with the most heinous suspects. And he could be kind, if he had to be. He reminded himself that he had no way of controlling what she wrote, so he may as well be himself. Still, her presence was a mosquito that attacked again and again.

Solange and Bertrand sat stiffly, backs straight in the hard chairs, locked in their roles of monarchs. Solange pulled a handkerchief from under her sleeve and blew her nose with such grace and refinement that Roche nearly smiled. Always the star, always on stage. Never out of character.

"We were very fond of Camilla," she said.

"Had you known her long?" He was relieved to be back on track.

Solange looked at her husband, knowing that he would supply the answer. When he seemed bewildered, she said, "I try not to think about time, Inspector. As Max says, time is never a friend."

"It would help if I knew." He waited, hoping she would fill in the gaps.

"Bertie," said Solange. "We worked with Camilla in that Ibsen play, do you remember?"

The old man looked up, his lips pursed. "Yes, now that you mention it, this was around the time we bought the flat in London." He glanced at his wife, who appeared surprised. "There are a few brain cells remaining, my dear. We told her about the flat and she gave us the name of a very good decorator."

"I remember!" said Solange. "That makes it, what, nearly fifteen years?"

"And how was your relationship with Camilla?" Roche asked, looking directly at Solange.

"Friendly, professional," she replied. "Not close, but I found her pleasant enough. Amusing."

"You never argued, disagreed?"

Solange laughed. "Disagreed about what, Inspector? We were a generation apart, nearly two. There was no competition for roles," she said. And then, almost as an aside, she added, "Certainly none when comparing talent." She gave Roche a long look. "I see that you want to ask me something more."

"Did Camilla want to play Gertrude?"

Solange opened her mouth, and then closed it.

"The queen," added Roche.

"I know who Gertrude is."

"And?"

"The question you really want to ask, Inspector, is *Did Camilla say anything nasty about an old woman playing a young queen?* After all, my role was the gem of the play. The answer," she added, with a glint in her eyes, "is no. Or if she did, it never got back to me. And that, in the theater, is rare. There's nothing we love more than cutting each other down by repeating juicy tittle-tattle."

Roche was about to respond when Aria gestured with her eyes toward Bertrand. He recognized the problem at once. The man had suddenly gone pale, the color in his cheeks almost ashen. He turned off the recorder. "It's been a long morning," he said. "I'm sure we could all use a break. Why not go to your apartment and rest? I'll come by this afternoon and finish my questions."

Solange stood slowly and then waited for her husband to rise. When he seemed to have difficulty, Aria came around the table and assisted him.

Solange said, "Aria, dear, would you tell Sashkie we're ready to leave?"

Aria rushed out as Roche helped the couple navigate toward the door. The old man leaned heavily against him.

Sashkie entered and placed herself between the two actors. "They're exhausted," she said. "This really is too much." She took a sweater from her shoulders and wrapped it around Solange. As the three of them walked out of the room, Sashkie hooked one arm through Bertrand's and the other around the old woman's waist. Gone was any lightness of step, any regal appearance. These were two elderly people anxious to return home.

Aria stepped forward and gave them gentle hugs. Roche saw kindness in her eyes, but also sadness.

"I'll come later…with the inspector."

Bertrand touched her face. "You will give Delphine our love, yes?"

As the three of them left the room, Roche followed as far as the door. He noticed a subtle change in the old man's step. It was more sure, balanced. Had he just been played for a fool? He told himself to listen to the end of the interview, particularly for anything that prompted them to leave so quickly. "We'll do this again," he said.

With that, Sashkie led them away.

Roche pulled out his cell phone and punched in a number. "Tenna, we need to talk to Linné Colbert…now." He checked his watch. "Damn, I'm meeting my son for lunch in ten minutes. Tell Anuj I'll swing by and pick you up. Say—one o'clock."

He ended the call and pressed his fingers against his eyes. "Meet me in the lobby in an hour," he told Aria. "That is, if you insist on tagging along."

She gave him a hard look.

It made him wonder what she was thinking. *Fuck you* came to mind.

Chapter Eight

Taverne rue Gabrielle was rumored to be one of those culinary secrets kept from tourists, but the food could have been slop, as far as Roche was concerned. The place was convenient: close to the theater and only minutes from his son's apartment.

He stood at the entrance and watched tourists descend from the steps leading down from Sacre Coeur. He checked his watch and wondered how late Luc would be. The boy was even born late, two weeks past his due date. An omen, to be sure.

He entered the café and was surprised to find him seated at a table. On time. That could mean one thing only: he was going to ask for money.

Luc stood and kissed his father on both cheeks. "The *steak frites* is delicious," said Luc. "And they make a nice cassoulet."

Roche put the menu aside. "Steak it is." He warned himself not to grimace. "So, life is good?" One question was usually enough for Luc to launch into his request. He used to feel guilty thinking of such things, but no longer.

Luc looked at him, his eyes so much like his father's. "Believe it or not, Papa, things are going quite well."

This was not the response he had expected. Where was the request for the loan? The promise to pay it back, as soon as he was on his feet? He was tempted to ask, but stopped himself. It would only create tension, anger, and then the big finish: Luc stomping out after accusing his father of sins real or imagined; the reminder that he had broken up the family, how it was a good thing that his mother was there for him.

"And work?" The one question that always led to battle.

"I quit my job," Luc said casually.

It was the tone of voice that goaded Roche. "The job at the bistro?"

Luc appeared amused. "That was two jobs ago. Since then, I sold art supplies and drove for Uber."

Nothing had changed. Luc was lazy, unmotivated, with two hard-working and successful parents. Roche had no idea how this had happened. He nearly asked, "Who are you sponging off now?" but a woman appeared, pad and pen at the ready.

She was motherly, older than Roche. He was tempted to invite her to sit down, have a meal with them. Keep the damned peace. Instead, she noted their orders and walked away.

"So, what will you do?" he finally asked. He didn't want to know the answer, but if there was another way to proceed, it escaped him.

The waitress returned and placed a large basket of bread on the table. Roche grabbed a roll, tore it open, and focused on applying a very large dollop of butter.

Luc picked up his knife and waved it in the air. "There's always something."

As much as he fought the comparison, Roche could not push away thoughts of Anuj. His young detective did not slouch. He held himself with dignity, back straight, chin up. As boyish as he appeared, he never backed away from a challenge. He sometimes paused, questioning his ability to handle it, but then moved forward, testing himself, pushing himself, always learning along the way. Why couldn't Luc have some of that? He had questioned Judith, and she suggested that Luc reacted to parental demands by ignoring them, and then feeling powerful, almost triumphant. "If we were failures in life," she told him, "our son would have become a neurosurgeon."

Roche spread more butter on the warm bread and shoved a large morsel into his mouth. He chewed, then chewed even more, following this with several gulps of water. When there was nothing left to prevent him from speaking, he launched into it. "Are you still staying at your friend's?" He knew the answer, but it felt like safe territory.

"House sitting," Luc corrected. "And yes. He won't return to Paris for another six weeks."

"And then?" He grabbed another roll, covered it with butter, and bit into it. There was more butter than bread. His own damn fault.

Luc stared at his father, one eyebrow cocked. "And then I'll rob a bank."

Roche picked up the paper napkin and unfolded it slowly before placing it across his lap. "Any particular bank?"

Luc leaned back, tipping his chair away from the table. He'd done this since he was a child, and he knew how it irritated his parents. When Roche said nothing, he tipped it back into place.

Their lunch arrived, and they dug in. Roche assumed his son was also relieved to have a break in the conversation. When Luc offered a spoonful of his cassoulet and was given a forkful of steak and fries in return, Roche felt hopeful. Not hopeful that Luc would suddenly announce his plans to return to school, but that they could make it through a meal.

When the time came to pay the bill, Roche was wondering if lunch was just that: lunch. He pulled out his wallet and handed the woman his credit card.

"Papa," Luc said, running the napkin across his mouth. "I have an amazing opportunity."

Roche nearly blurted out, "How much this time?" but said nothing.

"The apartment where I'm living? My friend wants to sell it. If I buy it directly, without an agent, the price is excellent."

Again, Roche reminded himself to pause, but not for so long that Luc translated this as judgment. "Tell me."

The change in his son's face was immediate; his deep brown eyes nearly danced. "One bedroom, a nice sitting room, modernized bathroom. The kitchen is small, but more than functional. Best of all, it's on the top floor, so no one's overhead."

"Elevator?"

"No, but it's only four flights, good for daily exercise, yes? Come with me now, I'll show you."

Roche checked his watch. "No time," he said.

Luc looked at him. "No time now, or no time ever?"

"Luc," he said, his voice suddenly sharp. "I'm in the middle—"

"You're always in the middle," said Luc, cutting him off.

The excitement in his son's eyes disappeared so dramatically that Roche regretted his tone.

"Fine," said Luc, dropping his napkin onto his plate and pushing it away. "I should've known better."

Roche felt the steak sauce rise to his throat. Would he ever learn to listen to his son? Perhaps Judith had been right: children are extensions of their parents. If they succeed, then the parents have done a good job. And if not? "I'm sorry," he said. "Of course, I'll take a look, but it can't be today. I've got this case."

Luc took another spoonful of cassoulet.

If there was going to be a truce, it would happen now.

"I saw it in this morning's paper," Luc said.

Roche felt relief rush through him. When was the last time they had dodged a conflict? So long ago, there was no memory. Hoping to make this good feeling last, he explained the case to Luc, and in more detail than he normally revealed.

The waitress appeared, and Roche signed the bill.

"So, we're in the middle of questioning the actors," he said. "The pressure is high."

"Camilla Rodolfo was a real beauty."

"You've seen her perform?"

"Not on stage, but in a few movies, television."

"And you understand how pressing this is."

Luc gave his father a dark little grin that said he'd heard this before.

Roche hoped to avoid sending this pleasant meeting into a death spiral. "What do you need from me?"

Luc sat with the question for a long moment before responding. "I need the down payment," he said, and then quickly held up a hand. "It's not much, honestly!"

"How much is not much?"

"Thirty thousand euros." It rolled so easily off his tongue that he might have been a child asking for lunch money.

"Thirty thousand? I'm a homicide detective, not the chief of police."

"I was hoping you could combine resources with Mom."

Roche felt a headache coming on. He checked his watch. "Damn!" He was late for the meeting with Linné Colbert and his team. Without explaining, he stood.

"Papa, please."

Roche looked at his son, a man who still thought like a boy. "I'll discuss it with your mother," he promised, and then felt relief when Luc seemed satisfied.

He rushed out before he could say something stupid.

A quick call to Anuj and plans were changed. "Pick up Linné Colbert and bring her to the theater." This would give him time to take a bit of a walk, sit someplace away from the station, and go over his notes. He needed to do a thorough review of the facts of this case, scant as they were. It would also eliminate the advantage people felt when being questioned in the safety of their home.

He entered the interrogation room, where Anuj, Tenna, Aria, and Linné were waiting. Anuj jumped up, offered his place, and then leaned against the wall.

"No, you stay there," said Roche. "Round up a chair for Madame Nevins."

Anuj rushed out and returned with a folding chair, metal, hard. He opened it and placed it close to the table.

Roche looked at Aria and then gestured towards the chair. She stood, walked around the table, and sat down. He saw defiance in her face. While Anuj was getting settled, she turned on her recorder and placed it on the edge of the table.

With everyone in place, Roche shifted his attention to the actress. His eyes lingered on her face. Not so much because he was curious, which he was, or that she was lovely, which she most certainly was. He looked at her because he was hoping to unnerve her, take away any sense of security she might be feeling, and remind her that this was not a publicity interview, and he was not a columnist for a fan magazine.

Linné Colbert was not the classic definition of perfection, not at all. Her mouth was a bit too large for her face, her teeth not perfectly straight. She was far from slim. He wondered if it was courage, or a heightened sense of confidence, that a woman who lived in the limelight didn't feel imprisoned by a culture that screamed for lean. He had learned from Judith that as much as a woman might aspire to feel comfortable in her own skin, social pressures dictated that she be thin as a model. Thinner.

He adjusted his chair, checked that his recorder was running, and reminded himself that he was a homicide inspector, this was a murder investigation, and Linné Colbert was on his list of suspects. "Thank you for coming."

She offered a wry smile. "I had a choice?"

He tipped his head.

"Do I need my attorney?"

He leaned back in his chair. "You tell me."

She leaned back in hers. "Do you think I killed Camilla?" There was no smile on her face now.

He saw how quickly her sparkle had slipped away. "I have a few questions," he said, looking directly into her eyes.

Her gesture invited him to proceed.

"Why would a woman who has achieved such admiration and respect accept a secondary role?" Before she could answer, he quickly added, "Your perfume endorsement alone must bring in more income than most of us earn in a decade."

Linné ran her fingers through her hair. To distract him? He wasn't sure.

Tenna quickly moved in. "You've been the star of a very popular *policier* and several films, so why an understudy?"

Linné shifted her gaze to Anuj, and a blush appeared on his cheeks.

Roche wasn't sure why he found this annoying, and then it came to him. Anuj was a handsome young man, so it was natural for the actress to ignore the women in the room, as well as the older man, and be flirtatious with the young man. Perhaps she thought he was more likely to cut her some slack, give her the benefit of any doubts that might arise. When she turned her gaze back to Roche, he chastised himself for making the assumption.

"I do know how implausible this might seem," she said, "but I really did have my reasons. There were at least two producers drooling to get the exclusive deal to document this performance."

"And that would have been—"

"Lucrative," she interrupted. "Very lucrative. I realize that not all documentaries are, but this one had success written all over it. So, even though I understudied Camilla, there was to be extensive focus on my part of the play. Especially," she added, "my willingness to be the understudy. It could've been a fascinating documentary."

"And what happened?" Anuj asked.

Linné said, "Camilla's agent threw a wrench into the works. He wanted an exclusivity that limited my visibility in the film. I'd never heard of such a request, nor had my agent."

"I imagine you were angry," suggested Tenna.

The actress looked at Tenna, her eyes flashing. "I certainly wasn't thrilled! It was obvious that her people were afraid that my on-screen presence would diminish hers."

"So, you resented this," Anuj said. "The possibility of losing publicity and a great deal of money."

"Wouldn't you?" she asked. "And to set the record straight, I wasn't alone. I'm quite sure everyone connected to this project thought it was unfair."

Roche noticed that Aria was watching with no small measure of frustration. Perhaps it was because she was not in charge, not driving the interview. Not in control. Too bad for her.

"Inspector," said Linné. "Before you consider this a perfect motive for murder, you should know that Camilla's agent backed down several days ago, and all the limits were removed."

"And now that she's dead?" He let the question dangle like a tease.

Linné laughed. "What would be my reason for killing her! Although," she added, her voice suddenly quieter and more serious, "with her dead, I'll be more in demand than ever. An actress couldn't buy the kind of publicity that will be coming my way."

That declaration struck Roche as unusually callous for someone proclaiming her innocence.

She might have realized this, because she quickly added, "I hardly knew her. And I liked her." Her hands trembled. "No matter what you think, I could never inflict such a wound. Such...mayhem."

Roche spotted tears in her eyes and reminded himself that she was an actor, able to turn the tears on and off. "And this documentary," he said. "Any idea where it stands?"

Linné shifted her attention to Aria. "I'm sorry, but who are you again?"

Aria opened her mouth to speak, but Roche cut her off. "Madame Nevins is a journalist."

The woman looked at Aria, and then at her recorder. "The last thing I want is a member of the press listening to my every word." She moved to stand.

"Madame Nevins is not here to report on you. She is here at the request of our department, documenting how we function."

The actress settled back into the chair.

"Now," Roche continued. "About the documentary."

"It will never happen. My agent can give you specifics, as can my attorney."

"Detective Berglof will get those names before you leave," he said, indicating Tenna. "Is there anything you'd like to add?"

Linné shook her head. "No, except everyone knows who should've had that role. I made the best of it, but I'm still not sure why Max chose her over me."

"You don't know?" asked Roche.

Linné gave a little shrug. "I suggest you ask him."

"I intend to," he said. He reached for his recorder, but he was stopped when Anuj spoke.

"Miss Colbert, when you learned that Camilla was dead and the play would continue, how did you feel?"

Good question! Roche thought, relieved that Anuj had pushed aside his gaga-eyed worship.

Linné tossed her head, hair tumbling forward and framing her face. "I walked onto that stage and delivered the best performance of my life."

"So, you were excited," Tenna said, her voice flat.

The woman reared back. "Are you serious?"

Roche was sure she meant to say *Are you crazy?*

"I was devastated! How would you feel?" Her voice rose in pitch until the words were a squeak. "What if you were told to take the stage minutes after someone was left on the floor, dead and bloody, with part of her face missing?"

"I'm sure it was difficult," said Anuj. "But when you say—"

She cut him off with a chopping motion of her hand. "It was the best performance of my life because I had to hold back a powerful sense of grief and shock to carry it off. And I admit it, fear."

The silence in the room lengthened. Finally, Roche stood, crossed to the door, and held it open.

Without a word, Linné Colbert rose from her chair and walked out.

The minute she was gone, Roche slipped the recorder into his pocket and stepped into the hallway, gesturing for the others to follow. "We need to drop in on the Gabriels," he said.

"Should I call them?" Aria asked.

Roche weighed the best approach. "No, the element of surprise might be more effective."

"What do you have in mind, Boss?" Tenna asked, hot on his heels.

"I need to know more about the relationship between Linné and Camilla. We can count on Solange not to hold back." He slowed his pace as they crossed the lobby, and then he stopped and turned to face Aria. "I need you to be there," he told her. "But you're to speak only when prompted by me, understand?" The words echoed back, and he heard harshness.

Aria's mouth shifted into a hard line.

"They expect us to keep to their schedule," he told his team. "It's time they adhered to ours."

"No prep time," suggested Tenna. "A good call."

"And no time to concoct responses," said Roche. "Or to learn their lines."

They arrived shortly before three o'clock. It was much like every apartment building in this part of the city: fashionable and highly protected. The exterior was watched over by a half-dozen security cameras installed above the entrance, along the perimeter of the building, and across the road. No one could come or go without being observed, whether through a door or a window. Roche tried to push aside a niggling resentment, knowing that such a lifestyle would never be achievable in his lifetime.

He was studying the electronic panel next to the front door when Aria reached around him and pressed one of the buttons. As much as he wanted to tell her to step back, he quickly saw that there was no list of owners, no codes to enter to announce one's arrival. When he turned to look at her, she offered a little smile and a shrug.

A man, elderly and slightly stooped, opened the large door. His uniform was wool, deep green, and with gold braid epaulets. Roche wondered if he was expected to wear this heavy outfit year-round. Summer in Paris could be brutal. He seemed to wear the uniform with pride. Perhaps he would request to be buried in it, his suit of honor.

"I'm here to see the Gabriels," Roche said, as if standing there alone.

The doorman moved aside so they could enter what had to be one of the most elegant apartment buildings in Paris. The lobby was a vaulted space, easily four times the square footage of Roche's place. The marble floors whispered wealth; the ornately painted walls made Roche think of a palace. A fitting home for the likes of the Gabriels.

The doorman led them to a large desk, its mahogany top reflecting the chandelier high overhead, nothing on its surface but a telephone. Behind it sat a man wearing what Roche recognized as Armani. He had the body mass of a weightlifter, his biceps straining the arms of the jacket. Roche immediately thought of *Rambo* and wondered if he was carrying a concealed weapon.

The guard looked at all of them with suspicion.

Roche was certain that announcing his name would not suffice. He pulled out his identity badge and gestured for Anuj and Tenna to do the same. "Senior Inspector Noah Roche," he said, handing the badges to the man.

"And these are my officers, detectives Kumar and Berglof."

The man studied the badges and handed them back. "And you?" he said to Aria.

"You can announce me as Aria," she said. "The Gabriels are my family."

He turned his attention back to Roche. "And may I ask the nature of your visit?"

Roche gave him what he hoped was a meaningful stare. "No," he said, "you may not."

The man was clearly surprised. He made a quick attempt to regain the upper hand by flashing a manufactured smile. When Roche did not respond, he reached for the phone and punched in a number. "Three detectives and Madame Aria," he said, and then waited for a response. "Very good."

Without a word, the doorman led them to the bank of elevators. He passed a card across the security mechanism, the door opened, and he stepped inside, the others close behind.

They rode up in silence.

The elevator stopped, and Roche found himself facing a private foyer. There were three hallways—one to his right, another to his left, and the third spread out before him and leading to rooms with closed doors.

"Straight ahead," said the doorman as the elevator doors closed.

They began to walk forward, their pace determined by Roche. Every few feet, he slowed to glance at a painting, a lithograph, sculptured objects lining the walls. Most people would never stand close to even one of these in a lifetime. Here, there were at least a dozen.

"I've never seen anything like this," said Tenna, her voice so low that Roche strained to hear.

"The apartment takes up the entire floor of the building," Aria said. "I remember running through these hallways with my brother. When I was a teenager, I stayed here for two weeks until I found a room close to the university."

"I've seen my share of wealth," Anuj said, "but nothing like this. This," he added, gesturing to everything around them, "is palatial."

It took a moment before Roche realized that a young woman had appeared.

She was as plain as this apartment was ornate, a contrast not lost on him, and he recognized her as Sashkie, Solange Gabriel's assistant.

"Madame Nevins," said Sashkie. "The Gabriels are waiting for you."

Aria smiled.

She turned to the others. "Sashkie Ferrer," she said, as if they did not remember her. "We met at the theater under the most unfortunate circumstances." With that, she turned and began to walk. She stopped to point out the ceiling adorned with a fresco of angels and clouds. "There are five bedrooms on this level," she said. "And six bathrooms."

Roche wondered why anyone needed six bathrooms. He could see that Aria was not impressed. Perhaps she was accustomed to living in such luxury.

They stepped into a room with floor-to-ceiling bookcases running along every wall. Perhaps thirty feet away, and seated on chairs that resembled thrones, their feet propped up onto matching ottomans, were the Gabriels. Two icons of the French theater—holding court.

Behind them were multi-paned doors leading to a roof garden with enormous potted trees. Beyond the trees was the Paris sky and an unobstructed view of Trocadero.

Larger than a parlor, Roche thought, *but smaller than an airplane hangar.* The carpet under his feet was plush, making him think he should be removing his shoes. Anuj and Tenna stood next to him. They, too, seemed uncertain what to do next.

Aria approached the old couple, and they struggled to stand, aged bodies fighting gravity and time. "Stay, please," she said, and they settled back into the cushions. She bent to kiss Solange on both cheeks.

Roche could only watch. He was so far out of his realm that he was willing for Aria to take the lead.

"Darling," the woman said, reaching for Aria's hands. "It is such a pleasure to have you here, but also a sadness. Your mother called earlier. Bertie and I are devastated that she was unable to join us."

"And it was so like your mother," Bertrand added, as Aria bent down and gave him a light hug. "She sounded quite fine, but you know your mother.

THE CURTAIN FALLS IN PARIS

Delphine could stand inside a burning house and mention that the weather had turned warm. She's always been a terrible liar."

Roche wanted to get this under control, turn it from a cozy family reunion to a murder inquiry, but he knew that caution must be followed.

"So many memories come flooding back," Aria said. "I remember being a little girl, and how my father put me on his lap in this very room. Perhaps on this same sofa," she added, indicating a couch that Roche calculated as fifteen feet long. "And he read to me."

Solange and Bertrand smiled sweetly.

"I can hear his voice, his lilting voice," Bertrand said. "And your mother's perfume—"

"Gardenias," Solange said. "But just a subtle hint. Anything stronger would have been tawdry."

Roche and the others sat on the sofa, lined up like children and facing the Gabriels. "I'm sure you know why I'm here," he began. "There are still questions with no answers."

Solange looked at him for a long beat and then turned to Aria. "Remember your mother's worries about the lamps?" She pointed to two table lamps, one on either end of the sofa.

Aria glanced at Roche, as if letting him know that he was in charge. When he said nothing, she gave a big smile to Solange. "I can hear Maman's voice, warning me, 'Ariadne, do not touch, my darling, they are Tiffany!' As a child, that meant nothing. Today, well..."

"Today," interrupted Solange, "they are easily worth fifty thousand dollars...each."

Roche saw Tenna cover her mouth as she suppressed a gasp. He quietly thanked her for her good judgment.

"Now," said Bertrand, as if about to make an important announcement. "The truth: how is your mother?"

"Maman is better," she said. "A cold that became bronchitis. The doctor swore he'd have her physically removed from the plane if she dared to make the trip."

"Well, you're here," Solange said, putting some effort into shifting her body on the chair. "And you were in the theater, so you can go home and tell her all about it…about…us."

"When did you get in?" Bertrand said.

"I took the red-eye, so I landed hours before the play."

Solange turned to her husband. "Bertie, we should have sent a car for her."

"Yes, why didn't we think of it, my dear?" he asked, concern in his eyes.

"Because we're old!" she replied, and they both laughed.

Roche watched this exchange and felt that little seed of resentment dissolving. These were universally respected actors living in what felt to him like extreme wealth, yet they could laugh at themselves, at growing older. And not only older…old. He doubted he would be as charming at that age.

Bertrand turned to Roche. "Bastion, heh? That glass monstrosity near Port de Clichy? I preferred it when all of you Brigade Criminelle folks were at Thirty-six. A classic place, to be sure."

"Deserving of the best French mystery," Roche said. "And I couldn't agree with you more."

"Maigret," Aria said. "I've seen them all."

"And now here's your flash for the day," Bertrand said with a mischievous grin. "That role should have been mine. Oh, yes," he added, waving his hand as if brushing away a gnat. "Bruno Cremet was fine, but I knew that character; I understood his inner strengths."

Solange patted his hand. "Yes, dear, we know." She looked at Aria. "Opportunities lost. It's the bête noir of the theater."

"You do understand why this little visit has to be short," Bertrand said to Roche. "At our age—"

"Don't you dare use the word *octogenarian*!" Solange declared.

"At our age," Bertrand repeated, "we need a good long rest in the afternoon."

There was a lull in the conversation. Roche looked at Aria and had the feeling she was suddenly on alert. He knew she had been living under a black cloud of suspicion and distress for several months, unsure of her future, her career, and her reputation. Did the Gabriels know?

"Aria, dear, it's tragic about your plight," Solange said.

Roche glanced at Aria, hoping the old woman's comment hadn't leveled her. He saw no emotion in her face. He shifted his glance to Solange. What was he seeing? A touch of—what—a smirk? He pushed that thought away. From what he had seen, Solange could be judgmental, sometimes harshly so, but not cruel.

"And how is Delphine taking it?" Solange asked.

"My dear," Bertrand said. "Perhaps Aria would rather not—"

Solange gave his hand a little slap. "Of course, she would, Bertie, she's with friends. We're…family!"

"The three of us are, yes," he said, making a show of looking at the others.

When she spoke, her voice was softer, kinder. "I don't judge," she said.

Roche had to suppress a laugh. He had been in Solange Gabriel's presence for a short time, but he knew that for her not to judge would be like a downpour leaving the ground dry.

Roche was afraid that Solange was turning this into some kind of verbal brawl. He had no doubts that she was pulling every trick out of the bag to distract him from doing his job. The last thing he could do was lose control. With one fluid gesture, he removed his little recorder from his pocket, placed it on his lap, and turned it on.

The conversation around him came to an abrupt halt.

Out of the corner of his eye, he saw Aria take out her recorder and activate it, but she kept it on the sofa, next to her leg and out of sight.

As he began to question the couple, he found their responses vague. In fact, it was only Solange who responded. Bertrand sat quietly, as if happy to leave the job to his wife.

"Do you know anyone who would want to hurt Camilla Rodolfo?"

"No idea, she was a lovely woman."

"Was there jealousy between Camilla and Linné Colbert?"

"Why? Should there have been?"

"Was there anyone in the theater who might have wanted to hurt Camilla?"

"Well, Bertie and I certainly did not. I can't speak for the others."

And on it went. Roche had hoped for some insight into the other members of the cast, but every twist and turn brought them back to the same conclusion: the Gabriels knew nothing that could help in this investigation.

"The relationship we had with Camilla was lovely," Solange insisted. "And yes, we knew about that documentary, but those problems were resolved."

"No conflict at all," Bertrand added.

"So, love and peace and friendship reigned," said Roche.

The Gabriels grinned in unison, bringing to mind matching Kewpie dolls.

Less than an hour later, Roche and Aria were standing on the sidewalk in front of the building. The doorman had returned to the stool just inside the entrance and was reading the latest edition of Libération. Anuj and Tenna had taken off for the precinct, sharing their boss's frustration with the stonewalling encountered upstairs. Thanks to the bodybuilder making a quick call, there was a cab waiting at the curb, its engine humming.

Aria opened the back door and tucked herself inside.

"Early to bed?" he asked with little interest.

"Since it's not quite five o'clock, it's a bit soon, but I have plenty of work to do." She patted her bag. "Lots of good stuff here."

Hackles rising, that's what he felt. And a pressing need to remind her that he, too, worked long hours, as did his team.

He was about to close the cab door, and then stopped. "I'm afraid the Gabriels have entered a zone of silence. I can only push them so far without appearing to be an ogre." Before she could respond, he said the one thing he'd tried hard to avoid. "You seem to be the only one who can make any headway with them." That sounded so pathetic to him. Or worse, like a man incapable of doing his job.

Aria looked up, her face pensive. "You have reservations about them."

Roche heard a warning bell. If he voiced doubts about their innocence, she could write something uncomplimentary about him. "Sometimes, even the most improbable suspects are guilty."

"But, really, the Gabriels?" Her expression was pinched, suggesting that his observation bordered on the absurd.

"Miss Nevins, it may be rare, but not unknown, for the elderly to commit murder. I can't cross them off the list, not yet."

She waited, saying nothing.

The best he could hope was that she remained neutral, professional. "My office in the morning, say nine?"

She grabbed the door by its handle and closed it firmly, leaving him standing at the curb.

He watched the cab pull away, certain that her only regret was that it wasn't raining, bucketing, leaving him drenched.

As he walked away from the building, he glanced back. The doorman was at his post, guarding the privacy of people who probably didn't remember this man's name, people who wrote nothing on the envelope slipped to him every Christmas.

Roche was certain the Gabriels had information that could help his investigation. What were they holding back, and why?

Chapter Nine

It was late, and Aria was trying to sleep, but she was worried about her mother's health. *The old order changeth, yielding place to new.* Perhaps this was not what Tennyson had in mind. But if it was, she found it unlikely that she could fulfill the expectations for the next Nevins generation. Better to skip this one and let her daughter, Lexie, take the reins. But this wasn't about her mother, or any family legacy. This was about her last meeting with Izzy Martinez, the jumping-off point for this wretched insomnia.

Izzy was more than her boss; he was her friend. They went back nearly twenty years, when he first arrived from Chicago to become one of the paper's political reporters. At their initial meeting, he had come across as standoffish, even gruff, but Aria quickly recognized that he was ethical and fair. And kind. Which is why, when she was sitting in his office only weeks earlier, his words had shaken her.

"It's a suspension," he explained for the third time, staring across the room at the cartons stacked on her desk.

"So you say, but am I coming back?"

He leaned back in a chair so worn its stuffing was escaping. He used the eraser of a pencil to scratch his balding head. "Give it time. The Aria Nevins I know has three lives, so you have two to go. It was a mistake, a terrible mistake. A lapse in judgment." His eyes were soft. "It happens."

"Not to me, it doesn't." She had felt both relieved that she might be given another chance, and terrified that no matter what she did, the damage was irreversible and her career was finished.

Now she was in Paris, and she was certain that Roche knew about her crisis, and she assumed that his team knew as well. As for de Charbonnet, he had made no effort to hide it. It was in his eyes, which she read as *I have you by the throat.* But no one needed to heap shame on her; she did that very well by herself.

She climbed out of bed and went to the window. Wind was gusting off the river and rattling the shutters; a police siren wailed in the distance. A quick glance at the clock told her it was just past midnight. "Oh, the hell with it."

She pulled on jeans and a heavy sweater, thick wool socks and walking shoes, the same shoes she'd worn during her treks across China when she was covering the government's crackdown on border crossings. The good old days, when she still had a job. And a reputation.

She grabbed her winter coat and cap and left the room.

As she passed through the lobby, she nearly ran into a man crossing to the reception desk.

"It's cold out there, Madame," he announced.

"A brisk walk and something to eat might help me sleep."

"Ah, well, then turn right at the quay, walk two or three minutes to the kiosk. Can't say much for the food, but it's hot and cheap."

She gave a little wave and walked out of the hotel, the promise of food giving her a resurgence of energy. Reflections of light on the river and the wind blowing off the water were invigorating. A tourist boat moved slowly past, rocking in the tumultuous water, and she pitied the people on board. Psychedelic lights shot out from the wheelhouse like shards of glass, bouncing off the buildings that lined the river, and throwing haphazard colors across the water.

There were a few late-nighters on the quay, but there was no way to tell if they were men or women. Everyone was bending into the wind, heads down, the boat's lights sweeping garish rainbow-colored patches across them.

The wind picked up, unleashing such a force that Aria nearly fell. She pulled her coat tightly around her and soldiered on. She was surprised to see a few booksellers along the banks. A man was using a pole to fetch a large poster from the water. "May I help?" she asked, her voice nearly lost in the wind.

Without turning around, he shouted, "Got it, thanks!"

No sooner had he spoken than the poster changed course, floated out of his reach, and disappeared into the black water.

She stopped to assist a woman who was placing blocks of wood on top of a pile of books. "It's wild!" Aria said, tying twine around the bin of posters. Their flapping sound reminded her of those days when she attached playing cards to her bicycle wheels with wood clothespins. The good old days.

"Thank you!" hollered the woman, locking down her display.

Around them, merchants were frantically folding their stalls into padlocked boxes and racing away.

Aria thought of turning back to the hotel. In the balcony of a nearby apartment, she saw how the rosemary, iris, and roses in window boxes were bending, and that most of the geranium plants were already stripped bare. Further along, she saw the light from a kiosk casting its glow onto the walkway, and she rushed inside. "Is it too late to eat?" she asked the teenage girl who greeted her at the door.

The girl called out, "Papa, are we still serving?"

A man stepped into view. "Two servings of tapas and then we're out."

"I'll take both," said Aria. "Any chance you have espresso?"

She waited for her food, a memory creeping into her mind. She was sixteen, and it was weeks after her father's heart attack and death. She and her brother had come to Paris with their mother, all of them exhausted. Delphine was in widow's black, grief-stricken, clinging to her children. They stayed with Solange and Bertrand in their villa north of Paris. Solange had been kind, even comforting, but something changed. Instead of pampering Delphine and her children, she became distant, chilly. Aria remembered feeling unwelcomed. Her mother explained that some people could not face grief, and that a childless woman might not understand what a child feels. Aria had been forgiving.

But here she was, nearly four decades later, and Solange was still running hot and cold. What did the Gabriels know about Camilla's death? Before she could pursue that thought, a voice reminded her that her assignment was to write about the Paris police. The murder, she felt almost ashamed to admit, was a bonus.

Roche had told her that she was needed to help with the Gabriels, which she interpreted as keeping them in line. Perhaps, in his eyes, she had crossed from albatross to colleague. It still begged the question: why were the Gabriels being so difficult? They were giving the appearance of speaking freely, but she sensed they couldn't be trusted. What were they hiding? Were they incapable of separating truth from lie?

The girl arrived with a plate of steaming tapas and a mug of espresso. Aria took a bite, but had to force it down. Ravenous only minutes ago, she could barely chew. She swallowed hard. It disturbed her that she thought ill of the Gabriels. Like this food, her judgment of them stuck in her throat.

She finished the espresso, placed fifteen euros under the mug, and stood. The wind was calming a bit. She might make it back to the hotel without being blown into the river. How perfect if the wind could blow away this penetrating guilt. But no, the damage was done. Her best hope was that she could disabuse herself of the feeling that she was standing in front of a firing squad, blindfolded, and waiting for the first shot.

Chapter Ten

Roche found Anuj in the corridor, standing outside one of the precinct's interrogation rooms.

"I'm waiting for Joseph," said the young detective.

Roche peered into the room, where Tenna and Aria were settled at the table. Men and women rushed about, a good number of them glancing into the room. Roche knew they were hoping to catch sight of a celebrity, and that most of them would drop everything to be part of this investigation.

"How about you take the lead?"

"Sure," Anuj replied, his voice calm, casual.

Roche could almost hear the detective's heart racing. He had put Anuj in charge of a questioning before, but never with such a high-profile case.

Tenna stepped out of the room. There was no grin, no cheery presence. Roche preferred it when she was cheeky. He had no time to commiserate with her private life.

"The sharks are circling," she said. "We all need to be more cautious than usual about what we say."

"And to whom," he added.

Just that morning, leaving his apartment, he had been faced with a mob of reporters. One of them pushed through the crowd and blocked his path. "So, who's this American journalist?" the man had demanded, holding a recorder within an inch of Roche's face.

He tried to back away; the odor of the man was overwhelming.

"Hoping to have a docudrama about you, Inspector? Or perhaps you've got her following you around to know you better—get it all right. That matters when you're negotiating film rights!"

Laughter ran through the group, but it wasn't friendly.

Sharks and chum.

"What's her name?" someone shouted.

He was able to slip back into the building and use the rear fire exit that opened onto an alleyway. From there, he made his way to a taxi. How long would this last? Even Judith had been approached. Her explanation that she and Roche were divorced and he no longer confided in her had fallen on unsympathetic ears.

And now here they were, in the station, and still accosted. Not by journalists hovering outside, but by the looks and whispers of fellow officers. Curiosity. The scourge of any complex investigation. He wondered if Aria's presence might be adding to the suspicions.

"Everything good?" Anuj asked Tenna.

"Couldn't be better," she said.

Roche heard sarcasm, but said nothing. They needed to focus on this case, and they were running out of time.

He stepped into the room, and they followed him. Aria placed her recorder on the table, quickly accompanied by Tenna's notebook.

"Before Joseph shows up," said Anuj, "what's your *Be-a-better-detective* lecture for today?"

Roche silently thanked him for getting back to business. The wise choice was to play along. "Today, it's about honing your skills, analyzing element by element all the evidence, both physical and psychological."

Anuj and Tenna looked at each other and laughed. Roche saw this as a *here he goes again!* moment, which pleased him.

He had another lecture, and it was far more important. "Never rush to judgment. Making a judgment based on little evidence can be disastrous."

His words came back to slap him in the face. He couldn't believe he had said that with Aria in the room. He couldn't bring himself to look at her.

The knock on the door was a reprieve.

Joseph Mardikian entered, and Roche gestured for him to sit. By the time the young man was settled in, Anuj had managed to leave the room and return with a chair. He pushed it to the head of the table and sat on it. "Thank you for coming," Anuj said.

"Did I have a choice?" Joseph's voice was pleasant, not angry or challenging.

"You always have a choice," Anuj responded. "Unless...you don't."

Roche watched this exchange, noting how Joseph's quick smile seemed to please Anuj, the young detective having conquered that challenge of connecting with a possible suspect. He thought of Max Formande, and how he would study his actors and give critiques. Perhaps a chief homicide inspector played the same role with his junior officers. That is, to observe, note how they communicate, and then offer suggestions.

"May I?" Tenna asked, directing her question to Anuj. He held out his hand, as if to say *be my guest.* "Joseph, is there anyone from the cast or crew you're particularly close to?"

Roche shifted in his chair and nearly spoke, but said nothing. Tenna knew her way around an interrogation, and often asked questions more comfortably asked by a woman. Or so he thought. He waited.

Joseph appeared confused. "When you say *close to,* I'm not sure I understand."

"Friends," she clarified. "Or more."

"It's not easy forming friendships during rehearsals," he said. "Especially in a situation like this one."

"Like this one...in what way?" asked Anuj.

"Rehearsals usually go on for weeks," Joseph explained. "Our lives become intertwined. We're together from morning to late at night. It doesn't matter if the production is ready or not; it has to open on the date announced. For *Hamlet's Father*, the pressure was much more intense."

"Intense how?" Aria asked, then glanced quickly at Anuj.

Roche wanted to remind Aria that her role was to remain silent, to do nothing more than observe, but Anuj had given her the go-ahead. He'd talk to him later.

"For one thing," said Joseph, "there were no previews." He looked at the others. "That's where an audience comes before the production begins and

95

watches rehearsals."

"Why would anyone attend a preview?" asked Tenna. "I mean, if lines haven't been learned?"

"That's exactly why," Joseph said. "People love to see the play in the making. They get to watch the actors forget their lines, sometimes give hilarious asides while making fun of themselves, even if it's someone like Solange or Bertrand Gabriel. There's always the problem of crossing to the wrong side of the stage and ending up speaking to a wall. Or a cue is missed and an actor is left there on the stage, waiting like some idiot." His face flushed. He had just described the night of the murder.

"So, you're saying that people come to these previews because they enjoy watching the actors flub their lines?" Tenna asked.

"A lot of people buy one ticket for the preview and another one for the end of a run. That way, they get to see how the play finally comes together."

"But there were no previews for *Hamlet's Father*," said Anuj.

None," said Joseph. "And only a few days of rehearsal, which were closed to the public. We had that one performance to get it right." He removed his glasses and rubbed his eyes. "We worked so hard. The performance was going so well, and then—"

A heavy silence descended, making the room feel dark and airless.

"I have a few questions," said Aria.

Roche wondered when she would understand that she was not part of this team, an interloper. He would tell her so later. For now, it was still Anuj's call.

She leaned forward. "Joseph, did you get acquainted with Sashkie? Or have a friendship with Laurene?"

Roche had to admit this made sense. A young man, two young women. Damn, he should have asked.

"I hardly spoke to Laurene," said Joseph. "She was always running around, fetching things for Max. But if you ask me, I think her main job is to clean up his messes."

"Messes?" repeated Tenna.

"Maybe that's not the right word," said Joseph. "His glasses are always missing. He forgets to take his meds. The names of people he's known for years get lost somewhere in his mind. I've worked here for nearly ten years, but recently he's been calling me Gerald."

"Who's Gerald?" Roche asked.

"Hell if I know. I corrected him several times, but it only upset him. So, now I'm Gerald."

"And the others," asked Anuj. "Are you friends with them?"

Joseph became very quiet.

"Joseph?" said Anuj. "Nothing leaves this room."

A pale flush crept into his cheeks. "Max's assistant, Laurene. I haven't spoken to her much, but I know she likes me. More than likes, I think, by the way she looks at me. But she isn't my type."

"Is there someone here who is your type?" asked Tenna.

Joseph lowered his eyes. "Sashkie."

Roche was perplexed. Laurene was attractive and stylish, with a strong personality, warm and charming. Sashkie, the assistant to Solange Gabriel, was mousy and dull.

"Sashkie is more than the old woman's assistant," said Joseph. "She's her dresser, her right hand. Sashkie does it all, and more."

Roche was always trying to gain insight into the personalities of suspects and witnesses. If there was one thing he knew, it was that people see more than they realize.

"What about Anton Delant?" Aria asked. "Or Laurene and the sound technician?"

"I'm not sure I understand your question," said Joseph.

"Would any of them benefit from Camilla's death?" she asked. "Perhaps one of them shared a history with her that should have remained a secret?"

"I can't see how," Joseph said. "I don't even know if they knew each other before this performance."

Tenna placed her elbows on the table. "Was there anyone who believed that her death would advance their career?"

Furrows appeared on Joseph's brow. "Can someone be so ambitious they'd commit murder?"

His response struck Roche as naïve. People did terrible things to get what they wanted, what they believed they deserved. He saw evidence of raw ambition in his own department. And not rarely, but daily. And what about resentment when a promotion didn't come through? Or when the wrong person received it? "Ambition can be ugly," he said. "And sometimes deadly."

While Joseph ruminated on that, Aria stepped in.

"Did something happen before rehearsals that might have triggered anger, or any kind of negative feelings against Camilla?"

Joseph pressed his lips together, his expression perplexed.

Roche knew that discomfort could yield results, revelations. He flipped open his notebook. "Where were you during intermission?" He felt Anuj's eyes on him.

"Where I always am," Joseph said. "Above the stage, adjusting the lights for the next act. With a small stage, the adjustments aren't major, but when you're working with the likes of the Gabriels—" He let the sentence linger.

"What do you mean by *the likes of the Gabriels*?" Anuj asked.

The way Joseph stared at the door, Roche wondered if he was considering making a break for it.

"Joseph?" Anuj prodded. "I know you're tired, we all are, so just a few more minutes. What do you mean by *the likes of the Gabriels*?"

"I mentioned that Madame Gabriel sometimes joked with me, and she can be very funny. But she's also demanding. At the dress rehearsal, I must've spent two hours adjusting the lighting to suit her. If she had stayed in that big chair most of the time, no problem, but she likes to move around the stage. If the lighting is off, the audience…"

Roche suddenly turned to Tenna. "Do you have that list of ticket holders?"

Tenna reached down, and then stopped. "The file is at my desk."

"Could you get it?" Roche asked. "Please. I want to go over that list with Max."

Tenna rushed out of the room, and Roche shifted his attention back to Joseph. "You were saying?"

"Some actors don't change positions much, or they're happy to move from one spot to another. Not Madame Gabriel. She wanted the first light to track her until she was under the second one, and then I'd fade the first one. It's not complicated, but it takes a hundred and twenty percent of my attention. Which," he quickly added, "is no big deal, unless there's another actor on stage at the same time. And if that actor also has special instructions, well, it can get challenging."

Aria leaned forward. "So, you didn't have time to run out for a bite during intermission."

"That's when I set up for the next act. And if I've screwed up during the first act, no one can yell at me if I'm in the rafters."

"Thank you," Anuj said. "I think we're done here."

Before Joseph could stand, Aria spoke, setting off an alarm in Roche's head. In his mind, she was a pit bull being let off the chain.

"Above the stage," she said. "You have a bird's eye view of everything below you. Did you notice anything strange? That is, during rehearsals, or even during the performance?"

Joseph tipped his head. "What do you mean?"

Roche saw how the young man's face had changed, hardened a bit.

"Tensions between actors," she said. "Arguments or disagreements."

"No, just the normal stuff."

"Normal," Anuj repeated.

"You know, little spats and jealousies."

Anuj checked to make sure this was being recorded. "Who was doing the spatting?"

Joseph glanced at Aria, his eyes again pleading. "There was something going on between Camilla and Linné, but I think they worked it out."

"What was it?" Anuj asked.

Roche thought it was probably the conflict already described by Linné, but perhaps not. His thoughts were interrupted when he noticed that Joseph was pressing his palm against his forehead, the way the inspector did when thwarting a headache. "Do you need a few minutes?" he asked.

Joseph shook his head, inhaled deeply, and released it. "I heard complaints about some documentary, and that Rodolfo's people were making demands."

"And this caused a rift between the women?" Anuj asked.

"For a time, yes. But then something happened and they were friends again."

"When you say *again*, does that mean they were friends before this play?"

Joseph shook his head. "No, because I remember how they were introduced the first day of rehearsals." He paused a moment. "What I mean is, there was something negative between them…and then it was gone. I think the problem was worked out."

Anuj flipped to another page in his notebook. "So," he said, glancing at his notes. "Other than this little problem, everyone got on well?"

Joseph gave the detective a long look. "If you must know, everyone steered clear of Solange Gabriel."

"You told us that she's demanding, and at the same time, how much you admire her," Aria said.

"I do! But she not only played a queen," he said. "She thinks she is a queen, and she expects everyone to treat her like one."

"And her husband?" asked Anuj.

"Demanding, expecting everything to run smoothly. But a sweet man, not a mean bone in his body. And a saint, if you ask me." Joseph leaned back and stretched his legs until they reached under the table, and his feet banged into Aria's. "Sorry," he said, pulling them back.

Roche asked, "Why a saint?"

"His wife may be a brilliant actor, but she can be a right nasty woman, as my father would say. How he's put up with that for nearly sixty years. Well, Christ Almighty, I couldn't take it for sixty minutes!"

Anuj thanked him for his time, adding that he was not to leave Paris until given permission, as there might be need for further questioning.

Joseph stood and left the room. Before the echoing sound of the closing door had stopped, Tenna blew in and placed the list in front of Roche.

He picked it up and ran his fingers down the names. "Nothing that jumps out at me," he said. "Not yet." He nearly turned to Aria to thank her for her questions, but held back. The image of the pit bull returned. Even with praise, the bite was just as ferocious.

"Thank you," said Aria to the team. "For letting me ask questions."

Roche acknowledged her with a nod. He turned to Anuj. "I said I'd leave you to run this, but—" It was part tease, part question.

"We were mesmerized by your technique, Boss."

Aria and Tenna stifled a laugh.

"You were all doing so well, I couldn't pull myself away." He stretched his neck and back. "I don't know about you, but I'm starving. How about we grab a crêpe near the Metro? Or," he added, "we could choose a real resto, something with great desserts."

"Le Grand Véfour?" Aria asked, her eyebrows raised in amusement.

Anuj appeared confused, and Roche nearly asked how she knew about one of the top restaurants in Europe. Then he remembered that she was the daughter of a famous designer. One day, he'd have to ask her about the restaurant's celebrated chocolate mousse. He shoved that thought away. He was a chief inspector. By God, he could afford to book a table and try it for himself! And then he warned himself to stay focused. "We've spoken to Linné, Joseph, Sashkie, and managed a partial questioning of the Gabriels," Roche said, eyeing the sheet with the names of actors, staff, and crew. "That leaves the sound technician and Laurene, Max's assistant. And Anton's understudy. Oh, yes, and then Max."

"It feels like we'll be swimming in these waters for days," said Anuj.

"There are a few we can cross off the list," said Roche, and then gave it another look. "The sound tech guy was in his booth, never left it. Max is too old, and I can't imagine him committing such an act. Maybe Tenna's list of the ticket holders will be more helpful."

"What about the Gabriels?" asked Anuj. "We seem to be giving them a free pass."

"At the moment, I'm not sure where they are, suspect-wise."

Together, they walked to a nearby café known for its onion blini and fast service. Roche was taking his last bite, and ready to order another, when he checked his watch and jumped to his feet. "Damn! De Charbonnet called me to a press conference, and it starts in fifteen minutes."

He rushed back to his office, grabbed his notes, popped a breath mint into his mouth, and rushed out.

He entered the large room just as de Charbonnet was approaching the microphone. He gave the inspector no more than a glance, but Roche recognized both relief and anger in the man's face.

The room was packed. There were journalists from every local, regional, and national paper, plus a few cable news reporters who provided stories globally. If anyone doubted that Camilla Rodolfo's murder was news, this crowd set the record straight. He looked from face to face and then saw Aria walk in, her press credentials hanging around her neck. Why would she miss the opportunity to watch him squirm? Anuj and Tenna were also there, standing in the back, leaning against the wall. He was surprised that their presence gave him a sense of relief.

Georges de Charbonnet tapped on the microphone. The sound filled the room, and he began to speak. He covered the basic information and turned to leave.

Roche gave a silent thanks to be spared the interrogation of the press, but before he could step off the dais, the room exploded into questions. For nearly fifteen minutes, men and women of the press verbally and sometimes physically pushed each other aside to get their question heard. De Charbonnet looked like a man trapped in an underground cave, the water level rising quickly.

"Do you have suspects?"

"What was the motive?"

"Is it true a large part of her face was cut away?'

"Why is it taking so long to find the killer?"

De Charbonnet responded, but Roche was certain he was inching away from the microphone.

He felt sympathy for the man. It wasn't easy being under verbal attack by dozens of people who believed they had the right to know.

"What's your next move?" called out a man from the rear of the room, nearly elbow-to-elbow with Tenna.

This time, de Charbonnet turned to Roche. "Chief Homicide Investigator Noah Roche will answer that one."

Roche stepped forward, replacing de Charbonnet at the microphone.

Before he said a word, sweat had already begun to form on his brow. He had held many press conferences, but this one was different. It was impossible to walk past a newspaper kiosk without noticing that nearly every edition had a headline screaming about this murder. It had only been two days, but the public was demanding an arrest.

"Inspector Roche," said a woman in the front of the room. "Just what are you doing to catch the killer? And do you have a suspect?"

He collected himself. "We are doing everything possible. There were nearly a hundred and fifteen people in the theater, including patrons, cast, crew, and staff. We're working around the clock."

"Are the higher-ups cooperating?" asked a man. "That is, are they giving you a free rein?'

He glanced at de Charbonnet. It was so tempting to be truthful, to mention the unceasing phone calls and texts he was receiving from this demanding, ambitious, and thoroughly annoying man. Instead, he said, "Yes, of course. Everyone wants this murderer locked away."

Before another question could be asked, Roche felt his phone vibrate. He ignored it, but when it stopped and immediately vibrated again, he yanked it from his pocket and checked the text. His face clouded over. Without a word, he spun on his heels and stepped away from the podium.

"Roche!" said de Charbonnet, his voice low, insistent, furious.

He ran from the room, certain that Anuj, Tenna, and Aria were close behind.

The minute they were out of earshot of everyone, he stopped. "Joseph has fallen from the catwalk," he said. "He's critical."

Tenna pulled the car keys from her bag.

"Anuj and I will take a taxi," Roche said.

He saw confusion on Anuj's face. What could he say? That the last thing he wanted was to be trapped in a car with Aria? But the truth was, he needed time to think and found this difficult in a car with three passengers.

He was relieved when Aria followed Tenna without question. They were barely out of the building when Tenna called out, "Sir, which hospital?"

"Pitié Salpêtriere," he said over his shoulder. He had no need to stress the urgency: this was where people with life-threatening injuries were taken.

The taxi driver seemed to understand the urgency and found a way to speed through the city and arrive at the hospital in good time. Roche paid him and rushed inside, with Anuj right behind him.

He was surprised to find Tenna and Aria awaiting them. "Our driver took shortcuts," he sputtered.

Tenna gave him a long look. "I turned on the siren."

They found Laurene and Sashkie in the lobby. Roche shepherded everyone into the emergency area and found a quiet corner. "What the hell happened?"

Laurene appeared stricken, while Sashkie's face was devoid of emotion. He wondered how Laurene felt, knowing that Joseph preferred the acerbic, plain-Jane Sashkie. Love was so complicated, and young love even more so.

"Who found him?" Roche asked.

"I was in the dressing room," said Sashkie. "To take inventory, so I'd know what went to the apartment and what belonged in storage. I heard a woman in the hallway shouting that someone was lying on the stage, and she wasn't sure he was alive. I ran there, and Max and Laurene were right behind me. We found Joseph. There was blood running from his head."

Laurene pressed her lips together and then whispered, "It was everywhere."

"What woman?" Roche pressed Sashkie.

She turned to Laurene.

"She's with the demolition crew," Laurene said. "Making sure nothing important was left in the building."

A nurse was passing by. Roche stepped away to confer with her.

She checked his credentials. "He's critical, Inspector, still unconscious."

"How critical?"

"You'll have to discuss that with the neurologist."

He returned to the others.

"A neurologist?" said Laurene. "That's bad." She grabbed Roche's arm. "It was no accident." Her voice quivered with emotion. "I'm sure he was pushed."

Sashkie muttered something. To Roche, it sounded like *drama queen*, but he couldn't be sure.

"Why do you think that?" Tenna asked.

Laurene stared at Tenna for a moment. "He knows every inch of that catwalk. Even when the theater is pitch black, he can move up there blindfolded." She began to weep.

Aria moved closer and touched her shoulder. "He's young, resilient. He's got that on his side."

Questions raced through Roche's mind. If Laurene loves Joseph, but he doesn't love her back, is that reason enough for her to attack him? No, it was more likely that Joseph's fall had something to do with Camilla's death. But what?

Aria suggested they find the cafeteria. "Nothing will be known for hours," she said, and then turned to Sashkie and Laurene. "If you're staying until something changes, you need to eat." She turned towards the door leading to the cafeteria, but the young women did not follow. Seeing this, she retraced her steps.

Roche thought of a mother duck trying to lead her ducklings.

"Good thing she's here," said Tenna, giving her boss what struck him as a stern look.

Aria spoke to someone behind the desk at the nurses' station and then gestured for the others to follow her.

They entered the ICU waiting room. Roche was certain the young women would not leave until they learned about Joseph's condition. He saw how Laurene was chewing on the inside of her cheek. He nearly told her to stop, but playing father to an adult woman could be seen as meddlesome. Or worse, disrespectful.

He saw how Aria leaned closer to Tenna. "We look like a Greek chorus," she said. The detective's brow furrowed. "Greek dramas had a chorus of women revealing the plot in one voice."

A doctor gripping a clipboard approached them. "He's holding on, but just," she said. "There's no certainty he'll regain consciousness; he took a heavy blow to the head."

"He fell from a theater catwalk," Roche said.

The woman gestured for him to follow her. When they were a good distance away from the others, she said in a low voice, "If I had to guess, I'd say he was struck hard, very hard, before he fell. The contusion here," she said, pointing to her temple. "That was caused by a direct blow, something small and round, like the head of a hammer. And there's a second point of impact. That's the blow that fractured his skull. It's consistent with falling from a considerable height." She checked her pager, excused herself, and rushed off.

"This isn't good," he murmured, returning to the team. "Go back to the theater," he told Sashkie and Laurene. "I'll let you know if there's a change."

Laurene passed her hand across her eyes. "Go back and do what?"

"There's nothing you can do here," he told her.

"Yes, there is. I can sit with him, and be here when he wakes up."

"I'll stay with you," Sashkie offered, although her tone struck Roche as half-hearted.

"Thank you," said Laurene. "But you go." She crossed to a row of chairs and sat.

The way Sashkie gave a quick wave and rushed toward the exit door made Roche think of someone being relieved of front-line artillery duty.

If Joseph had been attacked—and everything pointed to that certainty—they now had a second crime to explore. "We need an officer in his room at all times," Roche instructed Tenna and Anuj.

His heart was pounding, and pressure was building in his chest. The words *heart attack* rushed across his mind. He pulled in a hard breath and held it for a long moment, and then released it slowly. "The doctor's certain he was assaulted," he told them. "We can't take the chance this will happen again. Tell Laurene that the minute the officer arrives, she can sit with Joseph. But not until then. We don't need to put her at risk, too."

Tenna repeated his orders to Laurene, while Anuj made a brief phone call. "Twenty minutes," he told Roche.

His heart was calm. Decisions were being made. "We need to rethink this. Anuj, go back to the theater. Tenna, have a forensic team there as soon as possible. They'll be able to tell if someone has tampered with the railing."

He saw Aria watching, and he expected her to speak, but she remained silent. A wise choice, considering he had no patience to spare. His conscience informed him that he was being unfair, but he ignored it.

"Anuj!" he called out, and the young detective backtracked. "Take Tenna with you. We need to be sure nothing is touched, either on or above the stage." He chastised himself for not doing this sooner. The last thing he needed was an unsecured crime scene. Anyone could have moved things, destroyed evidence. He should have demanded this the moment he learned of Joseph's fall. It had to be fatigue; it was getting to him.

"It's been done," said Tenna.

He looked at her, confusion furrowing his brow.

"I called after we left the press conference. Two of our people are at the theater, and the forensics people should have arrived by now."

Roche stared at her for a moment. "Well done."

"Maybe we should all go back to the theater," suggested Anuj. "There's nothing we can do here."

Roche thought about this for a moment. "I need to see Joseph first."

It took his badge and firm persuasion before the head nurse would allow him into the dimly lit room. When her back was turned, he marshaled everyone inside.

They stood around the bed staring at what had been, only hours earlier, a robust young man, now a gaunt figure with tubes running into his arms and snaking out from under the bedclothes. An oxygen mask covered most of his face.

Roche learned close enough to get a good look at the massive swelling above his right ear and extending to the crown of his head.

Aria touched the blanket draped over his leg. "Somewhere," she said, "a mother is frantic."

Roche swung toward her. "A father, too. That is, if they've been told."

"Yes, certainly, a father," she quickly agreed.

Laurene hovered over Joseph, her hand resting on his shoulder.

"I think he'll make it," said Roche, his voice gentle, hopeful. "He's young and strong."

Laurene gave him a weak smile.

The officer arrived. Roche took him aside and spoke quietly. He could not have been older than his mid-twenties, but he seemed self-assured, like a veteran of the force who had seen it all.

Roche led Laurene to the nurses' station. "Other than your staff, the police officer, and Miss Froberg here, no one is authorized to be in that room. The officer knows to remain during all procedures, no exceptions. If there's a change in Joseph's condition, or any visitors try to gain entry, call me at once." He handed her his card.

The ride back to the theater was made in silence. This suited Roche. He needed a few minutes of respite from death and injury, and he was worried that Aria was feeding information to Charbonnet. He had no proof, but the suspicion would not leave him. Why couldn't she write a hard-hitting exposé on a murder investigation, start to finish, and avoid focusing on his team? First Camilla Rodolfo, and now Joseph. He imagined her chortling because a second major news event had landed in her lap.

"It's viral," Tenna informed him as they entered the theater, holding up her phone.

"Camilla's death?" he asked. 'Isn't that old news?"

"Joseph's attack," she said. "It takes one message and then…viral."

For Roche, *viral* conjured submicroscopic organisms carrying rumors and accusations from house to house. It was bad enough that his name was already appearing in fan magazines and newspapers. What bothered him far more was the proliferation of guessing, articles based on supposition and falsehoods. Weren't journalists notorious for that—guessing?

In the middle of these thoughts, he reminded himself that Aria was the only journalist with full access to every interview, every lab result, and every forensic analysis. Up to now, she had asked good and reasonable questions. But her presence was wearing thin. How much longer would she be willing to take a back seat, and not jump fully into the fray? Or was she already feeding information to the press? How else was the public learning the specifics of this case, and almost in real time? The way she kept close to Tenna and Anuj added to his suspicions.

Tenna's voice cut into his thoughts. "We're watching the internet," she said. "Chat rooms, blogs, whatever we can infiltrate. Our cyber experts are on the prowl."

Roche disliked technology, yet understood its importance, especially when searching for individuals and groups that did everything possible to hide from the law.

They entered the lobby of the Théâtre Junot. Anuj rushed into the performance area, and the others followed. Roche watched him scramble up the ladder and thought he could navigate that climb, but it would be one rung at a time, slowly and cautiously.

Overhead footsteps echoed through the space. Within a minute, Anuj was standing with them. "No question," he said. He pointed to the stage. "Joseph was found there." Blue tape outlined the shape of his body. "Directly overhead, the railing shows fresh scratches. He wasn't just struck; he was forced over. Follow me," he added, stepping onto the stage. "I'll show you."

"I'll take your word for it," said Roche with a sheepish grin. He turned and headed toward the street exit, certain that his team was close behind. His team and, of course, the journalist.

The precinct was in sharp contrast to the eerie silence of the theater. For a moment, Roche felt assaulted by the din of ringing phones, energetic discussions between officers, footsteps rushing here and there. On a good day, he was comforted by the racket; it was an indication that everyone was engaged. Today, it grated like white noise.

He escaped into his office and closed the door. This was as close to silence as he could expect. He wondered if he looked as grim as he felt. He derived some satisfaction from shutting everyone out. There would definitely be a backlash after walking out of the press conference. Was de Charbonnet lurking nearby, waiting to pounce?

Roche picked up a file and slipped out the list Tenna had compiled of everyone inside the theater when Camilla Rodolfo was murdered. He tried to read it, but de Charbonnet was on his mind. Wouldn't the man love to see Roche thrown out, leaving a space for one of his cronies!

He settled back into his work, which included shuffling through a stack of messages. He put aside the three from a man identifying himself as the attorney of Solange and Bertrand Gabriel. He alone would dictate the course of this investigation, not some octogenarian couple or their shark of an attorney.

There was a light knock on his door, and then it opened. Tenna and Aria stepped in and sat. Not for the first time, he wondered how women bonded so quickly. He had seen it with Judith and her friends, and here it was again, like one person divided into two bodies. Men seemed to sidle into a friendship, always testing, weighing, but never sure quite how to proceed. They trust, we don't. He needed tea.

He signaled to a rookie officer who was standing near the door, and the young woman rushed in.

"Sir?" she asked, her eyes shining with anticipation.

Roche looked at the others. "Anyone want tea? Coffee?"

Three people, three different orders. Sugar, no sugar; milk, no milk, both.

"There are proper mugs above the microwave," he told the officer. "No paper cups."

The young woman rushed off.

"Just watch," said Roche with a lamenting sigh. "I'll get milk in my tea."

"Judging by your commanding presence," said Aria, "the poor woman will equate that with death by hanging."

Roche gave her a long look. He was tempted to respond, but what would that serve? Instead, he opened the file marked *RODOLFO* and read the latest notes. He was halfway into the first page of the coroner's report when Anuj walked in and plopped into the last available chair.

"So," said the young detective. "Anything?"

Tenna shifted in her chair, pulling her skirt over her knees. "Finding Joseph's attacker will lead us to Camilla's killer."

"Let's see what the forensics gurus come up with," Roche said. "If Joseph regains consciousness, we'll get important answers." After a hesitation, he repeated, "If."

They sat together; no one said a word. It was as if they had an agreement to speak only when necessary. Roche knew they were all exhausted. Frustrated,

110

too, by the dead ends they were encountering.

During this shared silence, he received two calls from de Charbonnet, neither of which he answered. "I don't need to be reminded how unhappy he is," he told the others.

"Walking out of that press conference?" Tenna said.

"Hardly your fault," Anuj added.

Roche looked at Aria, certain she couldn't resist sharing her opinion, but she said nothing.

Tenna suddenly stood and rushed out of the room. He liked that her mind was always active and that she rarely ran ideas by him until she had done her research. He wondered what was on her mind now.

Just as he picked up the phone to return de Charbonnet's call, Anton Delant appeared. He was looking confident, polished, every hair in place. He even wore an ascot wrapped rakishly around his neck. The leading man, the star. "I gather you want to see me," he announced, flashing his red-carpet grin.

Chapter Eleven

I f an actor's entrance could be likened to food, then Anton Delant's was maple syrup. He oozed into Roche's office, making Aria think of liquid from a jar. Sweet, gooey, unctuous.

On his heels came Tenna, her arms wrapped around at least a dozen folders. When Roche looked at her questioningly, she moved closer and whispered, "More data than we ever imagined."

His expression struck Aria as humorous, but she knew better than to laugh. As much as they could use a bit of comic relief, this was, after all, a murder investigation. And she knew that Roche was not finding anything humorous about her position on this team. She sensed that he was suspicious, what with all this information being leaked to the press. Did he think she was the leak?

She watched Tenna unload the files onto a table shoved against the wall. She liked Tenna and felt a friendship growing. She was nearly old enough to be Tenna's mother, but that didn't seem to create a problem. Her thoughts were interrupted when the actor spoke.

"And what can I do for you?" he asked Roche.

Aria knew that Anton Delant was the darling of daytime melodramas, and it was clear that he knew this as well. There was a smugness about him, a sense of self-importance. He had starred in several forgettable movies and was getting a bit slack around the jowls, yet he seemed to think himself irresistible. He was handsome, she would give him that. His kind of tall, slender build usually appealed to women. But his eyes, they were hooded, a man who needed to paint himself as mysterious. His smug expression reminded her of the boyfriend who couldn't ditch her fast enough after the story broke. She knew what men were capable of doing. She didn't include Lexie's father, her ex-husband. He was never devious, just a man lacking the one characteristic she most admired: curiosity.

Did Anton Delant care about the world around him, or about having his face on the covers of celebrity magazines? She had heard a few of Roche's officers chatting at the coffee machine about Delant dropping from public view, with speculation ranging from hiding out in a rehab clinic to having been kidnapped by thugs holding his IOUs. When he finally appeared in public, reporters fell all over themselves to get to a truth that was never revealed.

Aria understood how gossip rags worked. Nothing was too tasteless or too cruel for their headlines. The bottom line was not truth, it was profits.

"So, what's the charge, Inspector?" Delant asked. "Organized crime? Peddling drugs?" He spoke with such a casual tone that he could have been inquiring about the weather.

Aria wondered why women loved men like him, the heartbreakers. Perhaps these women had too much lonely time, or empty and unfulfilling relationships. From a safe distance, they could fantasize about France's rendition of Hollywood's bad boy. She liked her men smart, confident, kind, and libidinous.

Roche's voice filled the room. "Mr. Delant, I have a few questions." He leaned back in the chair, his posture relaxed.

Delant spread his arms, plopped into the chair vacated by Tenna, and announced, "Ask away!"

Anuj shifted just enough to be able to see the man's face. "Mr. Delant," he asked. "Did you kill Camilla Rodolfo?"

The actor stared at the young officer and then announced, "Good delivery! And you got right to it. No dilly-dallying around!" And then he laughed. "Why in the hell would I do that?" He directed that question at Roche, the man in charge. "I liked her. And what would I gain? It's not like we competed for the same roles."

"Perhaps you were jealous of her talents," Roche said.

"Limited as they were," he mumbled, and then waved the comment away. "Unkind, sorry, mustn't speak ill of the dead."

"Do you know anyone who resented her?" Tenna asked. "Someone who harbored jealousy? Old feuds, rivalries?"

"If you knew how to do your job," the actor responded, all humor suddenly gone from his face, "you would have the answer. That's the trouble with your kind."

Aria nearly demanded to know who *your kind* was, but held her tongue. It wasn't easy. Why weren't Anuj or Roche jumping in to defend Tenna?

"And if you ask me," Delant continued, "I believe that—"

"No one is asking," Roche said. "Answer the question."

Delant stared hard at Roche, making Aria think of the evil eye. And then his face softened. Jekyll and Hyde, was that his game? "Please repeat the question."

This time, it was Aria who jumped in. "She asked if anyone resented Camilla."

They waited for the actor's response. He gave Aria a long look. Was he trying to make her feel uncomfortable? She returned the look, unwavering.

"Resented her? That's something you should ask Linné," he said. "Can you imagine someone with her gifts playing second fiddle to a less accomplished actor? But who knows? Maybe she did it so she could put the moves on me."

Aria nearly snorted.

"And does this happen often?" Anuj asked. "A woman manipulates and schemes so she can take you to bed?"

"More than I care to admit," he said, pride in his voice.

"So, you're saying that you have a history with Linné," Tenna said.

"History?"

"Like a love affair, a dalliance."

"Nope, never happened. Never will."

"You don't find her attractive?"

"Well, yes, but there has never been electricity between us."

"And with Miss Rodolfo?" Anuj said.

"Friends," he replied. "Long-time friends, nothing more."

"And yet you have this reputation," Roche said.

The actor grinned wolfishly.

"A regular Don Juan," Roche added.

"Or perhaps a Lothario," Anuj interjected.

Delant shook his head. "Never a Lothario. He was a seducer, but there was something evil behind it. When I seduce a woman, it's because I'm attracted to her, to the possibilities that we might share a future. Or, at the least, one memorable night."

Aria wanted to slap him. At the same time, if she could sell this interview to a major paper or magazine, she'd never have to work again.

"I've read about your busy schedule with women," Anuj began.

The actor bristled. "You can't believe everything you read! According to those rags, I'm the world's worst parasite."

"So, you're not a parasite," Anuj said.

Tenna's eyes widened.

The actor sat upright, nostrils flaring. "You have no right——"

"On the contrary," Roche said, "we have every right. This is not an audition; it's a murder investigation. And you, sir, are one of our suspects. So, the sooner you put your righteous indignation aside, the sooner we can complete what you seem to feel is a personal attack."

"A vendetta is more like it," Delant said, his voice petulant.

"We harbor no grudge against you," Roche said. "Our job is to determine who had a reason to kill Camilla Rodolfo."

Aria's eyes never left the actor's face. It was pale, with a sheen of perspiration appearing on his forehead.

"I did not kill her," he said. "I could not, I swear."

Aria believed him, although she wasn't sure why. She saw pain. Actors could do that—play whatever role was required—but it was the eyes that could most easily give them away.

Delant pushed his fingers through his hair, giving Aria her first glimpse at the marks running across his scalp. Hair plugs, no doubt about it. It made sense that an actor, and a sex symbol at that, would fight signs of aging. She guessed that he was in his early forties. When those first wrinkles appear, when the abs are no longer as tight, it is a short, painful step from leading man to the role of someone's father.

Aria assumed that Roche was about to terminate the interview, and she was disappointed. She had expected him to bring in the bulldozer, but it seemed that he was letting Anton Delant go without even scratching the surface. Her judgment was short-lived.

"Oh, and one more thing," said Roche, so casually he could have been discussing the weather. "What can you tell me about this morning's attempt to kill the lighting technician, Joseph Mardikian?"

Aria was certain that no actor on earth could fake such utter disbelief, and then shock.

"My God," he said, his voice a whisper. "My…God."

"You may leave," Roche said.

"But—"

Roche exhaled loudly. "We'll be calling you in again."

Anton Delant may have arrived like syrup, slowly and smoothly, but he departed as if shot from an arrow, the door slamming behind him.

"Not our man," Anuj said.

"I concur," Roche replied. "That man could never kill."

"A man afraid of his shadow," Aria said.

Roche turned to Tenna. "You arrived with a large stack."

"A few hours of late-night digging in the data mines," she said.

"That's my partner," Anuj said. "She doesn't emerge from the cave until she strikes gold." Before he could continue, he glanced at his humming phone.

From the way his eyes came alive, Aria knew who was calling.

"Maryam!" he declared, stepping out of Roche's office.

Aria wondered if she would ever love like that again, with such joy and trust.

Roche stirred sugar into a fresh mug of tea. "Hopefully, we'll have this solved today."

Aria turned to face him. "You think the case is wrapping up?"

He took a tentative sip. "I'm not sure if this is tea or coffee." He took another sip, confirming his worst suspicions. "Not wrapping up," he said, setting the cup on the desk and nudging it away. "But I think we're done at the theater. I doubt the building has more to tell us. We can question everyone here, or in their homes."

They were about to disperse when a policeman appeared. "Boss," he said, "there's an old couple to see you."

Before he could stand to meet them, the Gabriels appeared. Sashkie was close behind. They paused at the door, a theatrical posture, and then made their entrance.

"We were meeting at your apartment," Roche said, his voice flat. "Three o'clock."

"They insisted on coming now," Sashkie said. "Max told us you were here." With her hair clipped back with barrettes, she resembled a child. Before anyone could speak, she rushed from the room.

Roche pulled out a chair and gestured to Solange. "And you, sir," he said to Bertrand, "beside your wife, please."

There were five people in the room and four chairs. Aria moved to give up hers, but Roche shook his head. She interpreted this as his need to have her seated as close as possible to the Gabriels.

"Shall we move into a larger room?" Roche suggested.

For a moment, Aria was surprised, but then she understood. He was offering them greater comfort, perhaps the sense that they were, after all, in control, and that Solange might finally let down her guard.

"That would be very nice," Bertrand said, rising from the chair.

"We'll stay right here," Solange said, her narrow-eyed stare never leaving Roche's face. As soon as her husband was seated, she offered a taut smile. "Humor me, Inspector. Tell me why we must do this again." She pulled her shawl snugly across her shoulders. "We've told you everything."

"And I thank you for returning," Roche said. "I was expecting to come to you."

"Yes, well, and what if we refused to answer the door?"

Aria knew what was coming.

Roche did not let her down. "I would've sent a police car to your apartment, all lights flashing, sirens at full volume."

Solange stared hard at him.

Aria felt sympathy for the old woman, but also satisfaction that Roche had put her in her place. He might not be a pleasant fellow, but he knew how to do his job.

Roche stared back. "That would be quite a spectacle, don't you think?" After a long silence, he leaned closer to Solange. "You know about Joseph." Not a question, a statement of fact.

"Of course," Solange said. "Sashkie told us."

"Such a terrible thing," Bertrand replied, with a shake of his head.

"And what did Sashkie say?" Roche said.

"That he fell and suffered a head injury," she responded.

Roche paused again. Aria wasn't sure if he was considering his next comment or working to control the anger he must be feeling. "Did Sashkie happen to mention that he was struck on the head first, and then thrown over the railing?"

Bertrand pressed his hand against his mouth, his eyes wide.

"And what has that got to do with us?" Solange demanded.

"Solange!" declared her husband.

She pulled the shawl even tighter around her shoulders. And then, just as quickly, her body relaxed. "Do you like this?" she said to Aria, indicating the shawl.

Aria wasn't sure how to respond. She looked at Roche, but found no clues in his face. "It's very nice, Solange. Hermès, yes?"

"I see you inherited your mother's eye," she replied.

"If we can move on?" Roche said.

Solange gave Aria a playful wink.

"Detectives Kumar and Berglof will join me in the questioning," said Roche, his recording machine at the ready. "Miss Nevins will observe." He announced the date, time, the names of those present, and their location. "These interviews seem to begin on the same note. We're told how well everyone gets along. No jealousies or tensions among the cast, the crew, or the staff." He looked squarely at Solange and then Bertrand. "But then, the stories begin to change; little cracks appear. So, could we please save time and pass over the warm and fuzzy parts, and cut to the truth?"

Aria saw that Roche was fed up, both with the slow pace of this investigation and Solange Gabriel's queen-like aura, and she was curious to see how he could speed things up.

Solange shifted in the chair, the corner of her shawl draping over the table. "What I will tell you," she said, and then turned to her husband. "Hush, Bertie."

"I didn't say anything," he protested.

"But you were going to." She turned back to Roche. "What I will tell you," she repeated, "is that there's tension. It's not only expected, it's essential. Tension keeps us energized, terrified of losing lines or looking foolish to an audience that expects perfection. Do I feel more than tension from my fellow actors? Of course! Anton, Camilla, Linné, all professionals, but none of them will ever be a Solange or Bertrand Gabriel, and they know this."

"So, they resent you," Roche said, his voice flat.

"I certainly hope so!"

"My dear," Bertrand said, closing his eyes. "This is no time for humor."

One wave of her hand and he was silenced.

"They resent us, envy us, wish they could be us," she said. "We took the plum roles, two old goats playing characters half our age, and the audience loved us."

Aria saw that Tenna was jotting down a few words. She noted that Solange was seeing this as well.

"So, you're saying there *was* resentment, jealousy, envy," Roche stated.

"And respect," Solange added.

Bertrand looked at his wife. "Perhaps we should mention the anger."

When Solange waved her hand through the air again, Aria thought of banishing an annoying insect. The hand was veined and wrinkled, an old woman's hand. Makeup and surgery on the face and neck can hide age, but the hands never lie.

"We have it in our contracts," Solange said.

Aria looked at Roche. He seemed to share her confusion.

"I believe we were talking about anger," Roche suggested.

"And I am doing just that!" the woman declared. "In our contracts: every afternoon, two hours of rest, no matter what."

"And the actors objected?" Anuj said.

"Youth, pure and simple," Bertrand told him. "They can go morning to night without a rest. But reach eighty…" His voice trailed off into a sigh.

"Max arranged interviews and photo sessions with the London Times and Le Monde," Solange said. "Without thinking, he scheduled them for the afternoon. We complained, but he insisted that the time couldn't be changed. Bertie threatened to walk out." She threw a look of admiration his way, and he reacted by sitting even straighter, pride visible in his upturned chin.

"I'm sure that got his attention," Roche said.

"I think everyone finally understood," she agreed. "No more was said."

"But there was anger," Tenna suggested.

"You might say that shutting down a rehearsal for two hours and running the risk of missing out on interviews with two of Europe's major newspapers could lead to a few protests," Bertrand said.

Aria watched the couple, sensing that something was not being revealed. This was the moment to ask questions, but would Roche ask them?

The room was again quiet, eerily so.

"And between the other actors?" Roche probed. "Was there tension or anger?"

"There was tension between the ladies, Camilla and Linné," Bertrand said.

"We weren't sure why Max gave the role of Ophelia to a woman twice Ophelia's age," added Solange.

"And yet you are twice the ages of the characters you played."

Solange looked almost coquettish when she answered, "One cannot be compared to the other."

"And why is that?" Roche asked.

"Because we are the Gabriels! When Bertie and I step onto a stage, we are timeless, ageless." Leaning back, she shot Roche a look that dared him to disagree.

Worthy of a standing ovation, Aria thought, and then wished her mother could witness this.

Roche seemed mildly amused, but said nothing.

"Camilla was a respected television personality," Anuj said. "So why—"

Solange cut him off. "Respected, perhaps, young man, but a nothing next to Linné. Whether or not you realize this, or even care, Linné Colbert is not only the real thing; she's the closest I've seen to an actor who might one day take my place."

"The future of French theater," Bertrand agreed.

Tenna glanced at her notes. "We heard about a rather heated disagreement about a documentary."

"Resolved," Solange said. "A short dispute, nothing to it."

There was a tap on the door. Anuj opened it and then slipped into the hallway.

"I told them not to disturb us," Roche said almost apologetically.

There were muffled voices, followed by Anuj's face appearing around the door. "Back in a minute," he said.

A silence hung over the room. Aria felt it, heavy with expectation and tinged with fear.

Anuj returned wearing the kind of gloves worn by surgeons and homicide inspectors. He was holding a large plastic sleeve containing several envelopes.

"What have you got?" Roche asked.

Anuj leaned close to Roche and spoke into his ear.

Aria could only hear "...arrived in the post...anonymous..." and then saw anger flood the inspector's face.

Roche glared at the two actors. "When were you going to tell me about these?" He held up the plastic sleeves. He was clenching his jaw with such force that his teeth made a grinding sound.

Bertrand reached for his wife's hand.

Anuj produced two pair of latex gloves from his pocket and handed them to Roche and Tenna.

Roche pulled them on and removed what appeared to be a page of stationery. He read it to himself, then handed it to Tenna.

"It refers to sins long past," he said, looking directly at Solange. "And the unpleasant consequences you'll suffer because of them." He fell silent.

Aria suspected he wanted this revelation to shake them up, give them a reason to put aside the theatrics and play it straight.

The Gabriels remained silent.

Roche leaned closer to them. "Explain, please: what sins?" When they refused to answer, he raised his voice. "We call this hate mail."

Tears came to Solange's eyes. "Oh, Bertie, I told you we should have said something. Now, the inspector thinks we're hiding things." To Roche, she said, "I swear, Inspector, we have no idea who has been sending these, or why."

"There's always gossip," Bertrand said. "Fodder for those magazines that don't differentiate truth from lie."

Anuj pushed his hair off his forehead. "There have been rumors for many years, Monsieur Gabriel, that you are Camilla's father."

Aria felt the air being sucked out of the room. Anuj was jumping into murky water; she hoped he wasn't about to drown.

"Could that be the sin mentioned here?" Roche asked.

"Utter rubbish!" Solange said.

"How can I be sure?" Roche shot back.

Solange looked at her husband for a long moment. Finally, he closed his eyes, as if giving permission to share something.

"Inspector," she said. "We've always told people that we were too involved in our careers to have children. That it would be unfair to a child."

"The truth is," Bertrand said, "we can't have children. That is, I can't father them." He looked at his wife.

She touched his hand. "We never felt the public deserved to know."

Aria tried to gauge the reactions of the others. Whether they were sympathetic or unconvinced, she couldn't say.

Roche sent Anuj to find Sashkie. In the few minutes he was gone, the inspector read the letter again, Aria checked messages on her phone, and the Gabriels spoke quietly among themselves. Tenna was making notes.

The minute Sashkie appeared, Roche stood. "You can take them home."

Without a word, they rose and followed Sashkie out the door. No grand exit. Just a tired old couple.

Anuj slipped his notebook and recording machine into his pocket. "Is that it, Boss?"

Roche gave him a *you must be kidding* look. He checked his watch. "One more."

Aria wasn't certain if he meant one more in this round of questioning, but she knew better than to ask.

Fatigue was draped over all of them like a heavy fog.

Roche turned to Tenna. "That *one more* is Laurene. Go to the hospital and question her. And take Aria with you."

"Are you sure?" Tenna asked.

"It can't wait," he said.

The ride was made in complete silence. Aria sensed that Tenna shared her discomfort about pressuring Laurene for information.

They found her in Joseph's room, her hand resting protectively on his arm. At first, she refused to leave his side, but then finally agreed. Aria was certain this was because Joseph, although unconscious, seemed agitated by the voices around him.

Tenna led them into the cafeteria and chose a table in the far corner.

Aria did a quick study of Laurene and thought of fragile objects that disappear in a gust of wind. At the same time, the expression on her face gave her the appearance of forced confidence.

Tenna placed her recorder on the table and waited for Aria to do the same. "In the room," she announced, "Detective Tenna Berglof, Aria Nevins, and subject Laurene Froberg." She gave time, date, and place, and then turned her attention to the young woman.

Laurene began to fidget with her hair. Aria was certain that the confidence she was trying to project was a mask, and this mask could be easily cracked.

"You've been Max Formande's assistant for how long?" Tenna asked.

Laurene stared at her, and blinked a few times. "Two years and four months."

Tenna offered a little smile. "Very precise."

"I started on my twenty-seventh birthday."

"And before then?"

"I was twenty-six."

This time, Tenna's smile was broader. "And your employment before then?"

"Assistant to the creative director of a theater in Lille."

"And now you're in the big city," Tenna said.

Aria had no idea where this was going.

"Actually," Laurene said, "I'm back in the big city. I'm Parisian. Lille was a stopping-off point, a place to learn more about theater. I never intended to stay there, believe me. And I never expected to live and work anywhere but Paris. But it was a good offer. Being the assistant to the creative director is not my goal. I'm looking for a bigger role. If not in Paris, then in London or New York."

Tenna moved a bit closer to Laurene. "Miss Froberg, where were you during the intermission?"

The young woman looked hard into the detective's eyes. "Is that when it happened?"

"Can you think of another possibility?"

"There were several minutes between Camilla's exit and the curtain coming down. The time it takes for Solange's closing soliloquy."

Aria pictured the murder board in the main room. Faces, names, timelines, all still preliminary. Considering the long hours they were putting into this investigation, she had expected to see more. More details, more possibilities.

"Oh, wait!" declared Laurene, throwing her hands up. "God, I'm so stupid! When I went to use the bathroom, the audience was still applauding. The toilet was occupied, so I waited, and it was Camilla who came out! So yes, she died during intermission."

Aria expected relief to cross Tenna's face, but she saw no sign of it.

"And where were you during intermission?" Tenna asked.

"I was with Max," she said emphatically. "I never left his side."

"How can you be sure?" Tenna shifted her weight in the chair.

"That afternoon, he received the final eviction orders from the city. He was desperately sad and angry. With his bad heart, there was no way I was going to leave him alone, even for two minutes, except to use the bathroom. And now," she added, rising. "Are we done here?"

Aria was surprised when Tenna ignored the question, and then reminded herself that this young detective had earned her place on Roche's prestigious team.

"Sit, please," Tenna said.

Laurene lowered herself into the chair.

"Perhaps you were also afraid that Max would…" She left the statement hanging there.

Roche had used that technique several times. It was used by journalists as well. They loved that dangling question. It left a door open, inviting unexpected and often revealing responses.

"Afraid he would what?" Laurene asked. When no one responded, she said, "Like, you mean, suicide? Never! Max was in despair, but he knew there was always another theater, another place to work his magic." She looked pointedly at the two women. "Being a creative director is like being a turtle. Your shell is your talent, your experiences, your reputation. Wherever you go, your shell goes with you. So no, I wasn't there to pick up the pieces of his broken soul. I was there to work out the schedule for moving him out of his office, where he had collected mementoes for decades, and making sure he took his meds."

"Do you recall anything else?" Tenna asked.

"We were hard at work at the beginning of the second act when Camilla missed her cue."

"How did you know?" Tenna said.

"Pardon?"

"That she missed her cue," Aria said. "How did you know, if you were in the office?"

Laurene looked at Aria for a long beat and then said, "We can hear the performance. It's piped into all the rooms, so the actors, waiting in their dressing rooms, can follow the script and then head for the wings before their cues. Over the speaker, there was absolute silence. When Solange repeated the line, we knew something was wrong. Max and I rushed into

Camilla's dressing room and found her. Now really—"

"We're done for now," Tenna said. Before Laurene stepped away from the table, she added, "One last question, Miss Froberg."

Laurene turned and waited.

"Any idea who killed Camilla?"

Her eyes widened. "I can only tell you who didn't," she said. "Max, the tech gurus, and me. Beyond that, I haven't a clue." She turned and rushed out.

"So, what's next?" Aria asked, turning off the recorder and dropping it into her bag.

"I wish I could say food, sleep, and perhaps more sleep," said Tenna. She checked her phone. "The boss needs search warrants. He's texting the list to me."

They took the elevator to the ground floor and walked out of the hospital. Aria marveled at how the lights of Paris threw a glow across the darkening sky. For one magical moment, it was easy to forget that people lived without food or shelter, that there were bodies in the morgue waiting to be identified by grieving families, or might never be identified at all. For her, those were the tragedies, the men and women, young and old, with no one to grieve for them, or even give them a name. "Camilla Rodolfo was somebody's daughter," Aria said.

Tenna closed her eyes, and Aria knew she understood.

As the taxi pulled up to the curb, Aria imagined her bedroom at home, her bathroom with its large soaking tub. But did she want to be there, and not here? There was no man waiting for her, no career reflecting three decades of hard work and commitment to the truth. Everything she had earned, everything she had cherished, seemed far away and so out of reach.

Chapter Twelve

Noah Roche arrived at the precinct early, greeted by the usual ringing phones and the hushed conversations of people completing their night shifts and leaving for home.

His first stop was the alcove that passed as the kitchen. He prepared a large mug of tea, his mind awash with witness statements, crime scene photographs, and the forensics reports yet to arrive. There was no need to read the autopsy notes: the cause of death was obvious. But now there was this attempt to kill Joseph. As if murder weren't enough, and mayhem needed to be thrown into the mix.

He walked into his office and found Aria seated at his desk.

She looked up and smiled. "Good morning."

A fitful night's sleep, what he knew would be a mediocre cup of tea, and now this. He remained silent as she gathered a few folders and moved to the chair facing his. He preferred that she leave, but he felt de Charbonnet hovering overhead and watching, judging.

In the throes of his pique, Anuj arrived. He, too, carried a large mug, and he looked as tired as Roche felt.

"Caffeine," the young man said, raising the mug. "English Breakfast, much needed."

"No sleep?" Aria asked.

"The sheep failed to materialize."

"Welcome to the world of homicide," said Roche, his hands wrapped around the cup for warmth. He looked at Aria. "Solve the case yet?" The minute he spoke, he regretted it. The expression on her face told him she wasn't receptive to banter. Did everyone want to be left alone this morning? She was weighted down by her own problems, whether she wanted to discuss them or not. And he hoped she did not, because he was far too busy to act as a therapist, or even a sympathetic listener. The word *friend* never crossed his mind.

"Any word on Joseph?" Anuj asked.

Roche released a loud sigh. "Unconscious, but holding his own."

Tenna arrived, and Roche stood. "Let's head over to the theater. Hopefully, this will be the last time."

"Considering it's supposed to be torn down tomorrow," Anuj said.

"Unfortunate," Roche said. "Max is coming in at nine, which gives us time for breakfast along the way."

"Bagels and cream cheese," said Aria wistfully.

Roche shook his head. "This isn't San Francisco, where everything opens at four in the morning. In France, we don't begin living until eight or nine."

Tenna slung her backpack over her shoulder and moved towards the elevator. "I happen to know a place that has fresh bagels. It opens early, and we pass it on the way to the theater. Why not ask Max to meet us there? I'm guessing he could use a breather, especially with demolition about to begin."

They walked into the café and ordered eight bagels, a large container of cream cheese, several butter croissants, and a baguette longer than the waiter's arm. All of this was accompanied by macchiatos, lattes, and a few straight shots of espresso.

There was one bagel remaining when Max Formande entered the café.

Aria stood and greeted him with a hug.

Roche noted how gaunt the man looked, the lines in his face etched deeper than the day before. He wondered if Max's obituary would celebrate his sixty years of theater triumphs, or dwell on this one terrible night.

Max looked at the bread basket. "Slim pickings."

"Let me order more," Roche said.

"No need." He removed the bagel and applied a large dollop of cream cheese.

"Were you able to sleep?" Aria asked.

"Sleep," he repeated. "I have a vague recollection of that word. As a noun, not a verb."

Roche was anxious to get moving, but rushing an old man might be seen as bullying. Also, why push? Max did not commit this murder, nor did he attack Joseph. Still, he suspected that Max knew something he wasn't sharing, and it related to the Gabriels.

Roche bit into his bagel, enjoying the burst of flavor on his tongue. He wasn't eating well, he knew that, nor had he enjoyed a night of uninterrupted sleep for some time. If he could just get through this case, deliver the killer, and be done with Aria. A voice in his head told him that Aria wasn't the problem, the obstacle, it was Solange. Everything seemed to begin and end with her. His thoughts were interrupted by Tenna's voice.

"Do you think it was Solange?" she asked.

"Solange?" Max repeated. "You can't possibly—"

"I doubt her guilt," said Roche. "And that's from the viewpoint of both motive and physical strength. But I'm beginning to believe that someone was resentful of her talents, or wishing to even an old score."

"Jealousy, resentment, rage," said Tenna. "Viable motives, yes. And throw in revenge—"

Roche pulled out his recorder. "A few questions, Max."

Aria's recorder suddenly appeared.

Roche glanced at Tenna, who produced her notebook.

He noticed how Anuj was staring at the two recording machines. Perhaps he considered them sufficient, because he left his in his pocket.

"You have a good team here," Max said.

Roche looked at Tenna and Anuj, his acolytes. "Heirs to the kingdom," he said, and then wiped the corners of his mouth, taking care that he would not be questioning Max Formande with cream cheese spraying onto the table.

He gave Aria a hard stare, hoping this reminded her to remain silent. She returned the stare, and he was taken aback. He rarely faced defiance, except from a suspect, and he was not pleased. He heard Judith's voice telling him that one day he would meet his match. That might be, but Aria Nevins would hardly qualify.

He hit the recording button. "Present today," he intoned, "are Chief Inspector Noah Roche, detectives Anuj Kumar and Tenna Berglof, Aria Nevins, and theater director Max Formande." He added the time, day, year, and location of the interview.

"We have a few questions," he said to Max, and then turned to Anuj. "Ready?"

He knew that Anuj hadn't expected to take the lead again, but it was time to let his team know how much they were trusted. Later, he would hand this role over to Tenna.

Anuj remained silent. Roche saw this as reticence, and it moved through him like a bad meal. He shot Anuj an inquiring look, but Anuj presented a blank face. Roche pushed his chin forward, urging him to get on with it.

Anuj surprised Roche by ignoring him. After a long pause, he leaned forward, his hands clasped together on the table. "Monsieur Formande," he began.

"Please, call me Max. We're beyond formalities, don't you agree?"

"Max. As a director, you have a very different view of how the actors relate to one another."

The corners of the old man's mouth turned up just enough to suggest an impish response. "If you mean that I don't compete with them, or share their petty jealousies, or try to sabotage their performances for my own benefit, then yes, you're right."

The old man turned to Aria. "Any news about Joseph?"

She shook her head. "No change."

He took a deep breath and exhaled loudly. "I guess that's good news." He turned back to Anuj.

Roche hoped they wouldn't have to play cat and mouse while in search of information, or use squeeze tactics to get answers.

"I'm accustomed to running the show," Max said. "So, let me take the lead here."

Roche nearly laughed, imagining the relief running through Anuj.

"Where would you like me to begin?" he asked. "That is, in what order should I rip to shreds members of my cast and crew?"

Roche saw that Aria was working to suppress a laugh. He knew that levity served no good purpose in an investigation, especially not when potential suspects were present. It prolonged the questioning, which none of them wished to do.

"How about starting with your crew?" Anuj suggested.

"Saving the best for last, heh?" He waved his hands from side to side, imitating a vaudeville singer. And then all attempts at humor fell away. "Let's start with—" He paused, searching for the name. Relief crossed his face. "Joseph," he said. "Sometimes, I forget."

"Take your time, Uncle Max," Aria said, earning a grateful smile.

"A lovely boy, Joseph. Good at his job, always on time, never complains. Absolutely incapable of hurting someone." Tears came to his eyes. "Why anyone would want to harm him—kill him—I have no idea. None."

"Are you aware of Joseph having a personal connection with any of the actors?" Anuj asked, his voice gentle.

Max shook his head. "Almost impossible. Lighting is demanding, his only focus. How the actors want it, what they want emphasized…or not. I can assure you that no one in that theater ever found anything difficult or unpleasant about him. If they did, I'd be the first to know."

Roche heard his voice drop, his confidence slipping away.

Anuj pressed on. "What about a relationship with someone on your staff? Did Joseph have one?"

Max chewed on his lip for a moment. "No doubt you're referring to my assistant, Laurene. Alas, she fancies the boy, but he has eyes for another. God knows why. Sashkie's as exciting as a sack of hair. She refuses to give poor Joseph a second glance."

"The Gabriels' assistant?" Anuj asked innocently.

Roche recognized the ploy. The more unknowing Anuj sounded, the more Max would want to educate him, show his expertise, perhaps flaunt his knowledge of something that, without his realizing it, might affect the case.

"She's more than an assistant," Max said. "She's Solange's dresser, driver, secretary, go-fer, protector, you name it. Without Sashkie, the Gabriel household would collapse into disarray."

"Do the Gabriels understand this?" asked Tenna. "What I mean is, do they appreciate all she does?"

"Bertrand does, yes. Without her, Solange would be a disaster, and he'd be left to clean up the mess."

"But Solange doesn't appreciate Sashkie, is that what you're saying?" Anuj said.

The director mulled over this question. "I'm not sure Solange appreciates anyone. Except, perhaps, herself." He quickly added, "Actors and the public fawn over her, and sometimes they even grovel. No gesture of admiration is ever grand enough to please her."

"Is it possible that she needs to be soothed because of insecurity?" Tenna asked.

Roche reminded himself that Tenna viewed others through her own veil of kindness. Early on, this had bothered him, but he soon realized how her soft heart served to extract information from even the most hardened witnesses. On occasion, criminals, too.

Max looked at Tenna. "Very astute, my dear. Solange expresses her thanks with a broad grin and an appreciative voice, but those of us who know her—that is, who are privy to her little stage whispers—we understand that her need to be loved and admired is a black hole that can never be filled. Bertie does his best, and he's an angel in the way he tends to her every need, but I've seen him bite back anger, and even pride, because he knows that fighting her could never come to any good, much less change her behavior."

"You've known the Gabriels for more than fifty years," Anuj said. "Do you think either of them is capable of murder?"

Max leaned back so abruptly that he could have been pushed. He opened his mouth to speak, and then closed it. Finally, he said, "Bertrand? Never. Solange? If she were driven to the brink, perhaps." He turned to face Aria. "What do you think, my dear?"

"She's an observer," said Roche. He felt Aria's eyes on him, penetrating and hard. If looks could kill.

"There was no tension between Solange and Camilla," the director said. "And yes, I know about the rumors of paternity and all that garbage. But they were just that, rumors. Bertrand was no more Camilla's father than he's the man in the moon."

Anuj pulled his notebook from his coat pocket and read his notes. Roche was certain that Anuj was running through his list of suspects, and Joseph wasn't among them. The poor man was fighting for his life. Linné Colbert? An unlikely candidate for a brutal murder. Anton Delant seemed to lack the inclination, much less the courage, to commit a crime. Except, perhaps, to steal a scene. He had to remind himself yet again that most of these people were thespians, trained to act mean or haughty. And when it suited them, innocent.

"Can you tell us anything about Anton's understudy?" Anuj asked.

"Elvis Presley?"

Anuj smiled. "If I'm not mistaken, he's dead."

"Only in mind, body, and spirit," said the director with a laugh. "Darwin McAfee does one hell of an impersonation. Uncanny, truly. Good enough for Vegas. He was brought into the cast with no thought of ever putting him on the stage. I didn't think an understudy was necessary, but Anton's agent insisted. It seems that having someone to back him up diminishes his fears."

A crease suddenly appeared across Tenna's forehead. "Why would a seasoned actor experience fear?"

"A role in television or film is one thing," said the director. "You learn your lines for that day's shoot, get through the scenes, do retakes if it doesn't work the first time or the second...or the tenth. In the theater, you're on stage, in front of an audience. Blow your lines and it's in tomorrow's newspaper. Anton is one of those confident television and film actors who find theater daunting, even frightening."

Roche thought about this for a moment. "If so, why did you cast him in such a pivotal role?"

"Did you not see for yourself what a damn fine job he did of it?" Max chided. "My instincts are good. Sometimes, they're brilliant. That combination of arrogance and insecurity that we see in his televised interviews? They convinced me that this role was perfect for him. Type casting, if you will." He shifted in his seat.

"May I ask the waiter to bring you a cup of tea?" Aria offered.

"Thank you, my dear, but your old Uncle Max will tough this out to the end." He reached over and touched her hand. "Please tell your mother how much she's missed, will you?"

Aria squeezed his hand.

Roche nearly interceded to remind them that this was a murder investigation, not a family reunion. He said nothing.

"One more question," Anuj said.

"And I have a few of my own," Roche said.

Max said nothing, but looked from one man to the other, eyebrows raised, as though saying *Be my guest, I've nothing to hide.*

"This understudy, Darwin McAfee," Anuj said. "Not exactly a French name."

"Born near London. French mother, English father. His father died when he was a boy, and his mother returned to France. He grew up speaking French. He thinks in French and is considered French by everyone he meets. And he's the perfect understudy."

"Why is that?" Roche said.

"Oh, didn't I say? Darwin is Anton's closest friend; Anton trusts him with his life and his career. There have been more than a few occasions when Darwin has had to step in for him, including after that terrible accident a few years back."

Anuj quickly flipped through the pages of his notes.

"You won't find it there," said Max. "The fool was riding his motorcycle, very much in breach of his contract. He hit something on the highway and broke his leg two days before his play opened in Avignon. Darwin stepped in and gave a good performance. Not great, but the audience was sympathetic to him." He paused for a moment, kneading his hands the way one does when arthritis is flaring up. "Anton saw this as an omen," he said. "A reason to stay away from the theater. And before you ask," he said, "there was no way he was going to turn down *Hamlet's Father.* The publicity has been priceless."

"Were there other occasions when Darwin had to step in?" Tenna asked.

This time, the director remained silent for quite a long time. "You probably know this," he finally said. "Anton has a gambling problem. He's often in debt. And not always to the nicest people. His agent has bailed him out on several occasions, taking over IOUs that needed to be paid. However, this has nothing to do with Camilla's death, I assure you. Or Joseph's attack. You've met Anton. Did he strike you as someone capable of murder?"

"About this Darwin fellow," Anuj pressed. "A temper? Perhaps thwarted advances towards Camilla?"

"Darwin is the stabilizer in Anton's life. He's a rock. Always there, the strong shoulder. I've known him for years—never closely, but certainly long enough to judge—and I have never seen him lose his temper."

"But might he have held certain affections for Camilla? Affections that she rejected?" asked Tenna.

Max shook his head. "Never."

"How can you be so certain?" Roche said. "Even the mildest soul can be pushed too far."

"Not in this case," Max said. "Darwin is gay."

"Any chance he loves Anton?" Roche asked. "And he was jealous of Camilla?"

Max released a loud sigh. "Inspector, these two men have been friends, like brothers, since they were kids. Brothers, not lovers. Darwin is fine with Anton being straight; Anton is fine with Darwin being gay. No tension, no competition, no jealousies. Let that one go."

"One thing I'd like to understand," said Tenna. "Well, actually, two things. First, why did you cast Camilla in a role that everyone seems to think was more suited to Linné? And second, when you chose Camilla, why would you cast Linné as her understudy?"

Roche looked at his young detective. He felt almost proud, like a father who, after many lectures, suddenly realizes that his efforts have paid off.

"Easy," said Max. "The public knows Camilla for her superb theater performances, so I knew we'd get great press before the tickets were sold.

And as for Linné: sheer genius on my part! She's the big name in film, not so much yet in theater. Having them both in the cast, on the billboard, would not only guarantee ticket prices going through the roof, but would close this theater with a splash of elegance, and the kind of publicity a director dreams of having. Of course," he quickly added, pulling a somber face. "I never anticipated a tragedy."

Roche felt more questions hovering around him, but Max was showing signs of wearing down. He turned off the recorder and slipped it into his pocket. "Thank you, Max, you've been very helpful."

The director smeared another large blob of cream cheese onto his bagel and took a bite.

"Monsieur Formande," Tenna said. "I do have one question about your assistant. Do you know where she was during intermission?"

Max did not hesitate. "With me, in my office, going over some very nasty documents sent by the evil bastards who will be demolishing this grand old dowager tomorrow. Tomorrow!" He took a moment to compose himself and then picked a morsel of bagel from his shirt. "Laurene never left my side, from the beginning of Act One to the time Camilla was found. You can cross her off your list."

Anuj asked, "Not even to, say, use the bathroom?"

Max studied the young inspector's face. "Everyone needs to pee," he said. "That doesn't make them a killer." With that, he swiped the paper napkin across his mouth, rubbed cream cheese from his fingers, stood, and walked out of the restaurant.

"Poor man," Tenna said.

"This is not the way he expected to end his career," Aria said.

"What do you think about Laurene?" Anuj asked, directing the question to Roche.

Roche paused before answering. "I can't see it. And she would never attack Joseph. No, we're looking at the same person for both crimes, I'm sure of that."

Anuj gave a little groan as he stood and stretched his back.

"Even the young," Roche teased, fighting against his own stiffness as he stood.

Tenna gathered her things. "When I'm working a case like this, I take it to bed with me. It affects my sleep, controls my dreams, even my nightmares. And it doesn't leave me in peace until the case is solved and the bad guy is locked away. I hope it's soon!"

"I experience something similar when I'm faced with a deadline," Aria said.

"Hardly the same," Roche said, his mouth torqued just enough for him to be aware of how he must look to the others.

Tenna laughed nervously, as though needing to restore humor, or at least civility, to the conversation. "My husband complains bitterly about the unfairness of his sleep being disturbed." Pushing a strand of hair behind her ear, her expression was cheerless. "Serves him right for marrying a cop."

Roche was surprised to hear this. It reinforced his concerns that her private life was falling apart, and it caused him no little pain that his own life seemed to be doing the same. At the moment, things weren't bad with Judith, both of them working to keep it civil. But Luc? They were always navigating rough waters, but he was beginning to think that it wasn't his son who risked drowning.

Chapter Thirteen

I t took Aria several days to muster the courage to visit her brother on the outskirts of Paris. *Biting the bullet* came to mind as she stood in front of Martin's house. Her younger brother, her beloved younger brother, who hadn't spoken to her with any warmth, and not much civility, for years. It was a source of sadness for her, and a cause of quiet despair for their mother.

Despite it being winter, the little garden near the front door was a burst of flowers. Martin had always loved to work in the garden, even when he was a child. The plants chosen were particularly dramatic, cold-weather plants awakening into a riot of color. The daffodils were profuse, screaming to be seen, and the tulips were bursting into rainbow clusters that formed a circle around the hyacinths.

Aria knocked on the door. Her hands were shaking. She heard footsteps, and then the door opened.

There he was. Not changed so much since she had last seen him. A bit grayer at the temples, new crow's feet around his eyes, but still looking fit, slim, athletic. "Martin."

His face revealed nothing. "Mom said you were in town."

"May I come in?'

He stepped aside.

The foyer was a palette of gray and peach, with a dash of black and teal. "It's lovely," she said, following him into a sitting room.

"Would you like tea or water?" he asked, sounding more like a waiter than her younger brother.

"Thanks, I'm fine."

"Danielle is away; Fleur is napping."

She had never met her niece. "Will she be up soon?"

His face relaxed into a sweetness she had not seen in years. "If you're ready to leave before she's up, I'll awaken her."

Gratitude moved through her. "I'd like that."

They sat in silence. There was a discussion she desperately wanted to have, and now was the time. "We've been estranged for years," she began, her voice level. "And I don't know why."

He studied her for a moment. "With you, it's always been about the limelight." After a long beat, he added, "This time, you've paid the price."

Of course, he would know. Either from their mother, some old friend, or that damned internet. Her stomach turned. "It was a mistake, Martin. A terrible and irretrievable mistake."

He looked at her, perhaps not sure how to respond, and then he said, "Mother tells me you're somehow involved in this murder at the theater. She's very concerned about Solange and Bertrand. You know her, she sees only the good in her friends, never the evil."

"I acknowledge that they're difficult, especially Solange, but evil?"

"You don't remember after Father died, and how cold she was to us?"

"I remember some tension, but—"

He interrupted her. "You, Mother, me. We were in Paris and the focus of everyone's attention. Solange couldn't bear that. The beautiful widow, the fatherless children. At first, she was kind, but then she became ugly."

"I do recall that she was dismissive."

"Just like Mother," he said, shaking his head. "Selective memory. It's how you survive. If you pretend, or convince yourself that it didn't happen, then you don't have to face it. Mother conveniently ignored Solange's cruelty. Which means she failed to protect us."

"Martin, she was grieving."

"Oh, I forgive her. Hers is a history I wouldn't wish on anyone. Paris, the occupation. Having to go into hiding. So many people she loved dying in the camps."

Aria sat for several moments, heat burning her face. Before she could comment, he spoke again.

"Solange was, and I'm guessing still is, a self-centered shrew. But," he added, "I'd say it's unlikely she murdered Camilla Rodolfo. She might have wanted her dead, but she's far too proud to wield a weapon."

Aria was hardly listening. A strange sensation was moving through her. Was Martin right? That she needed to be the center of attention? Is that why she had jumped to conclusions and accusations? Rushing that article seemed right at the time, despite her voice telling her it was wrong. "What did you mean about the limelight, Martin?" She saw anger in his face. Or was it resentment?

"It was never enough for you, being an honor student. No, you had to be first in your class. And if you weren't, you were miserable. And you made all of us miserable. You can thank our mother for that."

"You blame her?"

"Aria, she pushed us to be perfect. I figured that out when I was a kid, that I would never do enough to make her proud. But you? You were determined to be second at nothing, and you usually achieved that. Mother never let me forget how perfect you were. Being the younger brother of super-achiever Aria Nevins was never easy."

Aria felt sadness engulf her. Perhaps he wasn't wrong. Before she could speak, a child entered the room.

"Here she is!" Martin declared.

Aria pulled herself together and gave the little girl her biggest smile. "And you must be Fleur!"

The girl leaned into her father.

"This is your Aunt Aria," Martin said. "She's visiting from San Francisco."

"You just had a birthday," Aria said. "That makes you six, yes?" She so desperately wanted to be given a chance with this child.

Fleur's face lit up. "You sent me my kitty!" She rushed out of the room and returned with a gray and white kitten, soft and huggable, green glass eyes and a big grin. "I call her Kitty Katty!" she declared, pressing the animal to her neck. "We sleep together every night!"

With that, she crossed to Aria and scooted herself onto her lap.

Aria held the child and inhaled her sweetness.

"She loves her Kitty Katty," Martin said.

They visited for nearly an hour before Aria checked the time. "I'm so sorry, I could stay all day, but I've been *embedded*." She used her fingers to indicate quote marks. "I'm still not sure why, but I'm beginning to suspect that the man who brought me here has some nasty motives." She turned Fleur around on her lap. "Please tell Mommy that I'm sorry I missed her and give her a kiss. Would you do that for me?"

Fleur wrapped her arm around Aria's neck and planted a loud kiss on her cheek. "Like that?" she asked, her eyes exploring the face of her newfound aunt.

"Exactly like that," Aria said, giving Fleur a squeeze.

The three of them walked to the door.

Aria touched the child's hair. "She's exquisite, Martin. And thank you for being honest with me. You've given me something to think about. You're right about my being an expert at avoidance. As for having to be the center of attention." She touched his arm. "I'm in town for a few more days. Perhaps we can meet before I leave."

"Perhaps we can." He gave her a quick hug and followed his daughter into the house.

Aria walked to the corner and hailed a taxi. She had just survived what she had feared would be a firing squad. It had gone well—better than well, brilliantly—and her strength was sapped.

Seated in the taxi, she fought the urge to close her eyes. Some of his words had landed hard, but there was a lightness she had not felt for too long. Like gossamer, she thought, allowing the warmth of relief and satisfaction to wrap itself around her.

She calculated the time change and figured that her mother was still sleeping. Pulling out her mobile, she texted Lexie: *Saw Martin. Met precious Fleur. Good visit. Please tell Grandma. Love you.*

She arrived at the theater and was assaulted by the din of jackhammers and heavy machinery. The building next to the theater was already being razed, with bulldozers scraping away a century of use. She had passed it a dozen times, yet had no recollection of what it had once been. An apartment house? A business? She searched her memory. We are here, she thought. We make our mark and are soon forgotten. Is that how it was for her? A lost reputation, a civil case yet to be resolved. Perhaps her legacy would be a recounting of her error. Like the loop of tape, repeating over and over the same message of criticism and guilt.

She had been surprised when Roche announced they were meeting here, cast and all. working around demolition crews. He had been adamant only hours earlier that they not return.

She stepped into the lobby and found Linné and Anton seated on the smaller of the two couches, with understudy Darwin McAfee standing at Anton's elbow and whispering in his ear. Max was pacing like a bad actor giving his interpretation of impatience. The Gabriels had taken the only high-back chairs, their postures erect. Sashkie hovered over them like an overcast sky. Roche, Tenna, and Anuj were standing apart from the others. The only people absent were Joseph and Laurene, and Aria assumed she was at the hospital.

"Thank you for your promptness," Roche told the group, raising his voice over the pounding noise. "I realize this is difficult, with this racket, but it's important that we meet here."

There were beeping sounds of a truck driving in reverse, followed by the crash of a wall coming down.

"I'm told they'll begin here at four," he said. "That gives us less than an hour. Any longer and we might become part of the debris." He waited. If he was expecting a laugh, no one complied. "In any case, thank you for agreeing to meet here."

Glances were exchanged among cast and crew, but it was Solange who spoke. "We didn't exactly agree; we were summoned. Did you think we wouldn't come?"

"Not at all," Roche said, slipping his recorder from his pocket.

"And if we hadn't?" she challenged.

Roche hardly missed a beat. "As I said before, Madame Gabriel, I would not have hesitated to send a well-marked police car to your door."

Aria saw how Solange's lips stretched across her teeth. She couldn't decide if this was controlled rage, nerves, or uncertainty. Or, perhaps, fear. She quietly removed the recorder from her bag, turned it on, and placed it on the little table at the end of the sofa.

"Is there any news of Joseph?" Linné asked.

"Holding his own, according to the neurologist," Roche said.

"With his faithful Laurene by his side." This came from Sashkie, but so quietly that only Aria heard.

Anton leaned forward. "How much longer must we do this?"

"I've summoned you here this one last time," Roche said.

The actor threw up his hands. "Good thing! I'm due in Berlin tomorrow afternoon. If I don't arrive on time—"

"I am not without sympathy," Roche said.

Aria sensed that, on the contrary, his sympathy was in short supply.

"But this is a murder investigation," he went on. "Nothing can be overlooked."

Darwin shifted in his seat. "So, you think it's one of us?"

It was the first time Aria had heard him speak. His French was perfect, and with those nasal sounds heard only in the speech of someone Paris-born.

"No one entered the dressing room area during intermission who didn't belong there," Roche told him. "That is, no one from the audience."

"As far as you know," Anton said.

"Yes," Roche replied. "As far as we know."

"And how far is that, Chief Inspector?" Solange challenged.

Aria watched this exchange and wondered if actors were ever at a loss for words.

"We were hoping to go to the country." Solange turned to her husband. "Tell him, Bertie."

Bertrand took his wife's hand. "A day away would be appreciated." Before Roche could respond, he quickly added, "But certainly we'll stay, if you wish."

Solange yanked her hand away. "My letters," she said to Roche. "I want them back."

Aria wondered why Solange had decided to open this can of worms in front of everyone. Was she hoping to strong-arm Roche into giving in to her demands? The air in the room was feeling heavier.

Roche stared at Solange for a long moment. "I would think you'd be relieved to be rid of them."

Solange shook her head. "I don't want them for my enjoyment; I want to destroy them."

"They're part of a murder investigation," Roche reminded her, his voice flat.

"Wait," Anton declared, eyes wide. "Are they...love letters?" He was clearly working to suppress a laugh. When no one responded, he leaned back. "Don't tell me it's hate mail. My God!"

A round of whispers coursed through the room, barely audible above the increasing volume of engines just outside the walls of the theater.

If anyone had previous knowledge of the letters' existence, it wasn't obvious. But then, Aria reminded herself again, this was a room of actors.

Solange was not accepting Roche's explanation. "How do I know you won't release them to the public?" Her voice dripped with accusation. "They'd make exciting fodder for the tabloids, don't you think? And they would certainly bring a pretty penny to the person who sells them."

"Madame Gabriel," Roche said, his voice even, controlled. "No one will release them, exploit you, or profit off your misfortunes. When this case is solved, and the culprit has been brought to justice, I will personally destroy them. And in your presence, if you wish."

The woman appeared not so much relieved as stricken. When was the last time someone had upstaged the great Solange Gabriel?

The mood was broken when Roche pulled out his mobile phone and pressed it to his ear. "You're sure?" he said. "Good work. Yes, we'll talk later." He turned to Anuj and then to Tenna. "Pascal."

"Who's that?" Anton said.

"Our forensics expert," Anuj said.

Linné leaned forward. "I'm guessing he didn't call to say hello."

Aria saw regret in Anuj's eyes. He knew better than to supply information, especially to potential suspects. A quick glance at Roche confirmed that the inspector wasn't thrilled either.

Roche gestured for his young detectives to follow him into the hallway. Without a second thought, Aria followed.

"Sorry, Boss," Anuj said in a low voice. "It won't happen again."

After an uncomfortable pause, Roche said, "As of this moment, everything changes."

Aria felt the hairs on her neck bristle.

"Meaning?" Tenna said.

"The makeup on Camilla's sleeve is identical to the shade Solange uses."

The facts were there, yet he sounded unconvinced.

"How likely is it…" Anuj said, then stopped.

Roche pressed his hand against the nape of his neck. "It's not."

"So, we bring her in?" Tenna said.

Roche shook his head. "Let's keep this between us for the time."

Aria saw a change in Anuj's face. Anger? She wasn't sure.

"But, Boss," he said. "What about—"

Roche cut him off. "I don't want the Gabriels, or any of those people, to know."

Tenna's eyes grew wide. "What if she's guilty?"

Roche shook his head. "We need to consider that the Gabriels are being set up. Whoever is doing this is very clever. For the time, let them think we've taken the bait."

Aria felt her heartbeat return to its normal rhythm.

"Meaning…we don't pursue this," Anuj said. "Even with solid evidence."

"Solid evidence that it's her makeup, yes. But did she put it on Camilla? Was she even in that dressing room? If someone's playing us, and we don't make this public, they'll wonder why."

That made sense to Aria. "Forcing them to show themselves."

Roche ignored her and turned to Tenna. "Have the background checks given us anything?"

"No more than what we learned earlier. Anton has two arrests for drunkenness; Linné has no priors, and Camilla's greatest sin seems to be a few unpaid parking tickets. The Gabriels have never been charged with a crime."

Aria followed them back to the lobby.

Anton jumped up from the sofa, his arms outstretched. "Connect me to a lie detector. Shoot me up with truth serum. Do what you must so I can get the hell out of here!"

Roche said, "Now, there's a good idea, truth serum. Why didn't I think of that?" When the actor glared, he added, "No lie detectors, and does anyone really use truth serum?"

"So why are we here?" Linné asked.

"I need you here so there's no doubt about your receiving my instructions. I could message you, leave emails, or phone messages, but where's the guarantee that you'll listen? And if you do, who's to say you'll comply?"

"So, what are you saying?" Solange asked.

"You may all go home. But you must stay in Paris, nearby if you're needed."

Anton turned to his understudy and mumbled, "A fucking waste of time."

"There will be no shackles," said Roche.

"And then what?" Anton demanded.

"And then we'll let you know."

A low rumble of protests ran through the group, but it was Bertrand who spoke up. "It's been two days, Inspector. Your people have checked every inch of this building. You've questioned all of us..."

"Don't you mean *interrogated*?" Anton said.

"I prefer *questioned*," Roche said.

"I'm sure you do," Anton shot back.

"I can't argue your point," Roche said. "The building was thoroughly inspected. But, if you recall, there was such chaos. Our forensics people were working until dawn. One more look is all we need, but you are free to go."

"And I can leave for Berlin," muttered Anton.

"Sorry, I'm afraid not," said Roche. "Until we clear you of all suspicion, you're not to leave Paris."

"Sorry about what? That I'll miss the first day of rehearsal? You damn well should be sorry!"

"The first day, yes," said Roche. "And perhaps the second and the third. The sooner you're cleared, the faster you can make your exit. But for now, more might be needed from you."

Anton pulled out his cell phone and hit a button. When he spoke, he made no effort to lower his voice. "I'm stuck in Paris. It's this damned murder thing." He listened. "Of course, I didn't kill her! But try and convince the cops of that. Yeah, a scene from a very bad movie. Darwin? Now there's the joke. He's stuck here with me."

Before anyone could question Roche further, a man wearing a business suit walked into the lobby. He was also wearing a hard hat in bright orange, and a heavy vest in garish green.

Aria said nothing, but she imagined her mother seated there, questioning why they could not provide safety gear that was color coordinated.

"You'll have to leave the building," the man announced. "It's nearly four."

"Soon," said Roche. "We're in the middle of a murder investigation."

"I'm aware of that," said the man. "And we're in the middle of a major demolition. We're nearly done with the surrounding buildings. We kept this one for last, at the request of the building inspector." He looked around. "Sorry to see this old gal gone. The wife and I saw our share of plays here."

Three workers entered. Their heavy boots sent echoes through the lobby as they stomped toward the dressing rooms.

"Absolutely not!" Roche announced. "Our work here supersedes yours. We'll leave when we're done."

The demolition crew ignored him and disappeared into the hallway.

Roche turned back to the others. "We'll check the rooms now," he told his team. To the cast, he added. "Go home. If we need to contact you, we know where you are."

"Welcome to house arrest!" Anton declared.

Roche gave him a rather acquiescent look. "More or less, but without the ankle monitor. Unless you prefer one."

Everyone stood, yet no one rushed out. Instead, they looked around, taking in the scene, their faces wistful.

Aria was certain they were storing images, their last views of an elegant building that had brought a century of artistry and joy to the public, and had been a second home to staff and crew.

"Let's do this," Roche said to his team. Without awaiting a response, he entered the warren of hallways now familiar to them all.

What they found caused Aria's stomach to churn. There was no demolition, at least not yet, but the hallway was piled with debris.

Tenna stood at the door leading into what had only days ago been Camilla Rodolfo's dressing room. "Oh, dear." Two words, but fraught with emotions.

Aria stepped inside. With the sink now on the floor, the walls were revealed as deeply stained. Broken shards of mirror were strewn about, and the ceiling plaster was cracked. It resembled more a slum than a place harboring a life of creativity and promise.

"I suggest we give a good look here, and then let it be," Tenna said to Roche. Before he could respond, she added, "There's nothing more to be found; every inch of the other rooms has been searched."

Roche looked at her. "I was hoping to find something, anything, we might have overlooked, but everything's been compromised." He glanced around, his expression bleak. "Let's go back to the station and see what we've got."

As they turned to leave, Aria spotted an old playbill among the debris. It was from a play performed twenty years earlier. "Look," she said, holding it up. "The Gabriels were in this." She turned to Roche. "Mind if I keep it? My mother would love it." When Roche said nothing, she tucked it into her bag.

They left the theater. The street was unusually quiet, the demolition crew awaiting their departure. A brushstroke of fading daylight bled through the misty fog.

Roche led them along a narrow road leading up to the basilica. "Some good bistros," he promised. "An early dinner and then back to the precinct."

"Or home?" Tenna threw him a wishful look.

Aria was too tired to be hungry. A hot bath called out to her. She quickened her pace until she caught up with Roche. "Anything on the agenda tonight?"

He shook his head. "I'll be working at my desk."

"Where he'll be making his famous lists," Anuj said. "Columns of the pros and cons of every suspect; notations about what's possible and what isn't. Who might be guilty…or innocent."

Tenna grinned. "Über-thorough, that's our boss."

"And yet," Roche said with a rather impish grin, "it works."

They neared the corner. "If it's good with you," Aria said to Roche, "I'd like to return to the hotel."

"As you wish," he said.

She tried to read his tone, but could not. If he was being dismissive or annoyed, she preferred not to know.

Anuj stepped off the sidewalk and raised his arm to hail a taxi. Several passed, but they were occupied. "Not so easy this time of day," he called out to Aria. Another half-dozen blew by, their roof lights dimmed to indicate a fare was inside.

"Keep trying," urged Tenna.

Aria knew the many steps required to descend, and that was to the Metro Abbesses elevator. And after that, there was the long ride deep into the earth before it reached the tracks.

Roche turned to Tenna, "I want you and Anuj in my office in an hour."

Aria had had enough of feeling left out. "Would you like me to disappear?"

He looked at her, but said nothing.

The air around them felt suddenly icy.

"I'm here at the request of de Charbonnet." Her attempt to hide her anger was failing. "If you're asking for my presence only when it suits you, that won't work." She saw his face shift, and thought that the controls he'd been exercising were failing him, too. "How about you do your job and let me do mine." With that, she turned and walked away.

There was no need to glance back to know that she had left Anuj and Tenna speechless. No one dared speak to their boss like that. Perhaps it was time someone did! There were footsteps behind her, someone walking quickly, but she was too angry to care. She had put up with the man long enough. De Charbonnet could take this assignment and shove it.

Roche caught up with her, his scowl so evident it was almost comic.

"Why can't you be honest?" she said. "The only reason you haven't sent me packing is because you'd have to answer to de Charbonnet, and you need help with the Gabriels. But we both know that if I weren't here, you'd find a way to deal with them. That makes me expendable. So, should I leave?"

He looked away. For the first time, she almost felt sorry for him. Was he afraid of the power de Charbonnet could exert over him and his career?

"I don't care how high you build that wall," she said, an edge of defiance returning to her voice. "Unless you throw me out, I intend to stick to you and your team like glue."

"There's no reason for you to be nasty," he told her.

She heard annoyance, and not the apology she deserved. That she had earned. "Oh, but there is," she insisted. "It's obvious that you want me gone, out of your hair. But what if Solange and Bertrand remain as suspects—or even Max? I'm sure you'll learn what you need to know, but my absence will make it more difficult." Before he could respond, she added, "And what will you tell de Charbonnet?" She had her own opinions about the man, and his motives for choosing Roche and his team for this little journalistic exposé, but she had no proof. Until she knew more, she'd say nothing.

Roche seemed about to argue, then his shoulders dropped. "We're all exhausted."

She was torn between assuring him that she would join them at the precinct, and telling him to go to hell.

Anuj appeared, his hands spread in frustration. "No taxi, sorry."

"Thanks, it's not a problem. I'll take the Metro."

"Come back with us," Roche said. "To the precinct."

Anuj walked away, leaving her standing alone with Roche.

"You're convinced de Charbonnet planted me in your squad so I'd leak information to him. Or write a scathing article about you. Just so you know, I'm not stupid. The man is transparent as glass. So back off, will you? Whatever I write will be fair and unbiased. And I'm doing it with or without your permission or support."

Roche said nothing, his face impossible to read.

When her mobile vibrated, she figured it was Lexie. It was six-thirty in Paris, which made it morning in California. Having a chat with her daughter lifted her spirits.

"Georges de Charbonnet here. My office."

She sat across from the man, watching him pick up items, then put them down. This was not the cocky man she had met at their first encounter. Was she the cause of his anxiety? A part of her hoped she was.

"How are you doing?" he asked. No inflections, no indication of emotion.

She had rehearsed possible responses to a variety of opening salvos, but not such a straightforward question. Perhaps this would be easier than she had expected. "I'm doing well," she said. "The team seems to have accepted me."

"Good, all good," he said, tugging on his lower lip.

"They're working nearly 'round the clock."

"And what were the odds you'd be so valuable?"

"A coincidence," she said. "A terrible thing, this murder. My presence seems to be helping with the Gabriels."

"I gather he's not bad, but she's a handful."

"That about sums it up," she said.

De Charbonnet leaned closer. "This case gives you an even closer look at the team. Any impressions?"

"A tight unit," she said. "A family."

"And Roche?"

A warning light blinked in her mind. "Fair," she said. "And demanding. As their mentor, he wants them to learn. They respect him."

"It must be a challenge for him, teaching acolytes during such a public case."

Aria studied his face. "His acolytes, as you call them, are seasoned detectives who work beautifully together. They've welcomed me into the fold. I'm sure you know that we were in Camilla Rodolfo's dressing room only minutes after she was killed."

His eyes locked into hers.

"I've watched Roche and his team inspect the evidence," she continued. "And then question actors, crew, and staff. The interrogations are still going on." She made a show of checking her wristwatch. She felt the tension around her. He was asking what seemed like harmless questions, but they were loaded with intent. Was he looking for fuel to ignite some hidden agenda? She knew that Roche suspected him of being on the lookout for anything incriminating to use against him. She felt squeezed between them, with an increased awareness of their mutual dislike.

De Charbonnet's voice broke into her thoughts. "So, you're finding Roche a good leader, fair and impartial."

The way he smiled made Aria think of a predator. "I take it you're not looking for criticism, just my impressions."

"Absolutely."

She had dealt with enough de Charbonnets in her career that she could smell a rat. "I'm so relieved," she parried, trying to sound innocent. "Because I wouldn't want to speak out of school."

"If you do pick up something that concerns you," he went on, "please feel free to share it with me. I'm always available to help my people improve their skills. Off the record, of course, all anonymous. Your name will never be mentioned."

Aria suppressed a laugh. "Monsieur de Charbonnet—"

"Please, it is Georges."

She stood and picked up her bag. "Forgive me, Georges, but I can't be late. The heat of the investigation, and all that. And thank you for your offer."

He walked her as far as the anteroom. She sensed there was something he wanted to say. If he was itching for dirt, a weapon to use against Roche, he'd have to find someone else to provide it.

She stepped into the elevator. It descended one floor and then stopped. The doors opened to reveal Roche, Anuj, and Tenna.

"We're taking a quick break," Tenna said. "Join us?"

Roche chewed on his cheek for a moment. "How did it go?"

She wasn't sure how much to reveal. That Roche's superior was fishing for dirt about his leadership? Or should she say nothing, remain neutral and safe? She understood why these meetings with de Charbonnet gnawed at him. The man held Roche's future in his grubby hands. She had to work hard to gain the inspector's trust. God knows she had been trying, but it wasn't going so well.

Chapter Fourteen

"I'm going stir-crazy," said Roche. "I've made a reservation at a café across from the Pantheon. We all need a break. Lunch is on me."

Feeling pleased with himself, he led his team, including Aria, through the garage, where they piled into an official car, one with emergency lights and all. "Gets around parking restrictions," he said, slipping into the driver's seat.

On days such as these, with the winter sun reflecting off cobblestones still damp from an early mist, Roche felt sorry for those Parisians wedged into Metro trains. Traveling by car meant traffic jams and burning expensive petrol, but it also meant avoiding the crush of bodies. Anuj had suggested he purchase a scooter, but the inspector couldn't see himself navigating Paris perched on what he considered a two-wheeled motorized golf cart. And was there anything more comical than a middle-aged man in a crash helmet?

As he drove, he thought about Aria, who was seated next to him. He had to admit that his initial resentment was softening, even turning into trust. Her meetings with de Charbonnet were irritating, unnerving, but now he was quite certain she wasn't criticizing him. He still felt the need to hold back comments that could be used against him, but her last dramatic outburst was giving him cause to relax.

They arrived at the restaurant. There were no parking spaces, including illegal spots, for a chief homicide inspector. He turned onto rue Cujas and inched along behind a garbage truck. The backup lights of a parked car gave him hope. He stopped and waited. Cars behind him honked, but he was unfazed. The only thing rarer than winning the lotto was finding a parking space in this part of Paris.

He maneuvered his way into the space and killed the engine.

"Well done!" Tenna broke into applause. "Not only finding it, but squeezing in, too."

Roche enjoyed a bit of humor after so much gloom. Perhaps this case would be solved soon and the bad guy locked away. He smiled to himself. Since he was creating this pie-in-the-sky wish list, why not add something about Luc getting a job and becoming financially independent?

They walked to the café. It was nearly empty. A waiter pointed to a table near the window, and they settled in. There were two people at the bar, where food was less expensive than if they sat at a table. A young man was working on a large glass of beer, and an elderly woman was chewing on a baguette.

Roche strained against the stiffness that normally didn't begin until later in the day. It didn't seem to matter if he slept or not, this fatigue was wrapped around him. The case was exhausting. In fact, the suspects and the non-suspects were exhausting. Was he running in circles, a dog chasing its tail?

He opened the menu, but nothing jumped out at him. Minutes earlier, he had felt almost carefree, but now the worries returned. The next meeting with the Gabriels would undoubtedly include their attorney. Harassment charges? He wouldn't blame them if they tried.

His cell phone buzzed. He looked at Anuj. "Would I be damned to hell if I flung it into the Seine?" He put the phone to his ear.

"Hey," said Luc.

No need to ask why his son was calling. "Hey to you, too." He gave his team an apologetic look.

"Have you and Mom talked. You know, about the apartment."

Roche felt a twinge of guilt. "Sorry."

"Dad."

"I know, Luc, but I'm in the middle of this case."

"He needs to know soon, or he'll hand it over to a realtor. That'll put it out of my price range."

Roche felt his jaw tighten. Whose price range? Not his son's, surely. Luc probably couldn't come up with the money to pay his EDF bill. What would happen when his power was turned off? But this was his son, and he seemed to be trying. "Tell him to wait a bit longer, will you? I'll talk to your mother tonight, I promise."

He slipped the phone into his pocket.

Anuj was staring out the window, a wistful look on his face. "Do you think Maryam is seeing the same sky in Addis Ababa?"

Before he could reply, the waiter arrived and they gave their orders.

"So, mon capitaine," said Tenna. "What's on the agenda?"

Roche's expression seemed almost playful. "What if I announced an imminent arrest?" He saw how quickly their faces shifted to attentiveness, and he immediately regretted his attempt at humor. "No, not really." He released a dramatic sigh.

Aria held up a finger, and Roche saw how quickly she had the attention of his detectives. He wondered if he had that same appeal.

"What if Camilla was flying high?" said Aria. "Getting great roles and making a lot of money. Who would resent her? Anton?"

"He certainly could have a motive, but only if he benefited financially," Anuj said. "I don't see how."

Aria said, "So maybe she loaned him money to cover gambling debts, and he couldn't pay her back." She turned to Roche. "And what about this hate mail? It began arriving weeks before Linné first met the Gabriels, so I'm guessing we can rule her out."

Try to be nice, he told himself. "She might have hatched her plan months ago."

Aria appeared confused. "But why? They'd never met."

"We've established that," he said. "But that's based on what she told us."

"You think she might be lying?" There was just enough wariness in her voice to raise his hackles. He was tempted to tell her yet again to mind her own business, to do her job, and let him do his. What goes around, he thought, remembering her recent demand, and in those very same words. He nearly asked her why she felt this way, but decided to let it drop.

Tenna pulled a folder from her backpack. "I've been working on the letter."

Her voice was upbeat.

"Good thing one of us is getting something done!" said Roche, again hoping to lighten the mood.

A pink blotch appeared on Tenna's cheeks. "Just an idea," she said demurely, unwilling to acknowledge the compliment. "Not much to hang onto."

Since Aria had joined them, Roche was getting a better sense of Tenna's private life. He knew Klemens wasn't easy, but now he suspected the man was a bully who seldom, if ever, praised his wife.

Tenna opened the file. "We've been quick to look at the actors, especially Camilla, as a possible candidate for writing these notes. But I had to ask myself—why would she send hate mail to Solange?" She looked at the others, her expression challenging them to come up with the answer. No one spoke. "Rumors about Camilla being Bertrand's daughter, or even Solange's, crop up with regularity, but they're not taken seriously, except maybe by the tabloids. And to be honest," she added, "two eighty-year-olds don't make for sexy gossip. So, I was thinking," she continued. "What if the Gabriels wrote them? What if something was going on between them and Camilla that we don't know about?" She turned to Anuj. "Has anyone checked with Camilla's attorney? Surely there's a will, but there might be other documents as well."

"Those letters began arriving long before Camilla was murdered," Anuj pointed out. "Why wait until now?"

"It doesn't wash," agreed Roche.

"Then let's take this a step further," said Tenna. "Solange told us that, as far as she knew, Camilla had never made nasty comments about her. That is, about an old woman playing a young queen. What if she was lying?"

"Even so," said Roche. "Could an elderly woman, or man, both so obviously frail, carry off not only a murder, but a vicious attack? And which of them climbed a steep ladder, bludgeoned Joseph, and then hoisted him over the railing?"

"My mother is in her eighties," said Aria. "She doesn't even use a stepladder, because it requires a balance she no longer has."

Tenna held up the photocopies. "There's more. See how the letters are formed? If Solange or Bertrand, or anyone of their generation, had written this, the script would be different."

Aria moved closer, with Roche looking over her shoulder. He picked up the scent of flowers, which he usually found pleasing. He was tempted to elbow her away.

"Here," said Tenna, pointing. "The letters 'a' and 'r' lack the old- fashioned model that children were taught decades ago in school. They're more modern, the kind of longhand my boys use."

Roche leaned closer. "What about the paper?"

"Definitely from Solange," said Tenna. "Forensics checked the fiber against her personal stationery, plus the watermark. They're identical."

"Which suggests that she wrote them," said Anuj.

"Easy enough to steal a few sheets here and there," said Aria. "Especially if she kept a box of stationery in her dressing room."

"Well, that's the thing," said Tenna. "She never brings her stationery to the theater. One of her great pleasures is to sit in the garden at their villa and write to her friends. So, whoever took them—if, indeed, they were taken—they had to have visited there."

"They always have visitors," Aria said. "Unless things have changed, flocks of them."

"I can't imagine what that place looks like," said Anuj, his voice wistful.

Tenna's eyes sparkled. "The villa? I've seen photos, and it's spectacular."

"It is," said Aria. "Lovely. The photos don't do it justice."

Tenna stared at her for a moment.

Color rose in Aria's face.

Their food arrived, but hunger seemed to have deserted them. A few little bites here and there, with no suggestion of enjoyment or satisfaction. It was almost a relief when Roche felt his phone vibrate. He pressed it to his ear and immediately signaled for the waiter. "It's not looking good for Joseph," he told them, dropping his credit card onto the tray.

Tenna slipped the photocopies into the envelope, and Anuj took one last bite of his croissant.

The moment Roche signed the check, they were out the door. They climbed into the car and raced towards the hospital, the posted speed limit ignored.

"Why did Joseph have to be silenced?" asked Tenna, the car nearing the imposing building. "If we can answer that, we'll get a handle on this thing. Also, why wait until the performance to kill Camilla?"

"She's right," said Anuj. "That rules out Linné, don't you think? If she wanted that role and was willing to do anything to get it, Camilla would have died long before this."

"So, we're back to where we started," said Aria.

"Not really," said Anuj. "If we rule out Linné, and we can pretty much rule out the Gabriels, who's left?"

"What makes you think we can rule out the Gabriels?" Roche asked.

Tenna gave him a wide-eyed look. "I thought we agreed that two elderly people—"

"—have the means to hire someone to do their dirty work," said Roche, cutting her off. "I'm not convinced they're innocent, but I understand what you're saying."

"And what about Anton?" asked Anuj. "I'm sorry, but can anyone see him handling a knife, much less cutting into flesh? The man strikes me as a—"

"Wimp?" suggested Roche.

Aria laughed. "Yes, Anton Delant is definitely a wimp."

"That pretty much says it all," agreed Tenna, and then she read out the names of the cast and crew.

"So, who is left as a viable suspect?" Aria asked.

"If we remove Linné and Anton from the list," said Anuj, "and accept that an elderly couple could not carry it off, then the list is shorter. What about one of the technicians working in the theater?"

"We haven't looked closely at Anton's understudy," Roche reminded him. "There's also Max Formande. Was the old man hoping for one last drama before his beloved theater was bulldozed out of existence? What could be more dramatic than a cold-blooded murder?" He didn't need to glance toward Aria to know that she was scowling. "This can't be easy for you, watching suspicion fall on people you've known all your life. But we have to explore everything."

She remained silent. Roche assumed she was working to control a blistering response.

"We can't discount Sashkie or Laurene," said Tenna. "But what could they possibly gain?"

"That leaves someone from the audience," said Aria. "Or even someone off the street."

"True," said Roche. "But how did the killer slip into Camilla's dressing room during the intermission, commit the crime, and then slip out unnoticed? If this was possible, and I strongly doubt it, then all of Paris should be under suspicion."

"And let's not forget that alley door and the way the lock was pried," said Tenna.

"Maybe it was the playwright," suggested Anuj with an impish grin.

Roche laughed. "As enraged as he might have been that a woman in her eighties was entrusted with a role that drips with intrigue, savagery, and sex, he's dead and therefore exonerated."

"What about another meeting with the pathologist?" Anuj said. "I'm wondering if they missed anything about Camilla's injuries."

"Where are you going with this?" Aria said.

Anuj thought about it for a moment. "I'm not sure, but what if there are bruises inflicted before the night of her death? A pattern of abuse we haven't seen. We don't even know if she was in a relationship when she died."

"Call now," Roche said. "Tell him to give it another look, and to do it sooner than later."

Anuj made the call, spoke a few words, then rang off. "Tomorrow afternoon, but he doubts he'll find anything. He said his autopsy was extremely thorough."

"Why isn't he doing it now?" Roche demanded.

"Some conference where he's delivering a paper."

Roche believed that nothing trumped a murder investigation. "De Charbonnet is breathing down my neck; we need to close this case quickly. And the more dramatic the outcome, the better. That man loves drama, headlines that drive home to the public not only that we know our job, but perform brilliantly—thanks to his guidance."

They arrived at the hospital and were informed that Joseph's condition had worsened, but he was holding on. Laurene had left before this reversal, finally going home to sleep. Roche thought of calling her, but nothing was likely to change soon.

After a few minutes, the team left.

Outside, they stood on the sidewalk. "How about we take a short break," Roche offered.

Aria immediately dug through her bag and pulled out a handful of euros. "I'll grab a cab back to the hotel, get a bite at the take-out, and go to work."

"Video chat with Maryam," Anuj said, his eyes bright.

"I'll run over to rue Rivoli and pick up sweat pants for the boys," Tenna announced.

"If you're pushed for time," said Anuj, "the street markets near there have everything you need, and for half the price."

While this discussion around economizing and the benefits of buying from sidewalk vendors continued, Roche punched a number into his phone. "Jean-Phillipe, my team is about to abandon me." He paused as his friend spoke. "You mean the one facing Saint Sulpice? See you in twenty. And if you get there first, order a double espresso."

He climbed into the car. Perhaps he would cancel his date with Jean-Philippe, go home, have a glass of wine, and then sleep. But first, he needed to discuss this apartment idea with Judith. He called Jean-Philippe and canceled their dinner. The kung pao chicken from the take-out joint near his apartment sounded perfect. Maybe there was a good mystery on television. He loved it when he guessed the killer. Sometimes, he got it right.

Chapter Fifteen

By the time Aria arrived at the Hotel Esmeralda, she was in a fog. She needed to get along with this moody inspector, but being polite, sometimes even charming, was making no difference. The man ran hot and cold, first inviting and then unyielding. If she behaved sweetly, she came across as unctuous, but if she expressed her true feelings, she risked being shut out.

She was about to enter the hotel's front door, and changed her mind. She needed to move, pull some of this brisk air into her lungs. Clear her head.

She walked down to the river and crossed at the Pont Louis-Philippe to the Île Saint-Louis. She had lived on the little island during her last year at the Sorbonne, in a studio apartment so small she couldn't burn wood in the fireplace unless the fold-out bed on the opposite wall was closed. Opened, the foot of the bed abutted the hearth and the mattress would have burst into flames.

She had loved that place, especially the string quartet that rehearsed every Sunday morning on a balcony overlooking her window. Music filled her little nest, often Vivaldi and Mozart. In the winter, it was the perfect accompaniment to reading the International Herald Tribune and attacking the New York Times crossword, with oak and madrone crackling in her little fireplace. It was so cozy, so…Paris. She could have been perfectly happy if she had never heard the couple below her. She was no prude, but being subjected to their rapture could be trying. When she finally dared to close her window firmly, she heard them laugh. As it happened, it was the beginning of a friendship that lasted for years.

She stopped at Berthillon for ice cream. She always promised herself she would order only one scoop, but often left the shop with two. If her hotel room had a refrigerator, she might have added several pints.

The shop was busy. There were a dozen people ahead of her, lined up on the sidewalk, and at least four languages being spoken. Everyone seemed to share the anticipation of moving into the tiny shop, standing at the counter, and making the selection.

When it was her turn, she ordered dark chocolate nougat and pistachio in a sugar cone. Stepping outside, she ran her tongue across the heavenly chocolate. She followed the little road that bisected the island, crossed the foot bridge, and passed through the gardens leading to Notre Dame Cathedral. The structure was magnificent, even more so now that the scaffolding erected after the devastating fire was removed.

Unlike many visitors, Aria knew of the concrete steps leading down to the memorial for the Jews of Paris. Around 76,000 were rounded up, sent to Drancy and then on to Auschwitz, including a dozen of Aria's family. Many of those deported were children, and less than ten percent of those 76,000 survived. It was a part of her mother's legacy that she could not, or would not, discuss. Over the years, Aria learned that this silence was quite common among those who survived, their memories deep and agonizing. She was certain this explained why her mother had never been as affectionate as Aria had desired, and why she kept people—even those she loved—at a physical distance. She sensed that her mother's wounds affected not only her, but her relationship with her brother Martin.

The ice cream dripping down her hand brought her back to the moment. It suddenly tasted too sweet. She dropped the cone into a trash bin and returned to the hotel.

In her room, she checked her email and found a message from Izzy, reminding her that the paper was behind her. "Easy for you to say," she murmured. "It's my name on that lawsuit, not yours."

She went to her bank's website and reviewed her finances. Money wasn't a problem, at least not yet. As for the lawsuit, the newspaper carried insurance for situations like this. Too bad her reputation wasn't insurable as well. Pay a yearly premium and be exonerated of all bad deeds, including notoriety and the loss of face.

The room was in a state of chaos. Clothing was thrown over the chair; papers were strewn about. There were containers of uneaten food, with several piles of clean paper napkins, compliments of the takeout restaurants. The housekeeper was coming in the morning. Pride pushed her to clean up the mess.

With everything straightened and two trash baskets filled, she checked her voicemail and found a message from de Charbonnet. He was the last person on her *Oh, I cannot wait to talk to you!* list. She took a long drink of water and called him.

"How's it going?" he asked. "Still enjoying your little foray into the world of Paris homicide?"

She had no idea why he was speaking to her so soon after having met. Was this a trap? "Far better than I expected," she said, the lie nearly catching in her throat. "Being able to watch every step of this investigation will add enormously to my articles. Very revealing."

"Revealing," he repeated, his voice suddenly flat. "So, Roche is still allowing you this bird's-eye view."

Not a question, an accusation, and it put her on alert. It was time for a little fun. "Monsieur de Charbonnet, as I told you at our recent meeting, Chief Inspector Roche and his team have been very accommodating." Before he could respond, she said, "Thank you so much for checking in! Talk to you soon!" and she rang off.

"Gutsy lady," she murmured. She retrieved one of the half-filled cartons of food from the trash and dug in, not caring that it was cold. After the last bite, she took out the recording machine and was soon lost in the threads woven through this case. After having to play the same interview with Linné three times, she gave in to the fatigue, slipped under the covers, and fell asleep.

She awoke with a start, not sure if it was day or night. She glanced at the clock: it was not quite eight and there was light coming through the window. She punched in Roche's number. He answered on the first ring. "What's the plan?" she asked.

"You mean now?" he said. "Not sure. Tenna's just arrived, and Anuj is getting tea."

"A nice meal with Jean-Philippe last night?"

"Ah, the best-laid plans. I grabbed take-out Chinese."

"I'll be there soon," she told him. "Within the hour."

The long pause might as well have been an ear-splitting gong. Without giving him the chance to tell her that she needn't bother, she uttered a quick good-bye and ended the call.

Ten minutes later, she was dressed and sitting in the back of a taxi. The driver was an elderly woman, and so small she could barely see over the steering wheel. Aria wondered about having to work at this age, which she guessed was close to eighty.

She gave the woman the address of the bagel shop. Perhaps food offerings would endear her to the inspector.

The cab waited while she ran into the café and exited with a dozen bagels and enough cream cheese to feed the precinct. She settled into the back seat, pulled a hot bagel from the bag, and held it up for the woman to see through her rear-view mirror.

The driver grinned.

"With or without cream cheese?" She got an energetic thumbs-up.

It took some dexterity to smear cream cheese on a bagel in a moving taxi, but she managed without making a mess. Perhaps the rest of the day would go well after all. She was a bit nervous, watching the driver nibbling away at the bagel while maneuvering through traffic, one hand on the wheel.

The taxi arrived at Bastion. Aria paid the fare, added a generous tip, and entered the building. She found Anuj and Tenna standing outside Roche's office. Neither of them seemed pleased to see her. "What?" she asked.

"He's waiting for you," said Tenna, her voice a warning.

Aria handed her the bag of bagels, squared her shoulders, and knocked on the door.

"Enter!" Roche called out.

She stepped inside. Tenna's voice of doom was confirmed.

He gestured towards a chair, and she sat. "Have you been playing me?" he asked, his voice without inflection.

Whatever she was expecting, it wasn't this. "Playing you?"

"I'm talking about de Charbonnet," he interrupted. "Are you working for him?"

How many times did she need to answer this question? "He's the one who brought me into this assignment," she reminded him. "So, yes, I am."

"I think you know that's not what I mean."

Could he see how fast her heart was beating? "Then say what you mean," she shot back.

"What are you planning to do with this information?" he asked, and then rushed ahead before she could respond. "Which tabloid is paying you? No, don't tell me." He stood, moved towards the door, and then his hand was on the doorknob. "Enjoy your stay."

She refused to budge.

He opened the door. "I've watched you recording everything, taking notes. Meticulous notes, I'm guessing. And not just about the murder, but about everyone involved, my team. All this time, I thought your objective was to be impartial."

She felt sick; she could taste the damn bagel. "I don't understand."

"I just spoke to him. And what do you think he wanted?"

Aria sensed he didn't expect an answer, so she remained silent. The door was ajar and she saw Anuj and Tenna, their heads cocked towards the office.

Roche closed the door and leaned against it. "He asked about you. How were you doing? Were you being observant? 'We don't want her to miss anything,' he said. It didn't take much for me to get his gist: you're here to dig up dirt on my team, anything to discredit me."

The burn of anger flooded her face. "Let's get one thing straight, Chief Inspector Roche. My objective is to watch and listen, to educate the public about what a homicide team does, and how the members of that team work together—or don't. When I joined your team, there had been no murder, remember?"

He said nothing. Had her rebuttal hit its mark?

"As for Georges de Charbonnet: digging up dirt on your team or, more

166

specifically, on you, may be his intention, but it's not mine. I'm following the three of you, step by step, as you unravel this tangle of a case. I'm looking at the logic and reasoning all of you count on to get from one point to the next; how you study the motives of possible suspects, and how your team works together. None of this has anything to do with him." She glared at Roche, and bit down so hard she nearly broke a tooth. "Do you think I don't know he's a weasel? Or that his biggest fear is your success?"

Roche looked away, but only for a moment. "He's accusing me of dragging my feet. What in the hell have you been telling him? That we're lazy?"

Aria saw his anger, that was evident, but also recognized defiance. "Do you honestly think I'm out to get you? Or is that the paranoid fantasy you manufacture when you're feeling exposed? Or worse, vulnerable."

She stood. "You want to make accusations founded on nothing? I can't stop you. But don't you dare pull me into your bullshit! I could've turned down this job, but I needed it, and we both know why."

There, it was said. Or, at least, intimated. It was his turn to reveal what he knew.

The silence lasted for what felt like hours. Aria exerted as much control as she could muster to say nothing.

The two of them stood there, closer than was comfortable for her, but she'd be damned if she would back away.

"Yes," he told her. "I do know why." He retraced his steps and sat at his desk.

She needed to organize her thoughts, decide what to reveal and what to keep locked away. A voice in her head told her that it was all or nothing. "Perhaps I should have told you," she admitted. "But I didn't lie."

"Omission is the same as a lie."

"If you've done your research, you know that I never write for the tabloids. Digging up half-truths and lies is not what an investigative journalist does."

"Is that supposed to make me feel better?"

She warded him off with upheld hands. "I didn't come here to investigate you, or anyone else. I came here to write about a homicide unit that's headed by perhaps the leading investigator in France. And no," she quickly added,

"I'm not flattering you. But I can say that I'm certain you and your team were not selected by accident. I don't know why, but he's out to make you look bad." Before Roche could speak, she said, "Which I have no intentions of doing, but he doesn't need to know that. One agreement I'm pushing for is that my articles will be published as they're written, with no editing on his part."

She wished the room had a window. Fresh air, a view to the street, people moving about while living their lives. Oxygen.

"And you believe he'll honor that."

She elbowed away her concerns. "As we say in the States, I trust him as far as I can throw him."

"Wise decision," he agreed.

There were footsteps outside the door, the low murmur of conversations, phones ringing. It was time. The moment reminded her of a postcard she had purchased at a bookstore in Amsterdam, the drawing of a man holding open a large book, its pages blank. He was vomiting onto the book, but it wasn't food coming out of his mouth, it was letters and words. And now here she was, vomiting her story.

Roche's expression hardly changed as she spoke. He seemed to be taking in every word.

She described it all: the opioid series, the fatal accident caused by Adele Jameson. How her contact in the police force was certain drugs were involved. "I pushed him hard to confirm that," she said. "Very hard. And even the pathologist agreed, to a point. I had a deadline, so I ran with the story." She swallowed hard. "The media ripped the woman apart, and she was labeled a murderer."

"A terrible thing to happen," he said.

"It's more than terrible, it's tragic. I'm sure you know that Adele Jameson hanged herself in her cell."

The expression that crossed his face caused her heart to clench. She saw sadness. Profound sadness. "I imagine she couldn't live with the guilt."

Aria wrapped her arms around herself. He knew part of the story, but not the part that counted most. "She had nothing to feel guilty about."

"Nothing except the drugs."

"There were no drugs. After the article ran, the toxicology reports were delivered, and her family insisted on another autopsy. Adele Jameson ran that red light and drove into the intersection because she was having a stroke. It was my article, my accusation, that led to her suicide."

He looked at Aria. "I'm not sure what to say."

"There's nothing to say. I've always scoffed at people who swear that the dead speak to them, but no longer. Adele Jameson is living in my head, and her voice is angry and accusing." She sat down and leaned into the chair, exhausted. "So, you need to understand: I'm not doing any of this to expose you, or to sell the story to some tabloid. I'm doing it with the hope that a few doors will open and I can return to what I love doing. If you want to know the truth, I'm doing this not to save my reputation, but to save my life."

"I'm sorry," he said.

She looked into his eyes. If he wasn't sorry, she didn't want to know. "I've been suspended, which will probably lead to being sacked. And now a lawsuit has been filed against me. My boss, Izzy, is doing his best to put out the fires, but it's not encouraging. The truth is, when you're writing a series that's got Pulitzer written all over it, and the story is so compelling that it's being picked up by papers around the country, and then it suddenly explodes—"

"It's a tragedy."

She looked him in the eye. "There are people who say I should go to jail for involuntary manslaughter. My attorney assures me there's no legal basis." She paused, the pounding of her heart fierce. "Thank you."

"For?"

"Listening."

He pressed his lips together. When he finally spoke, his voice was modulated. "I've made mistakes, Aria, we all have. A killer not identified until after he's killed again, someone I helped send to prison who was innocent. The rush to judgment can cause terrible things. I'm sorry for what happened to you, but you're human, fallible, like all of us."

She hoped she wasn't sounding bombastic, but she was nearly desperate for him to understand that she would not be deterred. "Despite what you might think of me," she said, "I put honor and ethics first. I always have. As for this," she added, her hand sweeping across the room and towards the world outside his window, "I'm not going away."

Chapter Sixteen

Everyone's patience was wearing thin. Aria's jaw ached from gnashing her teeth, reminding her of those nightmares that inevitably arrived during times of extreme stress. The dreams were always the same: her teeth were falling out and tumbling onto the floor, and she couldn't gather them fast enough to keep them from disappearing. She would force herself awake, run her tongue across her teeth to confirm that there were no bleeding gums, no gaping holes where teeth once had been, and try to get back to sleep.

But she wasn't in bed; she was in Noah Roche's office with Tenna and Anuj. Judging by their faces, she was sure they shared her wish to get this case solved.

Tenna exhaled loudly.

"You okay?" Anuj said.

"I need a vacation," she said, pressing both palms against her eyes. "Or, at the very least, tea."

The three of them moved to the break room, where Aria turned on the kettle and Tenna checked the cupboard for goodies.

Anuj tossed tea bags into three mugs. "Maybe we can convince the boss to buy a villa outside of Paris and invite his detectives for weekends."

Tenna held up a bag of cookies. "The expiration date has long passed, but I'm quite sure they're not toxic—yet."

Something Anuj said broke through Aria's thoughts like a low flame that suddenly comes alive. "That's it!"

"That's what?" Anuj asked.

"We've taken apart Camilla's dressing room, and her house in Paris, right? But what if there's another place? What if she has a retreat? A place to escape from her fans and the paparazzi."

Tenna appeared to be mulling this over, and then she said, "Yes, you're right, entertainers have those."

Anuj rushed out of the room and returned only minutes later. His eyes were dancing with excitement. "Camilla's attorney says she has a villa."

Ten minutes later, they were in Roche's car and heading out of Paris.

The streets were crowded. Roche maneuvered deftly, his face a study in determination.

The hum of the car's engine lulled Aria, and she had to command herself to stay alert. It helped that her gut was telling her that this could be the turning point in their investigation.

It wasn't until they were zipping along the Periferique—the giant round-about road encircling Paris, the road from which all parts of Europe could be reached—that anyone spoke.

Roche handed Aria a map. "You can co-pilot." He looked through his rear-view mirror. "Which of my brilliant detectives thought of this villa?"

"It was Aria," Tenna said.

Roche gave Aria a terse nod, which she found far from acknowledging. And yet, what did she expect?

They followed the highway northwest, beyond Amiens and toward a place that might reveal secrets that could break this case wide open.

After two hours, they arrived at a security gate. It appeared to be the entrance to a private neighborhood. A new Mercedes was parked at the mechanical barrier, blocking other cars from entering. The guard's kiosk was unmanned. A woman climbed out of the car and walked towards them. Roche lowered the window and flashed his badge.

"Nice outfit," Tenna said, keeping her voice low.

"It should be," Aria said, studying the classic Chanel. "That puppy goes for more than five thousand euros."

Anuj gave a low whistle. "That would cover my rent for three months."

Even in stiletto heels, the woman was so short she hardly had to bend to peer into Roche's face. Her fingernails were long, manicured, and matched her deep-red lipstick. "I am Florence Agnelli," she said, handing him a business card through the window. Her words were as crisp and impersonal as her suit, her voice flat as a desert mesa. "I'm not sure what you want. I doubt you'll find anything of importance." Before anyone could respond, she walked away.

"Charming," said Tenna.

They watched the attorney return to her car and touch a device attached to her dashboard. The barrier rose, and soon they were following her up a steep roadway leading to what appeared to be the front of a house.

"Impressive," said Anuj.

"That's not the villa," said Aria. "I'm guessing this is where the staff lives."

"Oh, my," said Anuj, his eyes wide as he took in the scene. "My family lives very well by Indian standards, but this—"

High above them, on a rise that overlooked everything, stood the villa. "You'd need a four-wheel drive to navigate this in heavy rain," said Anuj.

"So that really was the servants' quarters," Tenna murmured, her voice filled with awe.

Aria thought she sounded like a child visiting Disney World for the first time.

They followed the Mercedes up another drive, this one threading through a forested area that allowed scant sunlight to filter through. Along the way, they passed more buildings, mostly cottages, each one carefully painted and with a small garden framing the front door.

The shadows thrown onto these houses from a panoply of trees lining the road suddenly disappeared, and they were driving through a clearing filled with sunshine. They turned onto a dirt road and found themselves in a vineyard with what appeared to be thousands of vines on either side. Acres of them, dormant until spring, when they would explode into dazzling greens and then produce the fat, juicy syrah grape coveted for its peppery bite.

"Come fall," Roche said, holding the car steady as it rolled over the bumpy road, "these fields will be swarming with pickers."

Anuj looked across the expanse of grape vines. "Hard work."

"Don't I know!" Roche said. "I worked the harvest from the age of ten, and it was backbreaking."

"Were your parents growers?" Aria asked.

"Hardly," Roche replied. "They were pig farmers. Other than throw slop and clean the sties, there wasn't all that much for a kid to do. I could make real money during the harvest."

"If my boys did that, they'd be buying hundred-euro sports shoes," Tenna said. "What did you buy, Boss?"

Roche pulled the wheel hard to the right, nearly missing the turn. The Mercedes was far ahead of them, kicking up clouds of dust that obscured the route. "Every centime went to my parents."

"Sounds like child labor," Aria said.

"And without any laws to protect us," he answered. "All the boys in my school were put to work. I don't know about the others, but my wages helped my parents buy feed for the pigs."

Aria wanted to hear more. In her short time with this elusive man, she sensed that it was a rare event when he shared anything about his private life, even to Anuj and Tenna. She was about to ask about his family when they arrived at their destination.

The villa sat like a castle on a rise, but without a moat or turrets. The sea was miles to the west, yet visible. Rooftops of the nearby village were also in view, with the ever-present church steeple at its hub. So many European villages had their growth linked to trade routes, but not so much in France. Here, hamlets, villages, and then cities sprang up around a Catholic church.

Roche parked, and they climbed out of the car. Aria followed the others up a flagstone walkway, taking them through a garden now brown in its dormancy. The attorney was standing at the top of the steps leading to massive oak doors.

"It's like a movie set," Anuj said, gesturing towards the palm trees on either side of the house.

The villa was a two-story stucco painted deep salmon, its terra cotta-tiled roof offering protection from the scalding summer heat.

"I don't know if I could live here," Tenna said, looking out over a seemingly endless sky. "It's so vast."

"And beautiful," Florence Agnelli added, sadness in her voice.

Aria was surprised by the woman's show of emotion. Her expensive clothes, the Mercedes, her very demeanor suggested someone cool, under control.

She gave a closer look at Florence Agnelli and saw grief. Her client was dead, and she cared.

Agnelli rang the doorbell and then immediately reached into her bag and retrieved a set of keys. She opened the door and rushed across the foyer to disarm the security system.

Something struck Aria as odd. She stepped inside. "Madame Agnelli, is there someone in the house?"

Agnelli looked at Aria as if she were crazy.

"You rang the doorbell."

The attorney shrugged. "Creature of habit." A dark cloud passed across her face. "Camilla will never answer that door again."

Aria felt sympathy, but uncertainty nagged at her: something wasn't right.

She watched Agnelli cross to a large window and pull back the curtain. Behind her, she heard Tenna whispering to Roche, "Do you think she'll let us work?"

"You mean as we rake callously through her client's personal effects?" he responded. He turned to Anuj and, in a full voice, said, "Start with the upstairs rooms. I'll search the main floor."

"And just what are you expecting to find?" demanded Agnelli, nostrils flaring as if assaulted by an offensive odor.

Roche faced her. "Madame Agnelli, I do understand this is difficult, but I'm conducting a homicide investigation, not a treasure hunt. Camilla Rodolfo was murdered, brutally murdered. My duty is to find the person who did this, and your duty is to protect her possessions. So, please, either stand back and let us do our job, or wait outside."

Aria decided to intervene before this clash of two egos got out of hand. "What can I do?" she asked Roche.

The inspector locked eyes with her. "As long as you're here, follow Tenna's lead. Work with her. Look for anything that ties Camilla to the cast, particularly the Gabriels. Look for fan letters that seem over the top in adulation or threats. Don't do anything without Tenna's permission, and remember to wear gloves."

"Inspector," chided the attorney. "You can't possibly think—"

"That she was murdered out of hate?" he answered. "Or by someone obsessed with her? Jealous? Fearful of what she knew, or thought she knew? This case will be solved by thinking of every possibility, no matter how shocking or improbable it might seem to you, or to us."

The woman's eyes narrowed. "Then you must suspect me as well!"

"Did you kill her?"

Her expression shifted so dramatically, Aria thought it almost comical.

"You can't possibly think," she repeated, although this time with more incredulity than dismissiveness.

Roche towered over the diminutive woman, giving him the appearance of an ogre. "I assure you that I can. You are Camilla Rodolfo's legal representative. You have access to her contracts, probably her bank accounts, and certainly her will. Someone in your position can easily perform all sorts of chicanery to benefit financially. So, I'll ask again: did you kill her?"

The severity of the situation was clear in the woman's face. "No, sir, I did not."

As if this issue was as good as resolved, he moved on. "Have you any idea who might want her dead?"

This time, she did not argue. Instead, she appeared pensive. "To be honest, no. However," she added, reluctance in her voice, "Camilla has a brother, Enzo, who has always resented her fame and her wealth. On several occasions, he has tried to bully her into loaning him money for one of his misadventures."

"And did he succeed?" asked Roche.

"No, she gave him nothing."

"Despite her enormous wealth?' asked Anuj.

"It wasn't that she couldn't afford to be generous," said the woman.

"Then what?" pushed Roche.

She shook her head. "If she loaned him money, it would open the door for him to ask over and over again. Enzo is a terrible businessman. He has a real nose for lost causes, financially speaking. But don't get me wrong," she quickly added. "Camilla often helped with his rent. Living expenses. But nothing that smacked of risk-taking. No scheme that he swore would make him rich. And, of course, make her rich, too. In all the years I've represented her, not one of those schemes came to fruition. Camilla wasn't stingy or selfish: she loved Enzo. Refusing his requests was her way of protecting him."

"Was he angry enough to kill?" Anuj asked.

She thought about this for a moment. "No," she said with certainty. "He's an opportunist, not a killer. And, in his own way, he was devoted to her. She never told me this—at least, not directly—but I've always suspected that he leaned heavily on her for emotional support. He is not a man who can be self-sufficient, if you know what I mean. Emotional problems."

Roche turned to Tenna. "Before we leave, get Enzo's address. He might not harbor murderous thoughts, but perhaps he knows someone who does." With that, he excused himself and crossed the foyer leading to the back of the house.

Agnelli pulled out her cell phone and scrolled down. She held it towards Tenna, who electronically transferred the data onto her own phone.

"He doesn't live far from Paris," Tenna told Aria, before heading into the first room on the right, a bedroom. She started to pull out drawers.

Aria stood and watched. "I'm not sure what I'm allowed to do," she said, feeling a bit like a child hoping for an invitation to a classmate's birthday party.

"When Tenna's on a mission," Anuj told her, appearing at her elbow, "the world disappears. Come with me. We might find something upstairs that only one set of eyes could miss."

"But Roche said—"

Anuj waved away the comment. "I need you, and he doesn't bite." He handed Aria a pair of gloves, then took another pair from his pocket and pulled them on.

They ascended the stairs and began in Camilla's office. It was small, elegant, with windows looking onto the vineyards and far beyond to the sea. Aria could just make out a cargo ship laden with containers, and an ocean liner, its white hull in dramatic contrast to the startling blue of the water.

"I'd like to be on that ship," said Anuj with a wistful sigh.

Aria stood at the desk. She ran her gloved hand across its surface, the mahogany almost cinnamon in color.

"My parents have something similar," Anuj said, opening one of the desk drawers. "If I ever have a place large enough, they'll ship some of their pieces to me." As he spoke, he moved objects around, inspected a few brochures. "So far, my décor is strictly spartan."

"No family heirlooms here," said Aria, opening a closet's sliding door and revealing stacks of documents. She leafed through several. "Mainly tax folders and documents, nothing of interest."

She picked up a loose piece of paper and called out, "Anuj!" She handed it to him. It was pale blue stationery, and of fine quality. Aria's eyes were wide with expectation.

Anuj took it and read it aloud. *Can't you let things alone? I know what you think, but you're wrong. Haven't I paid the price long enough?*

"What do you make of it?" she asked, taking it from him and holding it up to the light. "It's the same stationery used to send that hate mail to the Gabriels. Those pages were ecru, and this is blue, but look at the watermark. And the quality. Do you recognize the writing?"

"So, it really is the Gabriels we're after? I would've bet against that." He took the letter and slipped it into an evidence bag.

"Either they're guilty," said Aria, "or someone is going to a great deal of effort to make us believe they are."

"Her brother? He was planning something illegal, and she knew about it?" He shook his head. "No, that doesn't feel right."

Aria began to speak, then stopped.

"What?"

"How could Enzo get his hands on the Gabriels' stationery? I don't know this man, and I certainly can't guess how he feels or thinks, but I have a brother who resents me, and I can't imagine Martin being so enraged that he'd kill me. Take a knife and slash away part of my face? That's beyond jealousy, don't you think? Or even revenge." As if she had never spoken, never revealed something so personal, she opened another desk drawer and began sorting through its contents.

She felt Anuj staring at her, and then he resumed his examination.

They opened and closed drawers and closet doors, emptied shelves and sifted through books and papers, until every surface and storage nook had been searched.

They moved on to Camilla's bedroom and then her upstairs sitting room, which was more a library. It had one wall of bookcases, floor to ceiling, with a section for scripts, several hundred of them, all neatly stacked and with titles hand-written along the spine of each. Another section was dedicated to mysteries, a smaller one to poetry, and there were a good number of books on feminism.

"It would take an entire team days to get through these shelves," he said. "Every book should be inspected." He moved towards the door leading to the hallway. "There's nothing here for us," he said. "Let's go find the boss and see what he's got. That letter may be the only thing of interest."

"I thought she lived a comfortable, uncomplicated life," Aria said. "And yet someone hated her enough to kill her."

Anuj remained quiet for a moment, and then spoke. "What if we're looking at this backwards?"

"I'm not sure I understand," Aria said.

"What if Camilla's death wasn't about her? What if she was killed for no other reason than to place the blame on the Gabriels?"

They went downstairs and found Florence Agnelli seated in the front room, her shoes off and her feet perched on a footstool. She was thumbing through a magazine. Roche was at the other end of the room, standing by a window and staring at the sky. His cell phone was clutched in his hand.

"Boss?" said Anuj.

He turned. "It's Joseph. They need to operate. His brain is swelling.

They're going to remove a section of his skull."

No one spoke. There was nothing to say. A young man, friendly, liked and respected by the people around him. One blow to the head and a life forever changed.

"Where's Tenna?" Roche asked.

"Upstairs," said Anuj. "I doubt she's found anything interesting." Before he could mention the letter on the Gabriels' stationery, Roche asked him to bring her down.

"I'll go," said Aria.

It was less than a minute before she returned, this time at full speed, her face flushed. "You've got to see this!"

Roche and Anuj raced up the stairs and followed her into a small sitting room, hardly visible from the hallway. Arriving behind them was Florence Agnelli, her stockinged feet deep in the plush carpet. Tenna was studying a framed photograph on the wall.

"Look," said Aria, taking the photograph off its hook. The man in the photograph was white-haired, moderately attractive, perhaps forty, his expression practiced.

Roche moved closer. He took the photograph from her and showed it to the attorney. "Who is it?"

"Enzo," said the attorney. "Camilla's brother."

Roche turned to Aria. "And?"

"He was at the play!"

He held the image closer, tilting it to catch the light. "Are you sure?"

"He sat behind you. At intermission, he was stretching his legs, and his feet were in the aisle. I nearly tripped over them. He apologized. I'm sure it's the same man. Short white hair, unusual for someone so young."

"Is it Enzo who's trying to put the blame on the Gabriels?" asked Tenna. "But why would he, if he's never met them? Or has he?"

"We need to find him," Roche ordered.

"Wait," Tenna said. "I've gone over the list of ticket holders. I'd remember if there was a Rodolfo on that list."

"He's not Rodolfo," said Agnelli. "He was Camilla's half-brother. Same mother, different father. He's Florino, Enzo Florino."

Roche looked at Tenna. "Well?"

Her eyes widened. "He's on the list."

Anuj shared her look of surprise. "What's next, Boss?"

"We'll do a quick inspection of the grounds."

Florence Agnelli stepped forward. "Really, Inspector, is that necessary?"

Roche gave her a look so fierce that Aria flinched.

"We can take the back staircase," suggested Tenna. "It leads to the garden."

Agnelli stepped in front of them.

It seemed that this was all the resistance Roche needed. He took her by the shoulders and gently moved her aside, then followed the hallway to a second stairway, this one leading down to another part of the house.

"The housekeeper's quarters?" Aria asked. Agnelli did not answer.

It was darker here, no carpeting on the stairs, no ornate lighting to show the way. They were nearly out the back door when a creaking sound, wood on wood, caused them to pause.

"It's coming from in there," Anuj said, gesturing towards a closed door.

Roche took one long step, opened it, and then stopped so quickly the others nearly plowed into him. What they saw left them unable to speak.

The room was inviting, its walls a creamy yellow, the hardwood floor painted with designs that included a map of the world. There was a rocking chair near a large window looking onto the garden. The chair was old, with turned spindles. It looked as if it had rocked many babies. Seated in it was a young woman, perhaps thirty, with a cap of blonde hair. Her brown eyes were large. In her lap, lulled by the steady rocking, was a sleeping child with curly dark hair and eyelashes so long they nearly brushed his cheeks. The young woman kissed the baby's forehead.

It was Florence Agnelli who broke the silence. "Forgive me," she said, her voice barely above a whisper. "Camilla swore me to secrecy."

Aria turned to face the attorney.

"Marco," she explained.

"Camilla's?" asked Tenna.

The nanny glanced at Florence Agnelli, not sure if she should respond.

181

"Yes," Agnelli said.

"And the father?" Roche asked.

To this, there was no response. Aria wondered if she did not know. Or was she not at liberty to reveal his name? She saw how closely Anuj was watching, his brow creased. There were tears in Tenna's eyes.

"They leave tomorrow for Genoa," said Agnelli. "Camilla's sister; it's all arranged. Germaine here will travel with Marco and stay with him until he feels at home."

"Just like that," said Tenna.

The boy stirred, gave a little cry, and then settled back. Germaine shifted so he was nested into her. He released a little sigh and continued to sleep.

Roche pulled the attorney away from the others. "I must know who the father is."

Agnelli stared at him, her expression shifting from ire to resignation. "It's Anton Delant. But he doesn't know, and you must not tell him."

Roche instructed the woman to cancel the flight. When she protested, he promised she could reschedule soon. Until then, there was work to do.

The drive back to Paris was long and slow, late traffic causing a tangled mass in the normal gridlock of cars and trucks inching towards their destinations. As tempting as it was for Aria to be lost in her thoughts, little Marco's face loomed. "What if Anton does know?" she threw out, hoping to engage the others. "And he killed Camilla out of rage."

"Or," said Tenna, seated in the back with Anuj, "he killed her because he wanted to be acknowledged as the boy's father, and Camilla wouldn't allow it."

"Both are possible," said Roche, glancing over his shoulder and changing lanes.

Tenna leaned forward. "Either one makes him a key suspect."

"He can't know," reasoned Anuj. "How can a father not acknowledge the existence of his own son? Tamim isn't my flesh and blood, but I cannot wait to be part of his life."

Aria knew that the woman Anuj loved, Maryam, had a young son, and that the boy rarely saw his father. When the time came that she and little Tamim moved from Addis Ababa to Paris, Aria was certain Anuj would joyfully assume that role. She thought of her daughter Lexie, now a grown woman, and she was certain that nothing could break their bond. When everything exploded around her and she was dismissed from the paper, Lexie's support never diminished. If anything, she was even more loving. Unconditional love. What every child should have. And every adult.

They entered Paris and drove directly to the police station. As they pulled into the underground garage, Roche informed them that their day was over. "We're all tired," he said. "A few hours away from this will give us a chance to think."

Aria tried to hide her disappointment. She preferred running around with the team to sitting alone in her hotel room.

"Home. Rest. Sleep. Trust me," Roche added. "We'll all feel energized in the morning. If my instincts are right, we're going to need everything we've got."

"What time and where?" Tenna asked.

"Eight sharp," Roche replied. "We're paying an unannounced visit to brother Enzo, and then to Anton." Before he could add to this, his phone rang. He listened for a moment, then activated the speaker phone. "I've got my team here, please repeat." To the others, he said, "It's the neurologist."

"Surgery went well," said the man. "A large part of Mr. Mardikian's skull was removed. I'm happy to say the pressure on his brain was greatly relieved."

The call ended, and there was a collective sigh.

Aria's back was stiff from four hours in a passenger seat designed for trips to the local market.

"Boss," said Anuj. "I've got some things I'd like to check." He rushed toward the elevator, and the others followed.

"Sheep mentality," Roche said with a smile. "One goes, we all go."

They were in Roche's office for only minutes when another call came through. He listened intently and then ended the call. "Interesting," he murmured.

The others waited. Finally, Tenna blurted out, "What!"

"That was Laurene, Max's assistant. She says she held off telling us because Max might accuse her of stirring up trouble. It seems he can be—"

"Testy?" Aria suggested.

Anuj gave a little shrug. "To say the least."

"Perhaps," Roche replied, "but this was an argument she overheard. There were strong words between Sashkie and Solange. Sashkie said she knew what Solange had done and that Joseph knew as well. Sashkie threatened to destroy her reputation and her career. So," he asked, "what could've made Solange so frightened or angry that she'd harm Joseph?"

"Could Laurene be lying?" Aria asked.

"Or was it Max who wasn't being honest with us?" Anuj said.

So many questions, but no one had an answer. Aria sensed that all of them were struggling with the same frustration.

"Max? But why?" Tenna asked. "What could he possibly gain from Camilla's death? And Solange? How could Camilla's death benefit her?"

"It all seems improbable," Roche told her. "But we can't brush it away."

"First Camilla, now Joseph," Aria said, her voice low.

"It makes you wonder who's next," Tenna added.

Roche checked his phone for messages. "Joseph's out of recovery and back in his room. Nice to get good news. We started this morning with no real suspects, and now we have several."

"We have to include nearly everyone in that theater," Anuj reminded them.

The inspector shook his head. "I don't think it was a ticketholder, unless perhaps Enzo Florino. No, we need to keep our focus on the Gabriels, Laurene, and Camilla's brother. And then there's Anton." He tilted his head from side to side, as one does when trying to ease muscles tight from too much tension and too little sleep.

"What's next?" Tenna asked.

"We check out Enzo and find out if he had any connection to the Gabriels. Or to anyone in that play, other than his sister."

"I can do that," Tenna told him.

Aria felt a warmth for this woman who would do anything and everything to prove her worth to her team. No matter how difficult the task might be, she was at the ready. But there was more. She knew that Tenna would gladly work well into the night, if it meant not having to go home and face her husband.

Roche shook his head. "Thanks, but no, we all need a break."

Aria wanted to give him a swift kick.

"On the other hand," he said, "if you think you can manage this tonight—"

The gratitude and relief in Tenna's face was visible to everyone. "Night, all," she said, hoisting her backpack and heading to her desk.

Aria followed Roche and Anuj to the elevator. They rode in silence to the garage.

"Want a lift home?" Roche asked Anuj.

"Oh, so tempting," he said. "Not having to deal with the Metro."

"It'll be packed," said Roche. "And I know how you hate that transfer at Chatelet."

Aria concurred. Chatelet was not only one of the busiest stations in Paris, but the walking distance from one line to another, through the catacombs and reeking tunnels, felt like miles.

"It's out of your way," said Anuj.

"It's not," said Roche. "I'll drop Aria at her hotel, then we can swing by your place."

Aria was surprised by the largesse, which left her feeling a bit wary. The edginess between them seemed to be softening, but still.

Aria was well settled for the night when she remembered her promise to Lexie. She picked up the phone and called her mother.

It was Lexie who answered, giving Aria a bit of a fright. Why was she there? Was Delphine too ill to be left alone? "Please tell me Grandma's okay."

"She's better," said Lexie. "Her doctor-slash-hopeful-suitor came by last night, and she's on the mend. How's it going with you? I hear you've had some excitement! Wait, Mom, isn't it two in the morning there?"

Aria was thinking about age, her mother's age, the inevitability of death.

"Mom, are you alright?" Lexie asked. "Mom?"

Aria pulled herself together. "I was worried," she admitted. "And feeling more than a little guilty for leaving her."

With her phone pressed to her ear, she walked into the bathroom and managed to remove the bottle of painkillers from the zippered makeup bag. Filling a glass with water from the sink, she swallowed two capsules.

"Hold on," said Lexie.

Aria heard the echoing background, signaling that she was now on the speaker phone.

"Darling!" enthused Delphine. "You saw Martin. My heart is singing!"

Aria felt warmth creep into her face. "And I met little Fleur. What a doll."

As her mother and sister listened, she described the visit, leaving out Martin's comments about Solange being a self-centered bitch. Or his observation about their mother's tendency to ignore anything unpleasant. Instead, she focused on a description of the garden, the décor of the home, and the perfection of Fleur.

"I'm so pleased," said Delphine. "Darling, it's time for a little rest." She voiced a warm goodbye, followed by the sound of her slippers slapping against the oak floor as she left the room.

"So," said Aria, "the truth: is she better?"

Lexie turned off the speaker. "Mom, I swear she is. I had to talk her out of catching a flight to Paris tomorrow. She's read about this murder, and she's worried about Solange."

A stab of cold ran through Aria. "Read about it? What has she read?"

Lexie laughed. "Grandma surfs the web with the best of them. Between PBS, MSNBC, and Libération, she gets it all. And believe me, this murder is big news here."

If it was being so widely publicized, who would publish the book she was tempted to write? She reminded herself yet again that she alone had access to information available to no one outside Roche's team. There was a silence on the other end that was unsettling. What was Lexie not telling her? "Lex?"

"You got a letter."

The cold air was suddenly stifling.

"From your attorney."

Aria closed her eyes. She had been expecting some action, had dreaded it. For her, there was nothing worse than being in limbo, that state of the unknown. At least now she would know. "Did you read it?"

"I hope that was okay. You asked me to read anything from your lawyer." She heard the rustle of paper.

"According to this, the Jameson family has filed a civil suit against you, and another one against the paper."

"Is there anything else mentioned?"

"Like what? Hold on, Mom, I'm reading."

"Like...involuntary manslaughter?"

Lexie gasped. "God, no! It was suicide."

"For which I am responsible."

Another silence. Was Lexie deciding how to respond?

"It's a civil suit," repeated Lexie. "The lawyers want you to come back in the next week, if possible, so you can meet with them and work out your defense."

Aria wanted to tell her daughter that she had no defense. "Could you call them, please? Let them know I'll be home soon, possibly sooner than a week. Have you said anything to Grandma about this?"

"Do you want me to?"

"She'll know soon enough."

"Mom, don't worry. It'll work out, I'm sure of it. I love you."

The call ended with Aria torn between fear and hope.

Chapter Seventeen

It was coming up to Day Five since Camilla Rodolfo's death. Chief Homicide Inspector Noah Roche was feeling all the pressure that results from a highly publicized and unsolved case. His appetite was off, and sleep was as rare as a Paris snowfall in July. In fact, sleep had become his nemesis, and he was wondering if he would ever again sleep through the night. He had never been a great sleeper, but this case was keeping his brain churning at all hours. Even during those years when he and Judith were at odds, just knowing she was in bed beside him—even if she was teetering as close to the far side as was possible—he was able to sleep. Bringing a woman to his bed for the primary purpose of enjoying a night's sleep meant either developing a relationship or having an occasional one-nighter. Neither was appealing.

His phone awakened him with a jolt. The bedside clock showed 5:42. His first thought was *Who's dead now?* He heard Georges de Charbonnet's voice and was disappointed. If someone had died, it wasn't this bastard.

"Glad I got you before you headed out," said the man, his voice upbeat and annoyingly perky.

"Good timing," Roche said, adjusting his head on the pillow. "I was just leaving. What's up?"

"Caught the bad guy yet?"

If ever there was a time to hurl the telephone through the window, it was now. "Close," he said. "Keep the vultures at bay for a bit longer, and we'll wrap it up." The hell with the vultures. The real question was how much longer he could keep de Charbonnet at bay. This man was going to attack him until someone was locked up.

They exchanged a few more words and rang off.

Noah showered and dressed quickly, forgoing the power-packed coffee he normally brewed. The moment he stepped outside, all momentum was halted. Blocking his path were at least a dozen journalists, their mobile phones aimed at him. "Why is this taking so long?" demanded a woman, white-haired and fearless, her voice like chalk scraped across the blackboard.

Roche recognized her, this fixture among Paris journalists. He wondered if her disrespectful tone secured her place in the royal kingdom of news-hounds.

Before he could respond, a young man stepped into his path and shoved a microphone in his face. "Is it true this case is being turned over to another unit? And if so, how do you feel about that?"

He nearly responded to the young man, but why bother? Whatever came out of his mouth would somehow plague him. And that was not paranoia, it was reality.

So many questions, accusations, demands. He ignored them all, sure that de Charbonnet had put them up to this. The strategy was simple: discredit Noah, name someone else to run the investigation, and then take all the credit when the case is finally cracked. He shook off what felt like a sense of doom and reminded himself that if he didn't get control, he would never solve this damn case!

Leading with his shoulder, he pushed his way through the bodies, wondering how long it would be before his neighbors lodged complaints about crowds impeding their comings and goings.

He arrived at the precinct an hour before the light of day and found Tenna bent over her keyboard. Had she worked through the night and slept at her desk? That is, if she had slept at all. She was saddled with the task of finding Camilla's brother, Enzo. He now understood how this nocturnal pattern kept her distanced from her husband, and he wanted to help, but what could he do? His relationship with Tenna was professional, and he intended for it to remain that way.

He approached her, ready to tell her that she was carrying too much of the load, and that he would take over the search for Enzo, but he was stopped by his own voice of reason. Taking away this task could be seen as a lack of confidence, and no one surpassed Tenna Berglof when it came to uncovering even the most deeply buried information. It was his job to support her, but also to make sure she didn't fall into that abyss of sleep-deprived ineffectiveness.

He stood there for a moment. She was so still she could have been sleeping. "Anything?" he asked, keeping his voice low.

She straightened slowly, her eyes meeting his. "The address Florence Agnelli gave us is no longer valid. According to the building's manager, Enzo moved out nearly a year ago."

"You must be exhausted," Roche said. "Been here all night?"

"One thing about internet search engines, Boss, they never sleep."

"They don't need to, but you do."

Roche walked into his office, with Tenna trailing behind.

"We're getting close," she said, dropping into a chair. "I can feel it in my bones." She checked the wall clock; it was nearly seven.

"Keep at it, can you?"

She gave a little salute. After a moment, she said, "Boss?"

That was the tone she used when she was about to probe into his emotions, which were rarely shared with his team. Or with anyone, for that matter. "Just tired," he responded, hoping that would satisfy her need to know.

"It's just that you seem—"

"Short-tempered?" he offered.

"I was going to say worried."

He sat there, waiting for her to tell him what was really on his mind. If it was related to work, he could handle it. But his family? His private life was off-limits.

"It's not easy, I know, having a stranger following us around. But," she quickly added, "for what it's worth, I like her. Call it a woman's instinct, but I trust her, too." With that, she walked out of the office and returned to her desk.

"Of course, you do," he said to the empty room. He had worked with

Tenna long enough to know that she was almost childlike in how quickly she trusted. At the same time, he had to admit that her trust was often justified.

Through the glass wall separating his office from the main room, he watched how she leaned close to the monitor and made notes. There were thousands of photographs of Camilla to be found, but how many where Enzo was included? Or were named as the man standing by her side?

Ten minutes later, she returned and dropped the print-out of a photo on his desk.

Roche picked it up and studied the image. "I don't remember him from the play."

The man in the photograph was attractive, in his forties, shorter than his sister by several inches, and a bit on the stocky side. There was a family resemblance: the broad forehead and square jaw, the shape of the eyebrows, more arc-like than straight. "So, where the hell is he?" Roche asked.

"Soon, soon," she swore. "But one thing I do know: Enzo Florino does not want to be found. No one can disappear like this without careful planning." She began to punch a number into her mobile phone. "I'm going to ask Camilla's attorney." And then she stopped. "The crack of dawn might not be the best time." She turned and stomped back to her desk.

Roche opened a folder that was double in volume from the day before. As much as it disturbed him, he focused on photographs, drawings, and descriptions of the wounds inflicted on Camilla Rodolfo. When he heard Tenna shout, he rushed to her desk.

She gave him a look of pure joy. "Tax records! We can't hide from the tax man."

Roche felt hope slip quickly away. "You checked last night, remember?"

"Oh, yes, I certainly did, Boss." She was laughing as she pointed to the monitor. "But now I've got every Paris resident whose landlords have filed complaints against them. And guess what? There are two against Enzo Florino. Same landlord, same address, same complaint: non-payment of rent. The last one was filed two weeks ago."

She jotted down the name and address of the landlord.

Roche glanced at it. "By the time you navigate the crush of bodies on the

Metro, it'll be after seven when you arrive."

"Too early?"

Roche gave her a playful look. "Not for us, it's not."

She grabbed her backpack. "If the landlord's not there, maybe one of the neighbors can help out."

"The local post office, is that our last resort?"

Tenna shook her head. "No, but it's the best place to find out if he's had his mail forwarded. The last address I have is not far from Metro Saint Martin d'Étampes. I could be gone all morning."

His nod was an invitation to get on with her plan. But before she could dart out of the office, he called after her, "Why should you have all the fun?"

They agreed that a taxi would be faster, but the train would give them time to devise a plan. They took the Metro to the Saint-Michel station, then transferred to the RER and rode the train to the end of the line.

The sidewalk outside the Saint Martin d'Étampes station was bathed in morning sun. According to the map, it was a mile to Enzo's last address. They crossed the road to the taxi stand and took their place in line.

A few minutes later, they were in the courtyard of one of those semi-modern apartment buildings constructed when architects were wild about glass, especially if it was held together by intricate aluminum skeletons.

Roche searched the electronic keypad and found the name *Florino*. He pushed the button. No response. He tried again. Nothing. Before he could decide on his next move, Tenna crossed the patio and knocked on a door with *Concierge* stenciled across it.

There was music coming from within. She knocked again, this time more forcefully.

An elderly man opened the door. He was pulling a bathrobe around his large belly, and squinting at what he clearly considered interlopers. "Yes?"

Tenna gave him what Roche knew was her most disarming smile. "Good morning, sir," she said. "I am so sorry to get you out of bed. We're looking for Enzo Florino."

The manager looked her up and down. "Another journalist?"

Tenna reached into her bag and pulled out her identification card. The man looked at Roche, who also produced his. Without a word, he disappeared into a hallway. In a moment, he shuffled back, this time wearing glasses. Leaning closer, he read the cards. "Police? So early?"

"We need to speak to Mr. Florino," Tenna said. "Do you know where we can find him?" It wasn't an empty question. The managers of apartment buildings knew more about the comings and goings of their residents than they should.

"At the crack of dawn?"

Tenna again smiled sweetly, perhaps sensing that this old man was enjoying his power. "We're hoping he can help us with our investigation. You do know that—"

He interrupted her with a brisk wave of his hand. "I'd have to be dead and buried not to know," he said. "Television, newspapers, chitter-chatter on the streets. Nasty stuff, this."

"Oh, yes," she agreed. "And we're counting on people like you to help us solve this murder."

He was suddenly alert, engaged. "Haven't seen him in a long time."

"Did he happen to tell you where he was going?" she prodded gently.

His face changed. It was a transformation that made Roche think of melting wax. "He's behind on his rent."

Roche held back from speaking. Better to say nothing and let this man fill the void.

"Not sure where he is."

"By any chance, did he have his mail forwarded?" asked Tenna.

"A nuisance," he said. "Got it stuffed in bags. Want it?"

Roche saw that Tenna could barely contain her excitement.

"I do, yes," she said, maintaining an even, professional voice.

He left for a moment and came back with a shopping bag spilling over with mail. A quick glance told Roche it was mainly advertisements, but there was always a chance that something important was tucked in among the clutter.

"We'd like to look at his apartment," said Tenna. "Perhaps something will lead us to him."

"Unlikely," said the man. "I've only been inside twice, and I've never seen such an empty place." He pulled open a drawer and removed a ring holding at least a dozen keys. He handed it to Tenna. "No idea which is his. Process of elimination."

The seventh key was the charm. Roche and Tenna entered a space so devoid of personal possessions that they questioned whether anyone still lived there. After ten minutes of going through every inch of the apartment, they gave up.

Tenna returned the keys, then took down the man's name and phone number. "If you think of anything," she said, handing him her card.

There was a café across from the building. "Smell that espresso?" Roche said wistfully. "There might even be a croissant or two."

The food came, but was nearly untouched as they sorted through the mail. Flyers were put aside, as were magazines and catalogs, until there was nothing remaining, save a few letters. Three of them were asking for donations, one offered a free massage, and there was a stern warning from local authorities that failure to pay the rent would result in eviction.

"Not much here," said Tenna. "At least, nothing we didn't already know."

They held onto the official letter, then dumped the bag and contents into a public trash bin.

As they rode the train back to Paris, there was no conversation until they were minutes from the terminus.

"If Enzo did this," Tenna said, "why would he go after Joseph?"

"Perhaps to make us think it was someone on the inside?" He looked at her and sensed that she had another idea. "What?" he asked.

"We know he was at the play, and perhaps he somehow found his way to Camilla's dressing room during the intermission. But wouldn't someone have seen him the day Joseph was attacked? Only staff and crew were there, so surely he would've stood out."

Roche thought about this as they whizzed by a string of grime-covered buildings.

"And this bombshell about the baby?" Tenna asked. "Florence Agnelli says Anton has no idea about little Marco."

"I don't see him as a killer," Roche said.

The ear-splitting sound of the train's brakes announced their arrival. They rose unsteadily, gripping the vertical poles.

"We have plenty of information," Roche reminded her, "but no real clues."

They sat in the station in silence, and didn't speak again until they were on the Metro. Even then, there was little conversation. *Thinking time*, that's what Roche called it.

When they arrived at their stop, they stepped onto the platform and followed the crowd toward the escalator.

"What we have...they're like floats attached to a fishing line," Tenna said. "They keep bobbing to the surface, but nothing happens."

"We're missing something," Roche agreed. "And when we find it, we'll see how obvious it is."

They returned to Bastion, and Roche forced himself to go over the transcriptions of the interviews yet again. "I should have these memorized by now," he grumbled to the empty office. He saw Tenna at her desk, immersed in her search. He hardly had time to look at the transcription of the discussion with Anton Delant when she raced through his door.

"One call to France Telecom!" she declared. "So, tell me, how long does it take to learn that a phone's been disconnected?"

"Meaning?"

She leaned forward, her braid draped over her shoulder. "Enzo's phone was cut off the morning after Camilla died. A coincidence? I think not. The way I see it," she said, "there are two possibilities: either he was overwhelmed by journalists and paparazzi, or—"

"Or," Roche interrupted, "he committed the crime and left town."

"Or," she continued, "he committed the crime and left the country."

"Yes, that, too."

"I love this job!" she nearly shouted. "I'll check with the passport folks now. If they have no record of him leaving the country—"

She was back in five minutes. "Enzo Florino has not used his passport in nearly two years." She chewed on her lip and tapped her pen against the edge of Roche's desk. "Someone has to know where he is."

"You're probably right, but—"

Tenna cut him off by pulling out her notebook. She flipped through the pages and made a phone call. "The concierge from Enzo's building."

Roche listened as she explained the urgency. He started to give her instructions, but she held up her hand to silence him.

"Please," she said to the man. "No harm will come to him, I promise." She turned on the speaker.

"I like him," said the old man. "But I've never been able to help him."

Roche was about to ask the nature of this help he couldn't provide, but Tenna spoke first.

"We need to find him," Tenna insisted. "He has to be somewhere, and we're certain he's still in France. If you know, and you're not telling us—" There was enough threat in her voice to make even the most headstrong person fearful.

"You have to understand," he said.

"I don't want to send a police car to your home," she told him, her cheeks suddenly red.

Roche listened with surprise. Tenna Bergloff strong-arming an old man?

"Is that what you want?" she added.

"An ambulance came," he finally said. "They had to sedate him."

Roche felt a new energy coursing through him.

"And?" she asked.

"I went to see him when I heard about his sister. I knew he was there, but he wouldn't come to the door, so I used my key. He was in a terrible state; I called for help. I hope it was the right thing to do. I was afraid he was going to kill himself. It's not the first time he's been like this. There was so much blood. So much. I cleaned up after they took him away."

Tenna's face softened with compassion. "You did the right thing, telling me." Before Roche could intercede, she asked, "Do you know which hospital?"

As soon as the man revealed the location, Roche was on his feet, gathering his recorder and mobile phone.

Tenna rushed out of the office, nearly bumping into Anuj and Aria.

"Found him!" she declared.

Aria shot a look at the wall clock.

"We've already been to Enzo's place and back," Roche told her, and then realized how much he sounded like a boastful child.

As the four of them worked their way through the labyrinth of desks and headed towards the elevator, Tenna gave Aria and Anuj a quick summary.

The elevator was in use, so they pounded down the stairs to the garage. Roche was moving so quickly he was nearly running. It wasn't until they were at the car that he turned to Aria. "We've got this," he told her. "No need to come along." The moment he spoke, he saw Anuj and Tenna staring at him open-mouthed and clearly unhappy. Even he was surprised by the harsh words. Where were they coming from? He reprimanded himself to get control of his anger.

"That might be, Inspector," Aria responded, her voice equally as angry. "My job is to stay with your team. If you have a problem with that—"

"You'll what?" he asked, his voice calm, but the taunt was unmistakable. What was it about this woman that brought out the worst in him?

"You and I will meet with de Charbonnet and clarify my assignment."

Roche knew he had erred, but he did not know how to extricate himself. "That won't be necessary," he said. He thought of apologizing, but that wasn't something he was accustomed to doing. And if he did it badly, without sincerity, that would be far worse than saying nothing. Rock. Hard place. Would it ever be easy?

They were barreling through Paris when Tenna finally spoke, breaking the tension that hung over them like a bad odor. "He was taken by ambulance to Sainte Anne."

"Oh, God," Anuj said. "The psychiatric hospital?"

"It could be the perfect hiding place," Aria said.

Roche knew this wouldn't be the first time a clever murderer had sought cover under a psychiatrist's care.

"According to the manager," said Tenna, "he collapsed early Saturday morning."

"Convenient," Anuj said. "So, he kills his sister, realizes he'll be identified, then hides at St. Anne's."

"Let me guess," Roche said, navigating the heavy traffic. "He's depressed and under suicide watch."

Chapter Eighteen

They pulled into the parking lot, scrambled out of the car, and rushed across an expanse of parkland to reach the entrance. A former farm, the facility was spread over more than thirty acres.

When they arrived at the reception area, all of them were breathing heavily. Roche showed his identification and asked for Dr. Silva.

"Is the doctor expecting you?" The man behind the desk picked up the phone.

"We have an appointment," Tenna said.

Roche looked at her, as if to say *we do?*

The man completed the call. "The doctor will be with you shortly."

Before anyone could question his definition of "shortly," a woman approached. She was of medium height and reed thin, which made Roche imagine her blowing over in a strong wind. But there was something about her styled silver hair, and eyes so brown they were nearly black, that announced strength and self-assuredness.

"Dr. Silva?" Tenna asked. "Thank you for agreeing to meet with us."

The woman extended her hand, and Tenna took it, and then she shook hands with the others. "I have to admit, I'm not comfortable with this meeting. My job here is discreet. I usually offer information only after I receive a subpoena. However, I do understand the urgency. Please, come this way." She led them down a corridor flanked by offices. They came to her office and squeezed into the small space.

"I'm sorry, but I'm short of chairs."

Aria removed the recorder from her bag. When the doctor shook her head, she put it away.

"So," said Dr. Silva, directing her comments to Tenna. "What do you need from me?"

Roche leaned forward. "As you know, there's been a violent murder. We know that Enzo Florino was at the scene while this crime was taking place. It's imperative that we talk to him."

"Tragic," Silva said. "As for talking to him—I'm afraid that won't be possible."

"And why is that?" asked Aria, her voice tinged with as much compassion as frustration.

"Mr. Rodolfo is under suicide watch."

No one on the team could miss the *I told you so* expression in Roche's face. Even he knew he was doing a terrible job of hiding it.

The doctor looked at him for a moment. "I'm sure you've run across the criminal who uses our mental health facilities to hide from the law. But I can assure you, his illness is real." Before the others could respond, she stood. "Follow me, please."

She led them along another corridor and through a code-locked door leading to a warren of passageways. She stopped at a door, the upper half a window so large that no one inside could move without being observed.

"Please," she said, gesturing toward the window.

Roche stepped forward. The room was small, the light muted. His breath nearly caught in his throat when he saw the padding—it covered every inch of floor, wall, and ceiling. There was a single bed in the middle of the room. On it was the man he recognized as Enzo Florino. He was on his back, a plastic ring clamped onto his wrists, and those rings attached to leather straps bolted to the bed. His arms were heavily bandaged, as was one side of his face. "He needs to be restrained?" Roche asked. "Did he try to hurt someone?"

"Only himself," she replied. "The manager found him in the bathtub. He was unintelligible and tearing at his skin. The morning newspaper was nearby."

Tenna turned to Roche. "Why do you think the old man left this part out?"

"He was clutching a photograph of his sister," said the doctor. She looked inside the room, her hands pressed against the glass. "Tragic," she said quietly.

Tenna looked again, and then turned to the doctor. "Please forgive me for sounding doubtful, but how do you know he's not faking?"

"His sister was cutting off financial support," Anuj said. "That could be a strong motivation to kill. With her dead, he might inherit everything."

"It could be," Dr. Silva agreed. "But in this case, I have to say that it's not only unlikely, it's nearly impossible."

"Because of what he's told you?" Tenna said.

The woman shook her head. "When the paramedics brought him in, he was delirious. I'm not usually called so early, but there was real concern about his condition. His heart rate was so fast it was nearly lethal."

"Drugs?" Aria said. "I know they can be used to make someone appear to be close to a heart attack or stroke."

"It happens," the woman said. "But in this case, no."

Roche was about to ask how she was sure, but he was interrupted by the doctor.

"I realize that tearing away his skin adds to the drama, but his wounds were brutal, deep, and far beyond superficial. They were vicious. Had he not been found by his neighbor, I'm sure he would have bled to death. He's suffering overwhelming trauma brought on by grief."

"Perhaps he was inflicting the same pain on himself that he had inflicted on his sister," Aria said. "What makes you think it was grief, and not guilt?"

The woman's eyes softened. "Forty years," she answered. "Always in psychiatry, and most of those years assisting the police." She took another look into the padded room. "Camilla was his closest relative. He feels abandoned, utterly and desperately alone. To tell the truth..." Her voice trailed off.

"What?" Roche asked, working to keep aggression out of his voice.

When she spoke, her voice was stronger, the professional coming through. "There may not be a day in his life that he doesn't wish himself dead. I'm no homicide inspector," she said directly to Roche, "but I'd bet my reputation that Enzo Florino is incapable of harming anyone. Except, tragically, himself."

Roche thanked the doctor and turned to his team. "We can't forget that Enzo was here when Joseph was attacked."

Before he could go on, the doctor pivoted and asked, "Have you spoken to his mother?"

Roche gave a quick look to his team. "His mother?"

"She's quite elderly, I believe an invalid. She lives somewhere just outside Paris."

Roche berated himself. How could he have overlooked this? Getting a list of family members was at the top of any inquiry. He could justify the lapse, saying he'd been caught up in this dramatic death, but even a rookie officer would not be convinced. Before he could instruct one of his juniors to dig deeper, Tenna stepped in.

"I'm on it, Boss," she said, and then turned to the doctor. "Can you please give me her full name and address?"

The woman did a quick scan of her cell phone and held it up for Tenna.

"Got it," Tenna said. "Thanks." And then to Roche, "Now?"

"As soon as we're done here, yes. Get a cab and take Aria with you." He nearly added something about her being particularly good with difficult old women, but he held his tongue.

Before they reached the car, Roche's phone sounded. "I really hate this thing," he muttered, pressing it to his ear. The call ended. "Linné Colbert can see us now. Her attorney will meet us at her place."

Linné Colbert lived in the 6th Arrondissement, a few steps from the Luxembourg Gardens. The streets around her were ancient, many of them too narrow for two cars to pass. With underground garages coming hundreds of years after many of these buildings were constructed, parking was restricted to emergency vehicles, delivery trucks, and dignitaries living nearby. Without a second thought, Roche pulled into a No Parking space.

Standing at the front of an old and elegant building, Anuj ran down the list of residents on the electronic panel, and then pressed the button next to LC. There was a crackling sound followed by a man's voice. "Yes?"

Roche announced his name, and the lock was released.

"Top floor," said the man.

Roche and Anuj stepped into a foyer with marble floors reflecting the deep-mustard walls, then took the elevator to the top floor. Standing in a doorway was a man who appeared to be in his sixties. His silver-gray hair was long enough to tuck behind his ears, and his deep tan made his gray eyes distinctive.

"David Denfer." He shook Roche's hand and ignored Anuj. "This way," he said. "Miss Colbert is in the sitting room."

They followed him into a room filled with sunlight. So many apartments in Paris look into other apartments, but not this one. The view from the floor-to-ceiling windows was a sky so vivid it sparkled like cut crystal.

Roche crossed to one of the windows. Below was the Luxembourg Garden encircled by lush foliage. There was a large pond, the wind causing its water to slap against stone. A boy was kneeling at the edge and struggling to keep his little sailboat upright, poking at it with a stick. A man stood behind him, calling out words of encouragement. It made something in Roche's chest ache. All those years when he wasn't here, at this miniature lake, urging Luc on. Being a father.

"Lovely, don't you think?" asked Linné.

Roche turned to her. He had met her several times, but in this light her beauty was pronounced. At nearly six feet, she stood eye-to-eye with him. The contrast between her alabaster skin and those dark eyes created a mystique. He sensed that she wore confidence with ease.

It wasn't until Anuj spoke that Roche realized his young officer was standing behind them.

"Maryam's boy would love that pond," he said.

Roche heard longing in his voice.

"He's with his mother in Ethiopia," Anuj told the actress, who was still watching the excitement generated between father and son as they worked to save the boat before the wind pushed it out of reach.

Roche noted how the man leaned over the low wall and used a pole to capture the large toy, but one big gust, and it sailed away. When the boy raised his arms in alarm, his father kissed the top of his son's head, pulled off his shoes and socks, rolled up his pant legs, and stepped into the water.

There were sounds of surprise, even alarm, when passersby realized the water was up to his chest. He grabbed the boat, made his way to the side of the pond, and hoisted it onto the cobblestones. As he pulled himself from the water, several people cheered.

Roche asked himself if he would have performed that same fatherly act for Luc. The response arrived immediately: Of course. That is, if had spent more time with his son.

"It's why I bought this place," said Linné. "Life is going on outside my window. I can stand here and feel a part of it. The horse chestnuts are glorious. And the orangerie! When the fruit is ripe, I'm tempted to sneak inside and grab a few pomegranates."

The conversation was interrupted by her attorney. "You have a rehearsal, remember?"

"We'll be out of here, as soon as we've had a look around," Roche said.

Denfer's face darkened. "And what do you expect to find?"

"It's fine, David," she said. She turned to Roche. "I assure you, there's nothing here that ties me to this horror. And until the play, I'm quite sure I never met Camilla."

Denfer pulled her aside. His voice was too low to hear, but Roche was certain he was instructing his client to say nothing.

"We have the right to go through your papers, your closets, and all your furniture," Roche said.

"That includes your personal things," Denfer told Linné, a quiet urgency in his voice. "Things you prefer to keep even from friends you trust." He turned to Roche. "Show me your search warrant."

"David, stop!" she insisted, a line forming across her brow. "Inspector, what have I done that makes you suspect me?"

Roche was expecting this question. He preferred not to have this conversation in front of her attorney, but that option didn't exist. "As we discussed, when a woman considerably older than you—and with less talent, I'm told—is given the role you want, emotions can be strong. Were you jealous?"

She stared at him, then ran her tongue across her upper lip. "Camilla was more than capable of handling the part," she said.

"I'm sure she was," said Anuj, "but that's not what he asked."

"Then what!" demanded Denfer, his face red as an overripe plum.

"Was your client jealous of Camilla?" Anuj repeated.

A silence hung over the room. Roche sensed that this question came as a slap across her face. He had learned early in his training that what he failed to ask was often more damaging to a case than the information he received. Sometimes, a probe sounded like an accusation.

Denfer took his client by the arm. When she gently removed herself from his grasp, his face hardened. "Linné—"

Roche saw it so clearly. She might still be in her twenties, but she knew her mind. Not even a seasoned attorney was going to stop her from doing as she wished.

"Linné," Denfer repeated through clenched teeth.

She looked at Roche. Her eyes were flashing.

Roche suspected he was about to witness drama at its finest.

"Of course, I was jealous!" she declared.

"My God," muttered Denfer, shaking his head.

"Oh, stop," she said. "Being jealous doesn't make me a killer." She looked at Roche. "I didn't kill Camilla, and I certainly did no harm to poor Joseph."

Roche wondered why she would refer to the dead woman as Camilla, but the young man as *poor Joseph*. An innocent choice of words, or was there meaning behind them? He warned himself not to look for villains where there were none. But he could see that Anuj was also curious, the way his brow was furrowed, his lips compressed.

"Start at the back of the apartment," he told Anuj. "Work your way forward. I'll take the bedrooms and the study."

"I realize how a woman's touch might make this invasion feel a bit less invasive," he said to her attorney. "Inspector Berglof is interviewing someone at the moment. If you wish, you may watch—without interference, and as a courtesy—while I'm handling your client's personal garments."

The search went quickly, with Roche and Anuj congregating in the foyer less than an hour later. They had searched every drawer and cupboard, all nooks and crannies and spaces where something, anything, could be hidden. They found nothing.

"Thank you," Roche said to Linné. He received a warm smile in return and ignored the prune-faced attorney.

The drive to the precinct went faster than expected. There was little conversation, other than the one taking place in Roche's head. He heard Aria asking why they were searching the homes of people no longer considered suspects. The answer was simple: they needed to be obsessively thorough, so no defense attorney could accuse them of sloppy investigating. Too many cases were thrown out for that very lapse.

He released a heavy sigh.

"You okay, Boss?" Anuj asked.

"I'm frustrated," Roche responded. "With everyone's resistance to being questioned. With barriers thrown across every route. And de Charbonnet's incessant phone calls, demanding I offer new information and threatening what will happen if we don't get this solved...and fast. There's so much uncertainty—I don't need his reminders. And let's not forget those damn reporters camped out in front of my building."

What he didn't say, and what he was certain Anuj knew too well, was that all of this uncertainty paled when compared to the headlines. Newspapers were questioning the efficiency of Roche's team, and de Charbonnet's calls only elevated the tension. Roche was itching with curiosity, wanting to know if Aria was also getting calls from de Charbonnet. And if so, what was she telling him? Friend or foe? As brilliant as he believed he was in getting into people's heads, she was still leaving him in a muddle.

"Where now?" Anuj said.

"Food," said Roche. "I think I forgot to eat today."

They found a quiet table at the rear of Léon de Bruxelles, a café chain known for its steamed clams. "Let's go over the list again," he said, after their orders were given.

Anuj leaned forward, elbows on the table. "Beating a dead horse, Boss. We've gone over that list a hundred times, and nothing has changed."

"So, we give up?" Roche asked.

"We improvise," Anuj corrected. The minute the words were spoken, he added, "And don't ask me what the hell that means."

Roche nearly spoke, but he was interrupted by his cell phone. He listened for a moment and smiled. "Jean-Philippe Mesur, come solve this case, will you?" He laughed. "I know, I know, but you're the theater critic; you have an inside track on everyone, yes?"

The call ended, and he turned to Anuj. "I was hoping he might have at least one morsel of information to blow this thing open. I have new respect for people who swear they're so perplexed or stymied they could tear out their hair. By the time this case is solved, I expect to be bald."

Their arrival at the precinct preceded that of Tenna and Aria by minutes. When the women entered his office, he could see they were upset.

"Nothing is worse," said Tenna, referring to Camilla Rodolfo's mother. "That poor woman. One child murdered, the other in a locked ward, restrained and fighting for his life."

"I can't even imagine," said Aria, her voice a raspy whisper.

Emotion rose in Roche's chest. Tenna and Aria were mothers; he was a father. The loss of a child, his son, was unthinkable.

"There's an ex-boyfriend," Tenna told him. "According to Madame Florino, her daughter had been seeing a Bruno Elian. She says he's a nasty piece of work. It did not end well. He's living somewhere near Marseille, but comes to Paris often."

The three of them returned to their desks, Aria's tucked in the corner where they put visiting detectives.

The mood was somber, reflective. Roche had to force his mind back to the evidence files. There was no need to tell Tenna to search for the boyfriend: she lived for this kind of work.

A few minutes later, she stepped into his office carrying several pages of computer print-outs. Her expression was one of uncertainty

"Whatever it is," he told her, holding out his hand, "it's more than what we've got."

She handed him the papers, but with such reluctance, he had to give a little tug to free them from her grasp. Before he had a chance to study them, Aria appeared at his shoulder. He found her closeness distracting and nearly asked her to back away.

Anuj joined them, settling into a chair.

"That's the police report on Bruno Elian," said Tenna. "Bar fights, a domestic violence complaint that was dropped, and a suspension of his license for driving while intoxicated. Enough there to make him a viable suspect."

"Stay on it," said Roche, while reminding himself yet again that there was no need to instruct her.

The other print-out was a photograph, a group shot, nearly all of the people in their twenties. Standing with them was Camilla Rodolfo, older by at least ten years.

"Very nice," said Roche. "Camilla as a younger woman. And?"

Tenna gave it a closer look. "Oh!" she declared.

"Oh…what?" There was exasperation in his voice.

"This was taken nearly six years ago, when Camilla was teaching a workshop for young actors."

"I still don't see…"

"Boss," she said, pointing to a young woman whose attention was directed toward Camilla. The expression on her face was pure adoration.

He looked closer. "Sorry, I have no idea—"

Tenna tapped on the image. "I'd bet my badge that's Linné Colbert."

Roche snatched up the reprint, gave it a closer look, then pulled open the top drawer of his desk and removed a magnifying glass. Holding it over the photograph, he shifted it from the faces to the list of names in the caption. "No Linné Colbert here."

Tenna scampered back to her computer, entered a few words, and returned. "Not then, no. She became Linné Colbert a few years later. Trust me, that's her. The same woman who swore she didn't know Camilla."

He stood so quickly that Tenna had to sidestep to avoid being knocked over.

"Now!" he hollered, and two of his men rushed in.

Tenna gestured to Anuj and Aria to follow her into the main room. While Roche was instructing his men, they waited for the next move.

"Looks like we were all fooled," Anuj admitted.

"What about the boyfriend?" Tenna asked. "Shouldn't we wait to hear from Marseilles before we drag her off to jail?"

"We need an arrest warrant...and fast," Roche told the older man, his voice loud enough to fill the outside room.

Tenna, Anuj, and Aria returned to his office, as though drawn by an invisible towline.

"Let's keep this quiet," Roche told everyone. "Not a word to the other detectives, and certainly not to those hovering vultures who call themselves journalists." He wrote down Linné's name and address and handed it to the older man. "Pick her up and bring her in. Her attorney will probably be there, so make sure the papers are in order. If he argues, tell him it's the price his client pays for lying to the police."

The men dashed out of the room and disappeared into the hallway. "Why not you?" Aria asked. "I'd have thought you'd relish this."

"It's more intimidating if the arresting officers are strangers," Anuj told her.

"And we certainly don't want to make them feel threatened by—what was it you called members of my profession?" Aria said. "Hovering vultures?"

"At this point, I don't give a damn who makes the arrest," Roche said. "As long as there's a light at the end of the tunnel and it isn't an oncoming train."

Tenna's phone sounded. She listened and ended the call. "It's not the boyfriend. The officer says he's in a wheelchair. He broke his leg weeks ago and is heavily into rehab." Before anyone could respond, she added, "I hope the bastard breaks the other one. When he was questioned, he told them, and I quote, 'The bitch got what she deserved.'"

Chapter Nineteen

Aria stood at the door of Roche's office. It was feeling like her home away from home, but without the coziness. He was on the phone, Tenna was at her desk filling out forms, and Anuj seemed so transfixed by his monitor that an atomic blast might have gone unnoticed. In the background, squad members were watching the same news report on their computers, a well-coiffed reporter announcing the arrest of Linné Colbert. From what Aria could hear, most of it was speculation.

Before she could step through Roche's door, her phone sounded and she pressed it to her ear. "Winnie!" She had contacted her dear friend two days ago, but hadn't received a response.

"Just got your message, darling. I arrived from Budapest early this morning. Interesting place, lovely city, but I am so glad to be home. When can I see you? How long are you here? Why are you here?"

Aria laughed. "Still the unending questions. How many years now?"

"Let's see, junior high, right? Which means we were around twelve. That makes it more than forty years, and I haven't seen you for at least three. How in the hell did that happen?"

"No idea. Time. Isn't it supposed to creep in its petty pace?"

"That's tomorrow, darlin'."

Aria made a little humming sound. Winnie's voice was salve. "I'm heading home in the next few days, so we need to meet soon. What works for you?"

"Where are you?"

"A little hotel near Notre Dame. I've been working all week with a homicide team, part of an article the French have hired me to write."

"I'll be near you tomorrow morning, at one of my rental apartments. I need to check it over before I list it. Can you be there at seven?"

She asked Winnie to text the address.

She ended the call and walked over to Tenna's desk. "Would you do something for me?"

Tenna looked up and smiled. "Sure, anything."

"I'm meeting an old friend. She'll be at one of her apartments. She has several rentals, and this one is about to be listed." She looked around, checking that no one else could hear, and then she leaned closer. "If I like it, I might rent it."

Tenna's eyes opened wide. "That would be amazing!"

Aria touched the woman's arm. "It's just a thought, but will you come with me? You know, moral support and all that."

Before Tenna could reply, Aria texted her the address.

"I'll meet you there, but it's very early—seven?"

Tenna laughed. "You're looking at the woman who never sleeps."

Aria arrived the next morning and found Tenna waiting on the sidewalk. "Thank you for doing this," she said, giving her a quick hug.

"Happy to get away from Berglof Prison," she said, half smiling. She looked suddenly stricken. Had she spoken out of school?

Aria pressed the button to alert Winnie of their arrival, and then she turned to Tenna. "Are you afraid of him?"

There was a long silence before Tenna answered. "Physically, no. But his anger is biting—he goes for the throat. I could never leave him. You don't know him. He'd threaten to keep me from my children, and then he'd try to destroy me in so many ways. But would he strike me?" She looked away, weighing her words. "Like so many bullies, he's a coward."

Aria pressed the button again.

The buzzer sounded, followed by "Third floor, darling," and the click of the lock being released.

They rode the elevator, and Winnie met them on the landing. Aria hugged her friend. "Like it was yesterday," she said, and they hugged again.

"And you're coming back!" Winnie enthused, her eyes alive with pleasure. "I'll have my Aria nearby. I called a few of our friends and they cannot wait!"

Aria made the introductions and then turned to Tenna. "We were terrors."

Tenna laughed. "So, you didn't spend a lot of time at the museums."

Aria looked at Winnie and giggled. "We did, actually, but only because it was a great place to make out with the boys! Oh, and smoke cigarettes."

It took less than five minutes for Aria to look around and know this place was for her. "Does any of the furniture remain?" she asked. The less she had to buy, the better. "I like what you've got here."

"For you, everything," Winnie said with a broad smile.

Without asking the price, Aria accepted the keys.

"When can I expect you?" Winnie asked.

The question came from friendship, but it turned like a knife in her gut. "I have some nasty business to deal with before I can leave the States." She noted how the sparkle faded from her friend's eyes. Before, she only suspected that Winnie knew, but now she was certain. It was naïve of her to believe that word had not spread through old classmates, wherever they were living. "It could be several months, but I insist on paying rent, beginning today."

"No need," said Winnie. "I'm thrilled to have someone here I can trust. And really, who's more trustworthy than a friend of the Paris police?"

Her face was filled with kindness, reminding Aria that good people lived in this world.

She said her goodbyes and they rode the elevator to the lobby. The air felt charged with energy.

They passed through the front door and stopped to give the building one more look. Suddenly, Tenna gave out a little cry.

Aria turned and saw a man standing only a few feet away.

He stepped forward and took Tenna's arm. "Did you think I wouldn't know?" His expression was smug, his mouth ugly.

"Know what?" asked Tenna, her face without color. And then her eyes flashed anger. "You're reading my text messages!"

He laughed. "Every day!" He tightened his grip.

Aria stepped forward.

"I don't know who you are," he said, "but this is not your business."

"Oh, but it is," Aria replied. "Tenna is my friend."

"Well, your friend is not moving out of my house."

Tenna's mouth opened, but she did not speak.

"The apartment is for me," Aria told him. She placed her arm around Tenna's shoulder and pulled her closer, at the same time grasping him by the wrist and forcing him to release his hold. "Now, if you'll excuse us, we're leaving."

He sneered at Aria, then turned to his wife. "Tenna, you're coming with me. It's time to stop this nonsense."

She looked at him, her eyes imploring. "Klemens, please."

But he would have none of it. "If you ever want to see your boys again—"

Aria turned on him with a rage that had been growing for too long. An innocent woman's suicide, public outcry, the loss of a career, the shunning, and now this vile man. When she spoke, she seethed. "What kind of a man threatens a woman with the loss of her children?"

"And you are?" he asked calmly. This was too easy, getting the upper hand on not one foolish and emotional woman, but two.

"Me? I'm someone who knows every major player in Paris. I'm the woman who can destroy you and your career with one phone call."

His expression became momentarily serious, but quickly returned to a smirk.

Aria pulled out her phone. "You're with NATO, yes?" Before he could respond, she was punching in a number. "Connect me to Monsieur Desarmes, please. Tell him it's Aria." The pleasure she felt watching his face shift to alarm was intoxicating. "Claude!" she declared, and then listened. "I'm well, thank you, and your family? Listen," she went on, "I have a situation here."

Klemens held up his hands and backed away. "You'll regret this," he told his wife.

Aria took the phone from her ear. "No, she won't," she said. "One move toward punishing her in any way, including her children, and you'll have a lifetime filled with regrets. And no career."

"Bitch," he muttered, then turned and walked away.

Aria dropped the phone into her bag.

"You just cut him off!" said Tenna.

"He was never on the line."

Tenna's brow creased. "But you know Claude Desarmes?"

Aria's expression was downright mischievous. "Never met the man. But I do understand how to deal with the Klemens Berglofs of this world."

They walked towards the Metro station.

"I envy your freedom, your independence," said Tenna.

Aria stopped in the middle of the sidewalk, forcing a young couple to walk around her. "I've changed my mind. I'm not taking the apartment."

"Oh, please reconsider. Having you here would be wonderful."

Aria held up her hand. "I'm not taking it, Tenna, but you are."

Her eyes grew wide. "I could never."

"Yes, you can. If the price is too high, Winnie will bring it down. I know her. She'll do anything to make this work." She waited a moment, allowing her comments to sink in.

Pink blotches appeared on Tenna's cheeks, making her look like a child coming in from the playground on a chilly day.

"It's your chance to be free, to have your boys in the next room, whether they're living with you or visiting. Say yes, please."

"Yes," Tenna whispered

Aria sat at her little corner desk, like a child being given time-out. The noise level around her was unusually low. The entire squad was drained of energy. There was a suspect in custody, but no sense of victory. She was certain that a survey would reveal that nearly everyone agreed they had arrested the wrong person.

The week allocated by de Charbonnet was coming to an end; it was time to book her flight home. She reached into her bag for her phone, but found the theater playbill from the Gabriels' dressing room. Unfolding it, she glanced at the names of the cast, crew, and staff.

"Anything interesting there?" Tenna asked, arriving with two mugs of tea.

Aria nodded her thanks and took a cautious sip. "No one from the original production, other than the Gabriels and Max."

"That's because the others hadn't been born yet. Anyway," Tenna added, "the boss says we've got our killer."

Aria heard forced light-heartedness tinged with doubt. She looked through the window of Roche's office. Without the dark clouds of strain, anger, and distrust, he was a handsome man. He was on the phone, and she heard animated snippets of his conversation. Was he talking to a woman? It had never occurred to Aria that he might have someone in his life. Or perhaps he was talking to his old friend, Jean-Philippe?

"I'm ready to go home," she told Tenna. "I miss my friends, my family. And I can cloister myself in my study, pull out all my notes, transcribe the interviews, and then write those articles." The part she left out, about meeting with the attorneys and hashing out a settlement they could all accept, was left unsaid. "But there's a glitch," she admitted, noticing Tenna's sudden alertness. "Until Linné Colbert confesses, or goes to trial and is found guilty, I can't name her as the murderer." She had made that mistake once; it would never happen again. "The best I can do is refer to her by name, but only as a suspect, or as the accused."

She held up the playbill. "I have to remember to get this signed by the Gabriels and Max," she said. "My mother will be so pleased. I always like this part," she added, showing Tenna the back page. "It's where the actors thank the people who influenced them." She glanced at it. "Bertrand thanks Solange."

"So sweet," Tenna said. "All these years later, and he still seems to be in love with her."

Aria read for a moment. "Solange thanks someone named Marie-Josette. I wonder who that was."

"Who-*who* was?" Roche said, appearing at the door of his office. He held out his hand, and Aria gave him the playbill.

He pulled out his mobile and made a call. "Jean-Philippe, do you know anything about Marie-Josette Lavalle?" He waited, listening. "And what happened?" Another pause, this one lengthy. He thanked his friend, rang off, and slipped the phone into his pocket. "As they say, the plot thickens."

Anuj walked in. "What plot is that, Boss?"

"Solange Gabriel fired this woman after forty years of employment."

"On what charge?" Tenna asked.

"Theft."

"It took her forty years to discover that a thief was working for her?" Anuj's face clouded with doubt.

"So, let's go talk to this Marie-Josette," Tenna said.

Roche shook his head. "We can't…she's dead. A few months ago, and in dreadful circumstances. The rumor was that there was no heat in her house, and it was freezing. She either fell or became ill. In either case, she was on the kitchen floor and unable to move. She froze to death."

"How does he know this?" Aria said.

"The theater community is small. Like a family, Jean-Philippe tells me. Word gets around."

"She froze to death?" Tenna gave a little shiver. "How gruesome."

"Does this change anything?" Anuj's voice sounded distant, as though he were wondering aloud.

"It probably doesn't," Roche said. "But loose ends must be dealt with. If we don't neaten them up, something is sure to explode."

Aria punched numbers into her phone. Max Formande answered. She pulled the recorder from her bag, activated it, and held it close to the phone. "Uncle Max? I have one quick question. It's about Marie-Josette Lavalle and her problems with Solange." She listened for a moment, noting that the recorder was running. "So, tell me, is there a link between Marie-Josette and any of the cast, other than the Gabriels?"

As she listened, she felt her heart accelerate and perspiration form on her brow. The others in the room seemed to sense that something was about to break.

"Thank you," she said, ending the call.

"Speak!" Roche insisted.

It took several moments before she could form the words. She held up the recorder, hoping it could speak for her. "Solange's assistant," she said.

"Sashkie Ferrer." She paused and swallowed hard. "She's Marie-Josette's granddaughter."

Roche stared at her without blinking.

It was Anuj who dared to ask, "Did we arrest the wrong person?"

The traffic was heavy as they approached a busy intersection. The light was red, which did not stop Roche from making an illegal turn and racing up the hill toward Montmartre. Minutes later, they were standing in front of the fallen theater. Facing them was Max Formande.

"Was this necessary?" asked the old man, his sweeping gesture taking in the debris.

"I needed to see your face," said Roche. "Hiding information from the police, especially in a murder investigation, is serious business. There could be charges brought against you."

The director's posture seemed to collapse, like one of those nearby buildings, only moments after the detonators were activated.

"Why didn't you mention this?" Anuj challenged. "That Sashkie is Marie-Josette's granddaughter?"

"Why would I?" he said, his voice belying any attempt at bravado.

Aria moved closer. "Don't worry, Uncle Max, you've done nothing wrong."

Roche threw her an angry glance.

"But surely the Gabriels knew," said Tenna.

Max shook his head, wisps of white hair falling over his eyes. "Sashkie asked me to keep it from them. She needed the job, and she was afraid they'd judge her by her grandmother's misdeeds."

"Are you saying you knew Sashkie before this play?" asked Roche. While speaking, he herded the group into a little bar and settled them at a corner table, away from the outside noise.

"Of course," said Max. "She came to me when Marie-Josette was let go, asking me to introduce her to the Gabriels. We're old friends, remember?"

"And she wanted to keep that relationship a secret?" Aria felt her stomach churning.

"As I said, the girl was certain Solange would never hire her, and she was desperate for that job. Sashkie's father died when she was little, so she and her mother had moved in with Marie-Josette. A few years later, her mother married and left France, leaving Sashkie with her grandmother. It makes sense that Sashkie was devoted to the woman, don't you think?" He looked at everyone. "When Marie-Josette died, she was devastated."

Aria felt a brief moment of pity for the girl and then pushed it aside. "If she was so devoted to her grandmother, where was she when the woman was dying?"

Max lowered his head for a moment, as if needing time to form his thoughts. "Tragically, Sashkie was in Leeds, part of a group of French youth participating in one of those language immersion programs. From what I gather, she and Marie-Josette exchanged a few letters, but the old woman never complained. Had Sashkie known..."

"Max," Roche said, kindness in his voice. "I need to understand everything that happened."

The old man looked confused. "I'll tell you what I know; that's the best I can do."

"So, Solange accused Marie-Josette of stealing, yes?" Roche asked.

"There was a very expensive shawl, and there were several pieces of jewelry."

A woman approached them with a menu, but no one was hungry. Roche flashed his badge. "We'll be out of here soon," he promised. The woman shrugged and walked away.

Aria took Max's hand. "Tell me about the shawl."

The old man looked at her, not comprehending the question.

"Uncle Max, was it dark, green-black, with orange and red, and yellow?"

"Possibly," he said with uncertainty.

Tenna was now up to speed. "Aria, wasn't Solange—"

"Yes," said Aria, cutting her off. "She was wearing it after the performance."

Roche said nothing, but Aria sensed that his mind was going full steam. He made another call, speaking quietly, and then ended it. "One last road trip. I hope to God we have this one wrapped up."

Aria felt his anticipation, but she was struggling with her own thoughts.

What if she had called Izzy? What if she had asked him to run a teaser, a kind of *look what's coming next* announcement about Linné Colbert's arrest? And what if it had been picked up by newspapers around the country?

"I'm beginning to feel like one of those car-chase cartoons," Anuj announced as they zipped through the region northwest of Paris known as L'Oise.

At the same time, Tenna was speaking into her phone. "Lavalle," she repeated. "Marie-Josette. Somewhere near Beauvais. Get back to me quickly, we're heading there now. And notify the local precinct. We don't want to get arrested for breaking in." She confirmed her mobile number and ended the call.

Aria tried to sort through what they knew, thoughts racing across her brain like a horse at full gallop. She saw Roche's face—brows pulled together, stern, how he looked when his mind was sorting through facts. Like a hunting dog catching the scent, eager to tree his prey.

"We should be close," he said, braking for a hay-filled lorry lumbering along in their lane.

Tenna checked her phone. "Got it. Another six kilometers."

Aria sensed the mood shift around her, the anticipation of being close to the truth.

They turned onto a typical village road, two narrow lanes flanked by cottages. All of them boasted winter gardens, flowers in muted yellows, hearty enough to survive the cold. They passed the boulangerie, windows displaying racks of bread loaves and colorful pastries. Next to that was the charcuterie, salamis, and slabs of prosciutto in full display.

They stopped at a traffic light. Aria guessed it was the only one in the village. On the corner was the flower shop, its doorway nearly obscured by planters overflowing with white narcissus, their yellow centers reminding her of egg yolks, and the mauve hyacinths that her mother adored. There were baskets of purple anemones and white tulips. It was winter, but everything made her think of warmth and sunshine. And the hellebores! She recalled those times in France, how she would go with her mother to buy armloads of this flower, and then come home, cut the stems very close to the bloom, and float the flowers in a large bowl of water. Aria loved to climb on a chair and push the flowers around like little boats, their pink-red petals glowing like garnets. The crowns of queens, her mother had called them.

They passed the market, doors wide open, the tables outside covered with fruits and vegetables grown by local farmers.

Aria felt sadness draping over her. This was where Marie-Josette Lavalle had shopped; where she had chatted with neighbors she might have known for much of her life. How comforting that must be, living in one place and feeling safe. Perhaps if Aria lived here, and not in the middle of a cosmopolitan city, she would be surrounded by friends, not competitors. But wherever she was, she could not hide. Not from the public, not from fellow journalists. And certainly not from herself.

The car pulled up to a little house. It was bleak in its neglect. Aria had a sudden reminder of Izzy's voice the morning she was emptying her desk. "You'll survive this," he had promised. She stared at the front door, its paint peeling, and wondered about the old woman who had not survived. Was Solange to blame? Would Solange blame herself? No, she would not. In that woman's mind, the blame was never hers.

Aria wished she had some of that gift of denial. She had spent the past months probing and dissecting all the *why* and *why me* laments until she was ready to choke, but it changed nothing. She needed to forgive herself. The problem was, she could not.

It came to mind that if Marie-Josette Lavalle's cottage were alive, it would weep from the neglect it suffered. Weeds had overtaken the little garden until they blanketed the picket fence. Everything was dead or dying; any former charm or luster was long gone.

A young constable was standing at the gate. The way he tugged on his uniform jacket told Aria that he had been warned that someone important was arriving, and he had better look sharp and act professional—make the locals proud. He stood tall, his flaming red hair tucked rather loosely under his cap. She wondered how many policemen, so early in their careers, were given the task of assisting a chief homicide inspector from Paris.

She climbed out of the car and approached the gate. How had Marie-Josette felt, an old woman on the floor, helpless, suffering the bitter cold? Dying alone.

"Officer Pellier," the young man said, extending his hand. "Charles Pellier."

Roche shook it. "Roche. Chief Homicide Inspector Noah Roche."

Aria half-expected Officer Pellier either to salute or faint. There was such a thin line between respect and fawning. She gave him a warm smile to let him know that he was doing fine, and his face relaxed into a sweet grin. She had just made a friend. For life.

The young man removed a key from his pocket and unlocked the front door, moving aside as the others stepped into a small sitting room.

Aria looked around. The furniture was threadbare, antimacassars covering armrests so worn she could see the stuffing. The walls had cracks running from the doorways to the ceiling, and there were signs of water damage from a roof in serious need of repair.

Pellier remained near the door, as the others walked through the cottage.

Aria took note of a crucifix in each room, most of them crafted from wood, a few in brass. All displayed the face of Jesus, one expression more tortured than the next.

The discolored rectangles spaced along the walls told her that photographs had once hung here. Now, there were only picture hooks left in place. Whose images had adorned those walls? And where were these people when an old woman lay dying? She knew there was a child, because there was a granddaughter. Where were her children? Then she remembered Anuj mentioning that Sashkie's mother had died.

Aria looked out the bedroom window to the fields, trees with no leaves, skeletal branches reaching upward and seeking sunlight, warmth, growth. It was a dramatic contrast to a sky so intense it could have been painted on enamel. She felt a presence behind her.

"She had nothing," Roche said, his voice low with emotion. "I can see her counting each euro and wondering how she could possibly go on."

Aria thought about this for a moment. "That's what I don't understand. From what we know, she worked most of her life, and yet everything here says poverty."

Anuj entered the room and crossed to the cardboard boxes pushed against the wall. "Someone's been packing," he said, opening one of them. It was filled with the framed objects that had covered the walls. He removed a few, holding them to the light.

Aria looked over his shoulder. "Solange was never far away," she quipped. In nearly every photo, the actress was present.

She reached into the box and removed a few more photographs. One of them was a celebration of some kind, a group of people in a restaurant. And not just any restaurant. The table was set with crystal and china, the floral arrays sumptuous, everything expensive. The Gabriels were the focus, and they were standing behind an elderly woman.

"Marie-Josette?" Aria asked. She called out for the policeman.

Pellier walked in and studied the photograph. "Her birthday party. We heard about this dinner for weeks. No one in the village will ever eat at Épicure, much less pass through its front door. I dreamed of taking my parents there as an anniversary present, but the tab would have been more than I earn in three months."

She studied the photograph. Marie-Josette was smiling broadly, looking almost blissful. A box sat before her, its top placed to the side. Solange was in the process of draping a large shawl over the woman's shoulders. Aria recognized it at once. "There it is again," she said.

Roche leaned closer. "Are you saying this is the scarf Solange accused her of stealing?"

"Solange was wearing it the night of the murder," said Aria. "I even commented on it."

"You're certain it's the same one?" asked Roche. "Absolutely certain?"

"Positive," she said. "It's Hermès. And a vintage Hermès at that. If I had to guess," she added, "I'd say it goes for somewhere around five hundred dollars. If a seller could prove it had once belonged to Solange Gabriel, then we're talking perhaps several thousand—fifteen hundred euros."

Officer Pellier released a slow whistle.

Aria studied the photograph again. "Why would Solange say it was stolen, when it was obviously a gift?" She was afraid of the answer, afraid of having enjoyed all those years of loving and respecting someone, only to discover they were undeserving.

Roche took the photograph from her. "Perhaps the question we need answered is when did Solange take possession of it."

Aria saw his point. If Solange had taken it before Marie-Josette's death, they would have to learn under what circumstances. But if it was after the old woman died, then Solange, or someone else, had entered the house. Aria thought of ghouls who prey on the dead.

She walked into the kitchen. The linoleum floor was thin from decades of wear. In some places, so worn that the wood foundation was revealed. The cupboard doors were out of alignment. The pots and pans were of good quality, now dented and discolored.

Sadness tumbled over her like water from a spilled glass. Was there anything about this home to love? It was all so bland, except for the curtains, which had been sewn from bright remnants of cotton and sported appliquéd poppies in red and yellow. This is where it had ended, where an old woman had died alone. Here, on cheap linoleum.

Tenna entered the kitchen, and they remained silent together. It took a moment for Aria to realize that Tenna needed to speak. It was evident in her eyes. "What is it?"

"This house, it has death all around it. And not just the woman. What about the death of dreams? Give me a week; I could transform this place into a real home."

"Are you wishing you had a place of your own? It's about to happen." Aria touched Tenna's arm. "There's nothing more powerful than freedom."

At that moment, Roche walked in. "Find anything?"

Aria looked at him and wondered if they could make peace. And if so, when? She was about to return to San Francisco, and until her legal problems were resolved, that was where she would remain.

Several minutes later, Roche announced, "We're done here."

They left the cottage and walked to the car. Roche turned to Pellier. "If you ever want to work homicide in Paris, give me a call."

Pellier's face went from professional to astonished. "Do you mean that, sir?"

Roche pulled a business card from his pocket. "Here's how to reach me."

The young man took the card. He read it once, and again, and then slipped it into his pocket as if it were a priceless object. After giving Roche a smart salute, he returned to his patrol car, a lightness to his step.

"That's more excitement than he's had in years," Anuj observed warmly.

"Village life," said Roche. "For anyone with a dream, it can be hell. He reminds me of me when I was that age, insecure and desperate to join the real world and make my mark. I fought and scraped to make that happen." He looked directly into Anuj's eyes. "Maybe we can ease the way for him."

Aria watched Pellier drive away. "You'll hear from him soon."

"We'll see." He turned to Tenna. "Call the Gabriels and find out where they are. We need to see them now." Before she could respond, his phone sounded.

"Are you ever tempted to throw the damn thing away?" Aria prodded.

He raised his eyebrows in mock terror and then answered the call. "Good news," he announced a few moments later. "Joseph is conscious. So, first the Gabriels, and then the hospital."

Before he had time to put the phone in his pocket, it rang again. He listened through a lengthy discourse, murmuring a few responses. "Thank you for this," he said. "It does make a difference, yes. I'll let the station know. And I agree, there's no reason to make this public." He ended the call and turned to his team.

"Tell us!" prompted Anuj and Tenna, almost as one voice.

"That was Linné's attorney. She admits she met Camilla years ago, but they had exchanged only a few words. It was some kind of drama weekend, a camp for aspiring actors, and Camilla was there to share her experiences and advise the group."

"I don't see why Linné needed to keep that a secret," said Tenna. "I mean, why the lie?"

Roche moved towards the car. "It seems that Linné developed a crush on Camilla and wrote her several letters. Camilla never responded. At the first rehearsal of this play, Camilla recognized her, and Linné panicked. So yes, they did have a bit of a heated conversation, because Linné wanted Camilla's word that she'd never make this public. According to Linné, Camilla was fine with that. And then Camilla was killed, the investigation began, we started digging into everyone's past, and Linné was so frantic that she lied to us."

"Does anyone really care these days?" Anuj asked.

"I can see why she's afraid," said Aria. "A film star, a sex symbol, her elegance and femininity splashed across magazine covers everywhere. It's tough enough for a woman in the film industry, but a gay woman—"

"This is France!" declared Tenna. "Free love, everyone's into sex and being sexy."

Aria's expression signaled bemusement. "No matter how the French talk the talk—and I can only speak from my life here—that's all it is: talk. This culture is very conservative when it comes to sexuality, and gender issues are near the top of the no-go list."

"Are you going to release her?" Tenna asked Roche.

He slipped the phone back into his pocket. "Yes," he said. "And nothing we've discussed here is for public knowledge…ever." He looked directly at Aria.

"I agree," she said, but the look on her face was far from agreeable. She was tired of his suspicions.

"Good," he replied.

There was something in his voice that was softer, even kind.

For Aria, kindness was at the heart of everything.

Chapter Twenty

They rode in silence for nearly an hour. There was a backup on the autoroute, a minor collision resulting in a major snafu. Roche was in no hurry. He needed time to think.

Aria was seated directly behind him. He swiveled the mirror a fraction and saw that she was texting someone. It galled him that she was getting into his head. Did she know what he was thinking? And what was *she* thinking? Figuring that out would take more patience than he could muster.

Linné Colbert was about to be released, which was certain to set off a firestorm among those damn journalists. He heard the click of a seat belt being released, and then Aria leaned forward until her hair nearly brushed his shoulder.

"I recognize these houses," she told him. "We're nearly there."

"In my country," observed Tenna, "we call them mansions."

They were indeed large, and protected by fences so high they could not be easily breached.

"Turn here," Aria instructed, indicating a narrow road.

Her proximity unsettled him. From their first meeting, his instinct was to hold her at a distance. American women were trouble. They wanted the knight on the white horse, the hero who pushed away dark clouds and revealed sunlight and rainbows. Perhaps they weren't all like that, but this woman was carrying a heavy load, and he refused to be the knight carrying her through the darkness. Not that she had asked…yet.

"There," she said, pointing to a driveway flanked by a towering wrought-iron fence.

Roche turned in and stopped at an imposing security gate. Before he could open his window and push the button, the gate swung open.

"The eyes of France are upon us," Anuj said.

Roche drove up to the house and parked.

"And I thought Camilla's was a palace," Tenna said, as they climbed out of the car.

Roche was impressed. He guessed there were at least three bedrooms on the second floor, as well as the third, and that was only on this side. He removed his attaché from the trunk and followed the others up the steps.

Aria lifted the brass lion's head and let it drop loudly against the massive door, sending an echo throughout the interior.

They waited.

"Sweet," Tenna said, looking at the little gardens planted on both sides of the steps. The mid-afternoon sun was casting a glow across clusters of hyacinths and tulips.

"Where in the hell are they?" Roche muttered.

"I think I know," Anuj said, descending the steps and walking around the side of the house.

Bertrand and Solange were seated on a patio protected by an ivy-covered pergola. There were gas lamps glowing red-hot around the table. With them was a man Roche assumed to be their attorney.

Roche could see himself enjoying the serenity of these gardens, the blush-pink peonies bursting with growth. He tried to get a quick read of the Gabriels. They appeared unruffled, but he could smell their fear.

The man stood and approached him, his hand extended. "Girard Bettencourt, the Gabriels' legal representation."

Roche shook the man's hand. "Noah Roche," he said. "Senior murder investigator and chief official arresting officer."

Bettencourt pulled his hand away, as if having been stung by a wasp.

Roche questioned the need for this man's presence. Was it an admission of the Gabriels' guilt, or their fear of being exposed? He reminded himself that this was an unannounced visit, making the attorney's presence happenstance. Still, he would have to step gingerly or he might find himself in the middle of a dance choreographed by this Bettencourt fellow. He'd be damned if he was going to let this man take the lead.

There was a pause while everyone settled around the table. Roche took the chair closest to Solange, placed his recorder on the table, and turned it on. "Now," he said, using a voice that might convene a committee to plan the next flower show, "let's clear up a few issues and save ourselves a bit of unpleasantness later."

He saw how the Gabriels and Bettencourt exchanged glances. He guessed they were in favor of anything that got him out of their home quickly. He saw Aria place her recorder on the table. Solange saw this as well, judging by the way she looked at her. Did Solange consider this a betrayal, the ungrateful Aria forgetting her history with this living legend?

Roche felt something hard form in his heart. The Gabriels might not have killed Camilla Rodolfo, but he was certain they had a hand in the old woman's death.

"Let's begin with this," he suggested, opening his attaché and sliding a photograph onto the table. It was the one taken at the birthday dinner, with the shawl in question draped over Marie-Josette's shoulders.

"What does that have to do with anything?" Solange demanded, and then laughed when the inspector pointed to the shawl. "For God's sake, we gave her a shawl! So what?"

"You were wearing this same shawl the night of the play," said Tenna. "How did you come to possess it?"

Solange looked at the woman, her mouth twitching. Roche realized that the grande dame had been given a new place in the spotlight, and she was enjoying it immensely. "It was a foolish purchase," she said. "It never occurred to me that someone like Marie-Josette would have no occasion to wear such a splendid thing. When I suggested she return it to me in exchange for what I paid, she was more than happy."

"And how much was that?" asked Roche, suggesting that no one in his position could possibly determine its value.

"It must have been around three hundred euros," she answered. "And she was lucky to get that, considering the thievery she had committed."

Roche was ready to remind her that three hundred euros would cover the cost of the gift box, but Tenna spoke first.

"So, you didn't accuse her of stealing the shawl," said Tenna, her voice flat.

"Obviously not, if she's wearing it," said Bettencourt.

Bertrand reached over and placed his hand over his wife's. "It was very unpleasant," he said solemnly. "To give such trust and generosity to a woman, and then discover she had been stealing from us for years…well, it was a painful blow, believe me."

"Why didn't you fire her?" asked Anuj.

"We aren't savages," said Solange, her chin raised. "And we were all she had."

Roche nearly refuted that with a mention of Sashkie, but he held off. He wanted to see how this was going to play out.

"So, there was never any kind of punishment," suggested Anuj.

Roche glanced at Aria. She looked suddenly ill. He suspected she knew where this was going and did not have the stomach for it.

"When Marie-Josette retired," explained Solange, "we terminated her pension."

Anuj leaned forward. "Did she retire? Or was she told to leave?"

Solange waved the question away.

"If she had no pension," Tenna asked, "how did she survive?"

"This is France," Solange said. "I'm sure our government took very good care of her."

Roche wanted to announce that the four people who had just come from Marie-Josette's house begged to differ. "What items did she steal?" he asked.

Solange's expression changed from passive to something resembling triumph. "Several rings," she said. "At least one gold watch, and a very expensive strand of pearls. I can't even begin to name the number of little things."

"A gold watch is certainly valuable," Roche said.

"And that was only one of the missing items," she said.

"What did it look like?" Roche asked.

"It was a Bertolucci," she said. "Stainless steel and eighteen-carat gold. It was very precious to me."

"And the pearls?" Tenna asked.

"I was devastated to lose them!" Solange declared. "They were a gift from Bertie."

"Perhaps that's what you did," suggested Aria. "Lose them. Leave them behind in a dressing room, or one of the many hotel rooms along the way."

Solange looked at first surprised and then annoyed. Clearly, she was depending on Aria to take her side.

"Is it possible?" Aria asked, her voice gentle, giving this old woman a way out of a difficult situation.

"I never left a dressing room or hotel without Marie-Josette making a careful sweep, top to bottom, under mattresses and beds, in every drawer, nook and cranny. Silly me for being so trusting, don't you agree?"

Roche was fairly certain that complicity was not something Aria accepted. But with such a long-time friendship, would she allow her fondness for this woman to get in the way? His thoughts were broken by Solange's voice. He turned to face her. "Excuse me?"

"It's getting chilly," she said, giving weight to this with a little shiver. "I suggest we move inside." Without awaiting a response, she rose and walked into the house, back straight, still playing the role of Queen Gertrude.

The others followed like acolytes, the attorney pausing to extinguish the gas lamps.

The sitting room was large, yet intimate. There were four upholstered chairs positioned around a low table. Solange and Bertrand sat, as did Roche. There seemed to be some jockeying for the fourth chair, until Solange indicated that her attorney should join them. The others took chairs from around a game table and positioned them nearby.

The room was filled with period furniture, large paintings that Roche suspected were not copies, and memorabilia from six decades in the theater that included framed playbills, photographs with presidents and kings, famous actors and writers.

He stood and walked over to a smaller photograph. Solange and Bertrand were standing with Helen Keller, her face beaming with kindness. What would she think about people with no compassion?

He turned back and noticed how Solange sat quietly, yet seemed very much in control. At the same time, her hands were shaking, and there was fatigue in her face.

For a moment, he felt sympathetic, but that feeling quickly passed. He was tired of being played.

He sat, reached into his case, and removed a manila folder. Opening it, he placed it on the table, revealing a sheet of paper. "This is your stationery," he said to Solange. "It was used for the hate mail." He removed a printed document from the file. "This is the chemical analysis confirming that it was your makeup on Camilla Rodolfo's body. How do you explain this?"

Bertrand sat straighter, head high. "Anyone visiting our home would have access to that stationery," he said. "As for the makeup—"

"Absurd," Solange said, interrupting him. "All of it! As difficult as this is for you to believe, Inspector, I have never set foot in Camilla Rodolfo's dressing room. Why would I?"

Roche sensed she was struggling to remain in control. But was she lying? He thought not. And yet there was something there, an undercurrent he could not define.

"There's been a terrible mistake," Bertrand said. "I don't know why, but someone is trying to make us look guilty."

"You don't know why?" Solange's voice was tinged with mockery. "My God, Bertie, anyone who's ever acted resents our gifts." With that, she stood and left the room, her gait surprisingly brisk, considering the belabored pace only minutes earlier.

Roche turned to Aria. "Please, bring her back. Tell her five minutes more and we're done."

Aria rushed out and returned with Solange on her arm.

"Five minutes," Solange repeated. "Not one minute more." She turned to her attorney. "You'll see to this, yes?" Without awaiting a reply, she took her seat.

"Anuj," Roche said. "Contact the local station. Tell them I want a policeman outside, day and night, until I lift the order."

Bettencourt jumped to his feet. "This has gone too far. You can't possibly believe that my clients are killers."

"Of Camilla, no," said Roche. "Nor did they inflict injury on Joseph. Now please, sir, sit down."

The attorney complied, but was perched on the edge of his chair, as though ready to pounce.

"Why are you doing this?" Solange said.

"Yes, why?" Bertrand asked. "And the police?"

Roche directed his response to Bettencourt. "They didn't kill Camilla, but someone did, and that person is determined to put the blame on your clients. When word gets out that we're close to resolving this, the hatred that's shining a spotlight on them might put them in danger. Are you willing to chance that?"

No one needed to respond. The glances exchanged, the way Solange grabbed her husband's hand so hard he winced, said it all.

"I want you to look at this," Roche said, placing a photograph on the table.

Solange and Bertrand leaned forward for a closer look. "Our opening in London," she said, pointing to the billboard in the background.

In the foreground were the Gabriels, Marie-Josette Lavalle, and two unnamed people.

"Madame Gabriel," said Roche, his voice so quiet someone might have described it as menacing. "Look at the watch your dresser is wearing." He pointed to Marie-Josette's wrist. "A Bertolucci, is it not?"

Bertrand snatched up the photograph. "My God, so it is!" He turned to his wife. "You told me Marie-Josette stole it."

"Would you agree that it's rare for a thief to wear a stolen watch in the presence of its owner?" Roche said.

Solange pressed her mouth into a hard line.

"And this," said Roche, placing a second photograph over the first. "Your dresser, your thief, the woman who lost her pension due to her dishonesty. I'm no connoisseur, but I'm quite sure the pearls she's wearing are valuable."

Again, Bertrand picked up the photograph. This time, he gave it a quick glance and tossed it onto the table. "What does this mean, Solange? For the love of God, what have you done?"

Solange squared her shoulders and stood up. "I will not be treated like this." She pulled herself up to her full height and gave Roche a hard look. "Do you have any idea who I am?"

Roche also stood, towering over the woman. "Madame Gabriel, you made false accusations against an old woman who dedicated her life to you. She made you comfortable, presentable, and answered your every need. And what did you do? You repaid her by leaving her penniless. Are you aware that Marie-Josette Lavalle died alone? She fell onto the floor of her shabby house, where she froze to death because she couldn't pay her heating bills. So yes, I know very well who you are."

Solange took one step back as one would when shrinking from something fetid, even dangerous.

Bertrand stood and gripped his wife's arm. When he spoke, his voice was more forceful than Roche imagined possible. "How could you?" he demanded. "She did everything for you, for us. My God, Solange, this is—you are—barbaric."

Solange shook him off. "Do you have any idea how much we were expected to pay her when she retired? And would have to continue paying until she died? She earned a very good salary, my dear Bertie. I saw no reason to continue because she chose to retire. Retire! No one retires from the theater!"

There were tears in the old man's eyes. "I've always known you could be cruel. I've seen it when you're angry, or when you've felt slighted, but this?" He closed his eyes. "I never imagined there was such depth to your cruelty."

Solange brushed away his words with another sweep of her hand. "Foolish man," she muttered. She faced her attorney. "He'll get over it."

The ringing of Roche's phone was jarring. He listened, ended the call, and turned to Bettencourt. "Where is Sashkie?"

The man appeared confused. "The assistant?"

"Where is she?"

"Upstairs, I believe," he said.

Aria stood. "I'll find her." She rushed out of the room and up the winding flight of stairs, Roche on her heels.

The second-floor corridor was lined with gilded mirrors, portraits of the Gabriels together and separate, and porcelain urns perched on man-sized pedestals at the entrance to each bedroom.

"Which room?" Roche muttered, trying not to be impressed by the opulence.

"Not this floor," said Aria, rounding a corner and heading up another flight.

The third level was in dramatic contrast to the second. No oak floors, no porcelain urns. This was utilitarian, bare bones, as if no one sleeping here was worthy of the finer touches.

One of the doors was ajar. Aria approached it, looked inside, and entered without knocking.

Sashkie was stretched out on her bed, a movie magazine opened and nearly covering her face. She looked over the top of it. "Yes?"

"A few questions," said Roche, coming in behind Aria.

"What now?" She tossed the magazine onto the bed.

Roche gestured toward the door and watched Sashkie slowly stand, her expression suggesting utter boredom, another waste of her time.

They were heading downstairs when they ran into Bertrand. Without a word, he joined them.

A chair was pulled into the circle for Sashkie. When everyone was seated, their faces reflecting a hodgepodge of emotions—fear, boredom, an expectation of something not yet defined—Roche was ready.

"I'm here," Sashkie said, her voice sullen. "Now what?"

He checked that his recorder was running, and saw that Aria and Anuj were recording as well. As for Tenna, she had her notebook and pen.

Roche picked up the photographs and passed them to Sashkie, watching closely for her reaction.

She looked at them, then tossed them onto the table. "And?"

"Really, Inspector," demanded Solange. "Are such theatrics necessary? She was hired long after those photos were taken."

Roche said nothing.

"You heard her," Sashkie challenged with a smirk. "Nothing to do with me."

"Look closely," Roche said, spreading the photos so all the images were revealed.

Sashkie made a show of bending forward and giving them a close look. "I still don't see."

Roche felt his heartbeat quicken, as it did when he was about to throw a wrench into the works. "Sashkie, we know that Marie-Josette Lavalle was your grandmother."

Solange shot Sashkie a look. "You never told me."

Sashkie smiled, clearly enjoying this game. "Would you have hired me?"

"Certainly not!"

Sashkie laughed. "Which is why I didn't tell you."

Bertrand moved forward, his brow creased. "I don't understand."

"Seriously?" Sashkie retorted. "It doesn't take a great mind to figure it out." She turned to Roche. "Does it, Inspector?"

"Not a great mind, no," he said. "But a devious one, perhaps."

Sashkie laughed again. This time, the sound was throaty, callous. "I almost got away with it, heh?"

"Oh, God," Bertrand said quietly, covering his face with trembling hands.

Roche knew he was steps away from the truth. "Sashkie, you told us you overheard a row between Linné and Camilla."

"Never happened," she said, her voice almost playful.

"So, you figured—" Roche left this hanging, certain she could not resist filling in the pause.

Before she could answer, Aria turned to her and asked, "But why Joseph?"

Roche wanted to silence her, but said nothing. Sashkie was going to tell him everything he needed to know, no matter what the others might say.

"Joseph," she said, her voice now filled with contempt. "He had a crush on me, even when I treated him like shit."

"But why did you attack him?" Anuj asked.

Roche glanced at the others. Bettencourt was watching closely, looking mesmerized by what was unfolding before him. Even Solange and Bertrand were still, the old woman's face contorted in a most unattractive way. The only person in the room who seemed unfazed by the severity of these events was Sashkie.

"Yes, why Joseph?" Tenna said.

Sashkie looked around her. "If you must know, in a moment of weakness—no, make that stupidity—I told Joseph about the Gabriels, my grandmother, and how she died alone and miserable, all because of what they did to her. Not you," she added, looking at Bertrand, "but your greedy old hag of a wife."

Bertrand's eyes filled with tears. "So, poor Joseph had to die?"

"He needed to be silenced," she answered, her voice so casual it triggered a gasp from Bertrand.

A stillness descended over the room—the lull in the storm. And then Roche said, "The good news is, Joseph is awake and talking. He's prepared to testify about what you did to him."

"If it makes a difference, I regret pushing him over the catwalk."

"And Camilla?" asked Roche. "Do you regret mutilating her?"

Sashkie let out a snort. "She was there, handy. Poor cow."

Roche paused before dropping the question he knew his team wanted to ask. "Are you saying that killing her was random?"

"Wrong place, wrong time. Linné doesn't know how close she came to dying."

"How so?" asked Anuj.

"I went into her dressing room to kill her, but she was in the loo. I didn't have much time, so I went to Camilla's. God, it was so easy! She looked at me, I slit her throat, she died. Poof!"

Roche leaned closer to her. "And then?"

"And then," she said, her voice rising to her dramatic finish, "I stuffed a towel into her mouth." She leaned back in the chair. "That's all I'm going to say."

"What about the letters?" Aria asked.

"Fun to write!" Sashkie enthused. "And fun to watch you squirm," she added, speaking directly to Solange. "Very entertaining."

Solange's mouth fell open in a way no actor would want to be photographed. When Bertie stood, she said, "Dear, as long as you're up, could you please bring me water, with a bit of lemon?"

He stared hard at his wife and then shuffled to the door. He glanced back once and then left the room.

Solange looked at the attorney and shrugged. "He'll get over it."

"Anuj, call Officer Pellier," Roche instructed. "Tell him to come with a squad car. We'll need it for our trip back to Paris."

It was nearly an hour before Pellier arrived. Roche watched the young man's face, quite certain he had never seen a home like this one. Except, perhaps, in a movie.

Roche took the handcuffs from Pellier and snapped them onto Sashkie's wrists. He found it satisfying, the sound of locks engaging. "You'll need a lawyer," he advised her.

She turned to Bettencourt. "How about it?"

Bettencourt stared at her for a moment and then smiled rather grimly. "I don't do criminal law."

"But what if I were a famous actress?"

He let a little laugh escape. "Ah, but you're not."

The group moved into the foyer, where they found Bertrand, a small suitcase at his feet.

Aria approached him and took his arm. There was confusion on his face. Confusion and grief.

Roche sensed that Aria shared the old man's emotions. He wished he could take her pain away. Someone she had known all her life, a woman who was part of her family, was now unmasked, exposed as vindictive and heartless. It surprised him that he felt Aria's misery.

"Bertie?" Solange walked up to him. "What is this?" She nudged her toe into the suitcase, her eyes flashing anger.

He said nothing.

"Bertie, you can't!" She began to weep.

The old man shook his head. "I thought I knew you."

Solange suddenly transformed herself from the abandoned wife to the feral cat. "Fine, leave if you must. But remember, when you walk out that door, I'll be here alone. I could fall. Or become ill. How will you feel then?"

"I've called the housekeeper. She's on her way. She'll sleep here until you make arrangements."

Solange opened her mouth, but no words came out.

Bertrand picked up his suitcase and gave his wife a long, backwards glance, his face etched with grief, and then he walked out the door.

Roche stood with Tenna and Aria. They stared at the police car. Anuj was in the front with the driver, while Sashkie and Officer Pellier sat in the back.

As the car pulled away, Sashkie turned and looked directly at Aria.

Roche had seen his share of psychopaths, but few had sent such a chill through him. He called his desk sergeant. "Tell Linné Colbert's attorney that the murderer is in custody and his client can go home."

Roche and Aria were heading back to Paris when the skies opened. It was late in the day, the deluge adding to the darkness. There was a kind of sinister presence in this storm, amplified by the rhythmic thud of rain against the car. Tenna was ahead of them, driving Officer Pellier's car, its wheels throwing fans of water against Roche's windshield, the wipers working hard to keep the road visible.

They entered Paris with the streets and gutters overflowing, many of the cars up to their hubcaps in rainwater. The sidewalks were also flooded, forcing shopkeepers to stuff rolled newspapers under their doors. A few of them had the advantage of sandbags. A flash of lightning illuminated the street and then disappeared, leaving behind utter darkness, followed several seconds later by a rumbling thunder.

Roche pulled into the garage just behind Tenna, the rain-driven cacophony suddenly silent. Eerily silent.

"That's what the Brits call bucketing," Aria said, getting out of the car.

"No place for man or beast, to be sure."

Tenna joined them. "Anuj just texted me," she said. "Sashkie's confessed to everything. Give her an hour and she'll tell us she's Jack the Ripper."

"Let's get this over with," Roche said, little joy in his voice.

A phone sounded. He didn't recognize the ring and then realized it wasn't his.

Aria answered. He heard snatches of conversation. Whoever it was, she was pleased to hear the voice.

"A school friend," she said.

"Winnie?" Tenna asked.

Noah looked at both of them, again reminded of how quickly women bonded in friendship. It was so easy for them, so natural.

"I won't have time to see her again before I fly out," Aria said."

Roche saw how she exchanged what seemed like knowing glances with Tenna.

Aria smiled. "But she's fine with the arrangement."

Roche suddenly realized that, only a day ago, this would have rankled. But today? Now, it felt as if a hard edge he had been honing had softened. For one thing, Aria had kept her word about not interfering. At least, not as much as he had feared. She could be brash, and she came off as far too confident, but he understood that she was struggling under her own heavy load. Perhaps that brashness was how she kept going, moving forward.

The squad car that had transported Anuj, Pellier, and Sashkie was parked near the door leading to the elevator. Anuj was standing outside the car, leaning against it. The driver, Pellier, and Sashkie were still inside. "I'll take her up and book her," he said to Roche. "Murder and attempted murder, for starters."

Roche turned to Tenna. "Go with them. I'll meet you at the booking desk. You go, too," he said to Pellier.

Pellier helped a handcuffed Sashkie out of the car, his hand never leaving her shoulder, as if acknowledging that she could not be trusted.

"I reached Anton," said Anuj. "He'll be here within the hour. And so will Florence Agnelli."

"Good job," Roche said. "It's time he knew about the boy. And if he already knows, it's time he took responsibility."

He watched Anuj, Pellier, and Sashkie step into the elevator. Despite Sashkie being handcuffed, she appeared relaxed, almost enjoying the moment. The elevator doors closed. With Joseph able to give a statement, there was little more to do than take her fingerprints, a few mugshots, and lock her up.

Roche looked forward to calling de Charbonnet. And if the bastard ended up eating a bit of crow, that was just fine. He smiled to himself, imagining the man grinning broadly before the news cameras, bird feathers stuck between his teeth.

He rode the elevator with Aria and Tenna, wondering how Aria would tell her mother about Solange. He didn't envy her. He wanted to believe that Sashkie would feel remorse, knowing that a little boy would live his life never knowing his mother, but he doubted she would feel anything.

The elevator door opened, and Roche found Anuj and Pellier at the counter filling out forms. Sashkie had already been taken to be photographed.

"I'm guessing your station handles these things differently," Roche said to the young officer.

There was a glint of humor in Pellier's eyes. "I'm not sure we've ever had a murder, sir. At least, not since I was old enough to know about it."

"Join us and you'll have more than your share."

The young man's eyes lit up. "I didn't think you—were you serious?"

"One thing about the boss," said Tenna, coming up behind them and handing Pellier the keys to his car, "he is always serious. Even when he thinks he's being funny."

Roche wasn't quite sure how to respond, so he smiled and said nothing.

An hour later, he thanked Pellier for his assistance and asked Anuj to accompany the officer to the garage. Before they took two steps, a mobile phone was heard.

"Can't we ban these damn things?" Roche said. "They run our lives, no matter where we are." When Aria nodded her agreement, he nearly mentioned that this included the bathroom, but thought better of it.

"Mine," said Anuj, pressing the phone to his ear. He held up a hand. "Sorry," he mouthed, and then stepped a few feet away. A moment later, he released a joy-filled laugh.

Roche was struck by the emotions in that laugh. It was, perhaps, the most melodious sound he had heard in years.

"We'll talk later...soon," Anuj said, his voice filled with sweetness. He pocketed the phone. "They got their visas. Maryam and Tamim will be here next week."

Roche gave him one of those man-bonding slaps on the back, and then Tenna pulled him into an embrace. Aria squeezed his arm, and then she, too, hugged him.

Anuj tried to speak, but there were no words. The wonder in his face said it all.

Tenna walked with him into the main room, leaving Roche and Aria alone. "Now what?" she asked.

He heard concern in her voice. He knew she was asking what their next step would be, but he sensed that, embedded in that question, was confusion. How would she explain all of this to her mother? And where was her life going. Was this it? Would she return to San Francisco, write about his squad, and then move on with her life?

They returned to his office. He called Max and informed him of Sashkie's arrest. He listened for a lengthy time, while the director expressed shock, anger, and then sadness.

"I'm happy to say that Joseph is awake and recovering," Roche added, relieved to share good news for a change. "And one more thing," he said, glancing briefly at Aria, his eyes practically twinkling with pleasure when he saw that she was puzzled. It felt good, getting the upper hand on her. "You know my friend Jean-Philippe Mesur? He tells me he'll be writing an article about the theater and your memorable career. He's going to say that, if France is lucky, there will be many more plays directed by you." He passed the phone to Aria.

He watched as she exchanged tidbits with Max about her stay in Paris, and her promise to convey his love to her mother. She extended an invitation for him to visit them soon in San Francisco. When she hung up, she gave Roche a look that he translated as gratitude.

"Better?" he asked.

"Much. Thank you for understanding. I was worried about him. And thank you for easing his fears."

One of the desk officers tapped on Roche's door. "Got a minute, sir? Just some final details before we book the suspect."

"Not a suspect," Roche corrected. "A confessed murderer. Give me five minutes." He leaned back and folded his hands together. "Are you really considering renting a place in Paris?'

"I have a problem I need to resolve," she said. "That means I have to return to the States. Believe me, being mired in a mud pit is the last place I want to be, but I can't run away from this. When it's resolved, then I'll decide."

Night descended, and Roche felt exhaustion taking over. It had been a good day, productive, one murder and one assault solved, and the guilty party brought in without his team having to resort to aggressive tactics. Top brass was reveling in the publicity, and de Charbonnet was putting on quite a show for the media. Roche had turned on the little television in his office, not wanting to miss his nemesis being interviewed on the evening news, his pearly whites sparking. He was certain that behind that joyful face was bitterness. "Try and demote me now, you bastard," he announced to the television.

Aria appeared at the door and took the chair facing him. "I guess this wraps it up. Good timing, because I need to be in San Francisco. Unfortunately, the civil suit is going forward."

He tried to read her face. "I'm sorry."

Her eyes softened. "Thank you. Until I meet with the legal team, I'll have no idea what's going to happen."

Roche weighed his words. "When the judgment is delivered—"

"That's what insurance is for," she cut in. "The paper has good coverage, which means that I'm covered, too. But the publicity—" Her voice trailed off into uncertainty.

He knew she was worried about her future. Who wouldn't be? But would this bring her career to an end? He tried to imagine how he would feel in her position. The thought struck him as improbable, but then that inner voice piped up, reminding him that no one is exempt, no matter how important they are—or think they are.

"My career is probably over," she said, her voice nearly a whisper.

He studied her face, trying to determine what he should say, if anything at all. "Living in a state of limbo is hell." He saw what he believed was gratitude in her eyes. "For me, knowing what's going to come next—even if it's not good—is preferable to the unknown."

He wanted to question her about her observations during this past week, but his thoughts were interrupted by the appearance of the duty sergeant, a man he'd known for more than two decades. He could see how hard the man was trying to suppress his excitement.

"Someone named Anton Delant to see you, Chief," he announced, his voice modulated to sound professional, even in the company of a famous man. Before the inspector could react, the man rushed out.

"I completely forgot," Roche said. "Agnelli is coming, too."

Moments later, the actor entered the office. "Ready to arrest me?" He held his wrists together, his eyes wide with humor. "I see that your journalist is here," he said, giving Aria a nod. "She can document my arrest and incarceration."

"Sorry, but we have our killer," Roche said.

Delant's eyes grew wide. "Please tell me it's that old biddy, her royal majesty."

"Sorry to disappoint you. It was her assistant, Sashkie."

"That mousy little thing? And Joseph?"

"Sashkie again," Roche said.

"Joseph is awake," said Aria. "It looks like he'll be fine."

"Good," the actor said. "Good."

"That's not why you're here," Roche said.

The change in the inspector's voice was so sudden that Delant reacted with a snap of his head. "I'm not sure I know—"

"Monsieur Delant, are you aware that Camilla had a child?" He watched Anton closely. If he knew about the boy, he was a far better actor than Roche had imagined. Delant seemed interested, curious, but nothing more.

"A little boy," said Aria. "Marco."

Anton ran his fingers through his hair. "And why are you telling me this?"

Roche waited for what he hoped was a dramatic pause. "The boy is yours."

There was no doubt that this man-about-town, Romeo, and overall bad boy was learning this for the first time. His face metamorphosed from curiosity to shock, and then to an emotion Roche could not define.

Roche gave Aria a brief glance, certain that if the actor declared this a mistake or denied the boy, she would give him a hearty slap. "Could this be possible?" Roche asked.

Anton stared at the wall for a moment. "How old is he?"

"I'm told he's around eighteen months."

Anton thought for a moment. "Then yes, it's possible."

There was a commotion outside the door. Roche excused himself and returned, followed by Florence Agnelli. Behind her was the nanny, and in her arms, Marco. With Anton and the child in the same room, the resemblance was unmistakable.

Anton walked over to the nanny, an expression of wonder and joy on his face. He touched the boy's cheek, stroked his hair.

"Marco is going to Italy this week," said Camilla's attorney. "His aunt wants to raise him."

At this, Marco reached out for his father.

Anton took the boy and held him close. "Do I have a choice in this? I mean, must he go to Italy?"

"You can apply through the courts for custody," explained Agnelli, her voice gentle. "Until a decision is made, perhaps staying in Genoa is best for him."

"What do you want, Marco?" Anton asked. "Would you like to visit your aunt while your papa works to make you mine?"

Roche looked around the room. Was there a dry eye?

The entire scene lasted less than ten minutes, but Roche was certain two lives were changed forever. A child had his father; a man had his son. He was willing to bet that Anton Delant's gambling and bed-hopping days were over.

After everyone left his office, Roche felt at a loss. So much energy had been expended this past week, and he was depleted. What he craved was one full night and day of uninterrupted sleep.

Aria appeared at his door. He was about to suggest they get something to eat, but was stopped by a ringing phone. He considered not answering. "What now?" he murmured.

She gave a little shrug and sat down.

It was Judith.

"We need to meet," she said, pushing aside any preliminary greeting.

"Can it wait? I'm heading out."

"Ten minutes, I promise. I'm at our bistro."

He wanted to remind her that it had stopped being their bistro when she asked for a divorce. Instead, he said, "Fine." But it wasn't fine, not at all.

He turned to Aria. "Judith," he said. "Ten minutes, and then we can get something to eat."

Aria pulled out a small notebook. "I'll be here."

Roche arrived at the café and was thrown off-kilter to see Luc seated with Judith. The duo always unsettled him, making him feel outnumbered. As he sat, the table wobbled. He emptied a few packets of sugar, folded the little paper squares into a wedge, and shoved it under one of the legs.

"Always the fixer," said Judith.

He looked at her. Was she being nasty? He doubted it was a compliment. At the same time, he had to admit she rarely criticized him. "So, what's up?"

"Our son wants to buy an apartment."

"He told me. And how does he intend to pay for it?"

Luc threw up his hands. "Hello, I'm right here. Why not ask me?"

Roche turned to his son. "Fine, I'm asking."

The look on his son's face reminded him to modulate his voice. As much as he thought of Luc as a boy of fifteen, he was a grown man. If only he would act like one.

"I realize that the only career I've pursued, as far as the two of you are concerned, is to aggravate you," Luc said. "And yes," he added, before his father could speak, "I've done that very well. And yes," he went on, "I have expected you to be my personal bank." His voice was turning raspy. He took a sip of water. "I'm sorry for all of that. I'm responsible for myself, or I should be."

His parents said nothing. Roche wasn't sure what to say. He looked at Judith and recognized the same wariness in her expression.

"Dad?"

Roche leaned forward. "Let's go over this," he suggested. When no one spoke, he was relieved. "To buy a place, you need to prove that you're employed. And what will you use for the down payment? As you said, it's not our job to act as your private bank."

This was where he expected to hear the arguments, perhaps a string of recriminations about his being a neglectful father. Luc's response shocked him.

"I agree."

Was that a clap of thunder? The gods calling out to him?

"I'm in therapy," Luc said, his voice low.

Roche was not prepared for this. "Therapy? You?"

"There's nothing shameful about it, despite what you believe."

"Did I say it was shameful?" He heard defensiveness creep into his voice.

Judith laughed. "You don't have to; we know you too well. Anyone who turns to someone for help is weak. My God, Noah, if you had a brain tumor, you'd probably insist on operating on yourself."

"Judith, I—"

"Anyway," she said, cutting him off. "I've explained to Luc that he can no longer manipulate us."

Luc looked embarrassed. "I'm not sure I'd say manipulate."

Roche felt an old tightness in his chest begin to soften. "So, tell me, what's your plan?"

Luc sat stiffly, hands clasped on the table. "How about this: you loan me the down payment. Charge me interest at the same rate a bank would charge."

Roche looked at Judith, who shrugged. "I'm hearing this for the first time," she said.

"And then?" Roche asked.

"I'll handle the monthly payments," Luc explained. "I know this sounds risky, so I've got another part to this. I have a friend who's an attorney. He'll draw up a contract that says that if I miss even one payment, I'm in default of the agreement."

"Meaning?" asked Roche.

"Meaning you and Mom immediately take ownership of the apartment, with the right to put it on the market. You'll take back the amount of your down payment."

"And if there's a profit when we sell it?" his mother asked.

Luc gave her what seemed to be an endearing shrug. "We can split it?"

Roche and Judith exchanged looks again. "That works for me," she said.

"And for me," added Roche. "Except for one thing."

He saw how Luc's posture suddenly slumped, as if victory had turned to defeat. Judith said nothing, but he recognized distrust in her face.

"Whatever interest the bank is charging you, your mother and I will charge half of that." He turned to Judith. "Agreed?"

Her stern expression melted into a smile. "Sounds perfect."

Luc straightened up, surprise and pleasure in his expression. "I'll get it in writing and send it to you for approval." With that, he stood, kissed his parents, and rushed out of the café.

Roche turned to Judith. "You do realize that this is the first time in years we've been able to come to an agreement with him…about anything."

"It's practically historic," she said. "But the part about getting a job?"

He stood, prepared to walk away, but Judith took his sleeve.

"Noah, there's something I need to tell you."

He sat.

She picked up a water glass and swirled the liquid. "I'm getting married."

He felt surprisingly pleased for her. And relieved, too. She seemed happy, and she deserved that.

She shoved a strand of hair off her face and tucked it behind her ear.

It was a gesture he had known for nearly thirty-five years. That shoulder-length hair, once light maple, was now streaked with white.

"Are you angry?" she asked.

"Not angry, no. Happy for you. You deserve to be happy."

"As do you," she said, her eyes kind.

They walked outside, shared a quick hug, and he watched her disappear around the corner. So many of their meetings ended in frustration, anger, or sadness. But not today.

He returned to his office, feeling as he often did when learning about someone else's happiness. He never wanted to take away their joy, but wondered when it would be his turn. And while he rubbed salve on that wound and reminded himself that being alone meant fewer complications, it still meant being alone.

Aria was waiting in his office, her concentration directed to an assortment of papers spread out before her.

"Ready?" he asked.

She straightened the papers, folded them in half, and tucked them into her bag. "I'm sorry, but I'm going to pass on dinner. I need to work on my notes."

"Of course," he said, unprepared for the disappointment he was feeling.

She hoisted her bag onto her shoulder. "To be honest, I'm ready for a good night's sleep, but there are so many interviews to review."

"You'll have ten hours on the plane," he reminded her.

They took the elevator to the lobby and stepped outside. The night was calm, with surprisingly little traffic.

The third cab Roche hailed zipped to the curb. He opened the door and watched Aria settle into the back seat.

"I may not see you before I leave," she said. "So, thank you."

"For?"

"Finally trusting me. Or nearly."

Her words triggered unexpected pleasure: he did trust her. "Is there anything I can do before you head home?"

She scanned his face, looked into his eyes. "There is one thing," she said, holding his attention with a penetrating stare.

He was almost afraid to ask, yet managed to mutter, "Of course, what is it?"

CHAPTER TWENTY

"You can come back to the hotel with me."

Without a word, he ran to the other side of the taxi and climbed in.

Chapter Twenty-One

Aria awoke with a start. She checked the clock. Nearly six. She needed to make sure everything was packed. That meant an obsession-driven search of the closet, drawers, spaces behind furniture, and under the bed. As much as she hated separating herself from the warmth of Noah's body, she needed to do this.

She took her cell phone from the nightstand and sent Lexie a text, repeating her arrival time. That done, she crept out of bed, showered, and dressed. And then she kissed his forehead.

He stirred, mumbled something incoherent, then sat up.

"If you'd rather sleep," she said, "I can take a cab."

He took her hand.

On his face, she recognized not regret, but confusion, and she imagined that it was not unlike her own. What had come over her last night? What had come over him? Twenty-four hours earlier, she would have bet on the lives of everyone she loved that this would never happen. Perhaps it was a way to release the stress that had built up over a week of tension. But that didn't feel right. It was more.

"I do plan to spend more time here," she said, answering a question he had not yet asked.

He began to slip on his trousers, and she turned her back.

"When this is settled—when all the legal issues are resolved—I'll come back. Winnie always has an empty apartment looking for a tenant, so I'm not worried about finding a place."

"You could always stay with Solange," he said straight-faced.

250

She felt sadness welling up, but pushed it away. There was nothing she could do about Solange, and she had no desire to get herself embroiled in the woman's drama.

"Sorry," he said. "That was unkind. And Solange is not your problem." He stood and pulled on his shirt. "Not to sound cruel, Aria, but she takes very good care of herself. I'm quite sure she's played the role of queen and stoic for so long that she can slip into that persona at any time. It's her built-in protection."

"Yes, you're right," she said.

He gave her a little grin. "As for us, I know you'll be back: I'm irresistible."

She looked away. What did she want? San Francisco, where she had friends, more time with her mother and daughter, or Paris?

"Aria?" he said.

"I'm not sure what to do." It had been easier when they had begrudgingly given each other breathing space. And now here she was, trying not to remember how it felt, sharing the night with him. She saw kindness in his face. "I'm not good at this."

"Who is?" he said. "I hope you don't regret—"

She cut him off. "I don't." She imagined herself standing beneath a dam, and it was about to burst and carry her away. She took his hand, and was comforted when he held hers firmly.

She checked the nightstand clock. "I need to call my mother. Knowing her, she's waiting anxiously by the phone."

Roche finished dressing, buttoning his shirt, and pulling on his jacket. He folded his tie and tucked it into his pocket. "Should I wait here, or do you want me to head back to the precinct?"

"You go ahead. I'll meet you there."

The minute he was out the door, she made the call.

Lexie answered and activated the speaker phone. "Grandma's listening," she said.

"Tell all," insisted Delphine. "I'm a prisoner here, and your daughter is a very efficient warden."

She gave them a rundown of the trip to Marie-Josette's cottage, and then the discovery that Sashkie was the old woman's granddaughter. "That's Solange's majordomo," she explained. And then she went on to tell them about Sashkie's casual, almost cheerful admission of guilt.

"Thank heaven Solange and Bertrand are out of the woods," Delphine said.

"Not quite," said Aria. "At least, not Solange." Before her mother could ask, she described the drama around Marie-Josette and Sashkie, the accusations of theft made by Solange, and the reason why the Gabriels were set up by Sashkie to look like murderers.

"That is so sad," Lexie said. "What a terrible thing to do. For Sashkie, but I also feel sorry for Solange."

It was a long moment before Delphine spoke, her voice breaking with emotion. "This isn't the Solange I know. But, yes, she can be difficult, even cruel."

"I'm sorry, Maman," Aria said. "I know how dear they are to you. I'm not sure there will be any legal action against her, but I do want to warn you that Bertrand had no idea. When I last saw him, he had packed a bag. He might be leaving for good, I can't say."

The silence was a black space into which lives plummeted. Aria could only imagine what her mother was feeling, but she knew it was pain, and it was deep.

She repeated her flight information and promised to drop by the house on her way home from the airport. As they said their goodbyes, Aria felt a sadness wash over her. The old friendship between her mother and Solange would never be the same. Not only because Delphine knew the truth, but because Aria had been part of the drama. Solange would never forget, nor would she forgive.

With everything packed, all drawers, shelves, and the space under the bed checked, she was ready. The plan was to go to the precinct and remain there until it was time to leave for the airport. The authorities insisted that everyone arrive four hours before an international flight, so the sojourn with the team would be short. Noah had offered to accompany her, and she had accepted.

In the lobby, she handed over the key to the manager, who received it with hardly a glance. She hung it on its hook and then slid a printout of the bill across the counter. Aria ran through the numbers and gave the woman her credit card. After the charge was complete, she turned to go.

"Have a safe flight home," the woman said. And then she smiled.

Not once during Aria's stay had she smiled, but now here she was, smiling. And it was almost warm, and not at all predatory. Aria wondered why *predatory* came to mind. The manager's name tag read *Madame Renard*. Renard: French for fox! Without thinking, she went around the counter, hugged the woman, and then stepped away.

The woman's face reflected shock. And then, as if a wall of ice had suddenly collapsed, she grabbed Aria and hugged her back.

Aria rolled her suitcase through the lobby and onto the sidewalk. Magically, as if Paris knew she was leaving and was giving her one last gift, a taxi pulled to the curb.

In the ride to Bastion, Aria ran scenes through her head. It seemed like months, not days, that she had first met de Charbonnet. How would she approach this project? It would start in that little shop in Chateau Rouge. And then the theater, a murder, the unexpected family connections that made some of her work easier, but in many ways far more difficult. As her mind created the outline, she stopped herself. This was the book she was planning, not the articles. None of them would be about her. Rather, they would explore Inspector Noah Roche, along with Tenna Berglof and Anuj Kumar. The team. How they worked; how they succeeded.

She was out of the taxi and rolling her suitcase into the building when her mobile sounded. De Charbonnet wanted to see her before she flew off.

She took the elevator to his floor and stepped into the foyer. The woman behind the glass gave no sign of recognizing her.

"He's expecting me," Aria said. If the old biddy didn't remember her name, she'd force her to ask.

Five minutes later, she was seated in his office. Before he had a chance to speak—perhaps intending to plant doubts in her mind about Roche, his team, and their methods of exposing the killer—she said, "The media loves you. A major case with international attention? You're the hero of Paris."

His expression of pleasure struck her as forced. What was he thinking behind that mask? What pressure was he getting from those friends hoping to shove Roche aside, or under a bus? She wanted to ask how he felt to lose yet again to the son of a pig farmer, but she held her tongue.

"I'm not a monster, Madame Nevins," he said.

Of all possible responses, this was not on her list.

"I know you think I've manipulated you to write in my favor, against Roche, but you're wrong. I don't like the man, never have, but I respect him."

Aria thought about this before speaking. "You seemed so—"

"Determined to bring him down? I'm sure that's how it looked."

His voice made her think that he was surrendering to the enemy.

"Several very important people have exerted suffocating pressure on me. They want Roche out. He's not one of them, if you know what I mean. Wrong family, wrong education."

"You brought me from San Francisco. Certainly, there are dozens of journalists around Europe who could have handled this assignment, so I have to be curious."

Now it was de Charbonnet's turn to say nothing for a long moment. "I knew about your trouble," he finally said. "Until then, your reputation here and in the States had been excellent. It made sense to bring you here. I knew you'd be scrupulously careful and honest."

"No rush to judgment," she said, unable to keep the sarcasm out of her voice.

"No rush to judgment," he repeated. "Exactly. And I was certain you'd never buckle under pressure. There are people in this building who'd think nothing of strong-arming you to get what they want."

"And the work?" she asked. "My articles about the team?"

"Can you send the first one next week?"

"No problem," she said, wondering if he would be this friendly if he knew she would be giving Roche and his team high marks.

She went to Roche's office, left her suitcase behind the door, and sat down. "I've just been to see good ol' Georges."

Roche said nothing, his face unreadable to her.

"He was surprisingly pleasant. And he complimented you for your skills, your integrity—just about everything." Before he could respond, she said, "I think he meant it. I also think he has to fight to keep the wolves from his door—and yours."

When it was time to leave for the airport, Aria embraced Anuj and Tenna, promising to stay in touch and inviting them to come to San Francisco. Anuj smiled sweetly when Aria told him how much she looked forward to meeting Halima and little Tamim.

She gave Tenna one last embrace. "Take care, dear Tenna," she whispered into the woman's ear. "And don't let him bully you."

Tenna placed her hand on Aria's shoulder and gave it a gentle squeeze. "I've already paid Winnie for the first month, and I'll be moving in this weekend. I told the boys. I was afraid they'd be crushed. You know, divorce, trauma, and all that."

"How were they?" Aria asked.

Tenna looked directly into Aria's eyes. "They were thrilled."

Anuj stood there saying nothing, but the look on his face told Aria that he was hearing this for the first time.

Tenna turned to him. "Some people are happy together; others are happy apart. Maybe I should've told you."

Anuj brushed away her comment. "Brava," he said, affection evident in his eyes. "Bravissima."

Aria turned and saw that Roche had joined them. Tenna repeated the news, and he gave her arm a squeeze.

"Good," he said. "Excellent."

They arrived at the airport two hours before her flight. Had she been with anyone else, she would have panicked. This was one of the busiest airports in the world, with security lines notoriously long, and the baggage inspection process even longer. Roche reminded her that his official status allowed him to escort her past the lines and directly into the boarding area.

"I need to have you nearby for all my travels," she said.

He smiled. "That can be arranged."

There were plenty of empty seats in the waiting area, but they stood at the window and watched airplanes from dozens of countries being directed to gates projecting from the building, or being towed in preparation for take-off. Everything was fluid, coming and going. One plane sat at the nearest gate, the plane that would take her home.

Home, where she would put her life in order. But how would that life look? She had no idea. What she did know was that whatever awaited her, she would survive. She would make it work. Her misdeed could not be ignored, nor could she reverse the tragedy that resulted from it, but she could move forward. And that meant forgiving herself. Not finding an excuse, but understanding that she had made a tragic mistake and was taking responsibility for all that resulted from it. Perhaps the rock-hard seed of shame she had been carrying in her heart would one day soften.

She looked at Roche. His attention was outside, where trucks and baggage carts zipped around, never colliding but nearly. She was calmed by his presence. Ideas floated around in her mind, changing shape like amoeba, redefining themselves, revealing the directions her life could be going—with or without him.

She would write this series of articles about the team, Camilla Rodolfo's murder, the attack on Joseph, the tragedy of an old woman left to die. But there was also a book to be written. This was where she would introduce all those characters whose lives were entwined during the investigation. From actors to homicide inspectors, a village policeman, a NATO employee who bullied his way through life, and a little boy whose father was aching to shower him with love. Part of the story would be her terrible mistake, her personal scrutiny of the decisions she had made, and how the repercussions of decisions can too easily be brushed aside. Especially when ambition takes the lead.

The flight was called, and First-Class passengers were invited to board the plane. She silently thanked her mother again for insisting on upgrading her ticket. She turned to Roche. There was so much she wanted to tell him, but no time. It would have to wait. For a brief moment, she considered taking his arm and walking out of the building.

"When will you write your book?" he asked.

"My book?" His way of getting into her head was unsettling.

"Aria, how could you not? Are you saying you haven't written the entire story in your head? Think of it: you're the only journalist in the world who not only witnessed every step of the investigation, but has full access to the three homicide inspectors, including all of our notes and recordings."

She laughed. "Well, I was certainly in the right place at the right time."

The last call to board rang throughout the terminal.

"I'll be in the States in a few months," he said. "New Mexico. Somewhere high in the mountains. Should be an interesting conference, all about new developments and procedures in forensics."

"That's a beautiful part of the country."

"But dull, don't you think? The conference, not the scenery. No murders."

"I'm guessing you'll do just fine without the excitement."

Roche laughed. "You never know." He paused for a moment, and then said, "It's a short flight from San Francisco to Albuquerque, yes?" Switching to English, he said, "A hop, a skip, and a jump."

"It is that," she said, taking his hand.

They shared a long kiss, and then she gripped the handle of her suitcase and rolled it onto the plane.

Acknowledgments

In 1996, seated at my computer and hoping to come up with the next clever sentence in some Silicon Valley high-tech brochure, I recalled pieces of a dream from the night before. Had I turned on my computer during the night to write it down? And there it was: a file named *MYSTERY*. Three single-spaced pages describing a murder that takes place in a Paris theater.

This is where I thank friends and family who never said, "Give up and write something publishable."

First and foremost, loving thanks to my sister, Michele Zackheim, the best literary sounding board imaginable. Her keen eye and superb storytelling gifts helped me get on track when I was certain I was losing my way. And I thank her husband and dear friend, Charlie Ramsburg. Together, they have listened to my tales of woe around this novel for nearly thirty years and have encouraged me to forge ahead. As artists, they understood my desire to bring this project to fruition. Their love and friendship are invaluable.

Caroline Leavitt has long been my cheerleader, pushing me forward and never allowing me to lose faith. Her editing insights are golden. Whenever I need to share a laugh… or even a good cry… Caroline is always there.

Aviva Layton is more than a loving friend. She's a gifted editor who put her life aside for a week and dedicated herself to this manuscript. I turn to Aviva when I'm seeking writerly advice, and when I need to be reminded that it's good and healthy to be able to laugh at myself.

I thank my dear friend Susana Franck for her loving support. And to her husband Guillaume Franck, for providing valuable information about the Paris police. My heartfelt wish is that Guillaume could still be with us so I could thank him in person.

My thanks to friend and fellow writer Risa Nye for her encouragement.

And to the wonderful Elizabeth Breslin for reading a draft and giving spot-on feedback. Perhaps, when you're reading this, we'll be eating sushi!

For my family, steadfast in their encouragement, my thanks and love: Alisa and Mark Askanas, Sophia Law and Olivia Law; and Matthew Sosnick, Lily, Joshua, and Liam.

When I became friends with author Anne Perry and told her I had been working on a mystery for years, she asked if she could read it. I told her no. Anne was an international bestselling mystery writer and I never wanted her to think I had befriended her so she could help me with this novel. After more than ten years of friendship, during which time I had become her personal editor, she announced, "Send me the damn book!" I let her read it, she gave some excellent suggestions, and we rarely discussed it again. Anne, I wish you were here to share the excitement with me.

My sincere thanks to Shawn Reilly Simmons of Level Best Books, for expressing such enthusiasm about this novel and for her thoughtful editing. And to Deb Well, marketing maven and Jill-of-all-trades, for her patience, humor and support.

I know so well how a literary agent must believe in a book in order to pitch it to editors. I am profoundly grateful to Darlene Chan of the Linda Chester Literary Agency for not only believing in this book, but guiding me through the last revisions. And perhaps even more, for her patience whenever my insecurities threatened to take over.

And to you, readers, thank you. I put heart, soul, and nearly thirty years into this book. I hope I've done the story proud.

About the Author

Victoria Zackheim is the author of the novels *The Bone Weaver* and *The Curtain Falls in Paris*. She is the creator/editor of seven anthologies, including the international bestseller *The Other Woman*, adapted to the theater and performed in several dozen theaters across the United States. She wrote the documentary *Where Birds Never Sang: The Story of Ravensbrück and Sachsenhausen Concentration Camps*, which aired nationwide on PBS. She teaches creative nonfiction (Personal Essay/Memoir) in the UCLA Extension Writers' Program and is a frequent conference speaker and writing instructor in the US and abroad. A freelance editor, Victoria has worked with many authors on their novels, including international bestseller Anne Perry and New York Times bestseller Caroline Leavitt, and the memoirs of Robb Forman Dew, Gillian Herbert, and many more. She is a San Francisco Library Laureate and lives in Northern California.

AUTHOR WEBSITE:
www.victoriazackheim.com

SOCIAL MEDIA HANDLES:
Facebook: https://www.facebook.com/victoriazackheimauthor/
BlueSky: https://bsky.app/profile/vdzack.bsky.social
Instagram: https://www.instagram.com/victoriazackheimauthor/

Also by Victoria Zackheim

The Bone Weaver (novel)

The Other Woman: Twenty-one Wives, Lovers, and Others Talk Openly About Sex, Deception, Love and Betrayal

Exit Laughing: How Humor Takes the Sting Out of Death

The Face in the Mirror: Writers Reflect on the Dreams of Youth and the Reality of Age

Faith: Essays from Believers, Agnostics, and Atheists

For Keeps: Women Tell the Truth About Their Bodies, Growing Older, and Acceptance

He Said What? Women Write About Moments When Everything Changed

Private Investigations: Mystery Writers on the Secrets, Riddles, and Wonders in Their Lives

www.ingramcontent.com/pod-product-compliance
Lightning Source LLC
LaVergne TN
LVHW041743020625
812801LV00031B/231